MAN OF HER DREAMS

Perhaps one day a man will wait at the altar for me—a man deeply in love with me.

Anne smiled at the ridiculous daydream. The most generous of friends would admit that she was firmly on that shelf to which spinsters were relegated.

She glanced around to see if anyone had noticed her grinning. A tall stranger stood a little farther on. Oblivious, deeply involved in his own thoughts, he ignored her, which was good, since it allowed her to continue dreaming silly dreams. Anne pretended to look beyond him.

A man to love me, she mused. *A man like that one.*

Surreptitiously, she studied the dark stranger even as she chided herself for playing the romantic fool. And then she told herself she didn't care if she was a fool. She'd been too busy when of an age to spin fantasies, first as a vicar's busy daughter and then as housewife, nurse, and surrogate mother.

Anne watched the stranger, carefully pretending to stare beyond him. The capes of his long coat flipped around him, emphasizing the width of his shoulders. He wore no hat and unfashionably long dark hair was flung into wild disarray by the wind speeding them across the Channel. . . .

—from *The Perfect Mother, Retired,* by Jeanne Savery

BOOK YOUR PLACE ON OUR WEBSITE AND MAKE THE READING CONNECTION!

We've created a customized website just for our very special readers, where you can get the inside scoop on everything that's going on with Zebra, Pinnacle and Kensington books.

When you come online, you'll have the exciting opportunity to:

- View covers of upcoming books
- Read sample chapters
- Learn about our future publishing schedule (listed by publication month *and author*)
- Find out when your favorite authors will be visiting a city near you
- Search for and order backlist books from our online catalog
- Check out author bios and background information
- Send e-mail to your favorite authors
- Meet the Kensington staff online
- Join us in weekly chats with authors, readers and other guests
- Get writing guidelines
- AND MUCH MORE!

**Visit our website at
http://www.kensingtonbooks.com**

A
COURTSHIP
FOR MAMA

Alice Holden
Julia Parks
Jeanne Savery

ZEBRA BOOKS
KENSINGTON PUBLISHING CORP.
http://www.kensingtonbooks.com

Contents

The Managing Mamas

Alice Holden

Prologue

In the night the river that meandered through the Whitlock and Blair estates had left its banks during a severe storm.

Fascinated by a circumstance he had never encountered in his seven years, Benjamin Whitlock shucked off his brown leather half-boots and his white silk stockings and left them under a birch tree. Barefooted, he ran back and forth, splashing in the puddles on the flooded grass in sheer delight, grinning from ear to ear.

Nearby, in his full view, three-year-old Jillian Blair's Irish nursemaid Bridget slapped playfully at the hands of Jess, the Whitlocks' young footman, who was doing his best to steal a kiss.

Left to herself, Jillian skipped toward the riverbank, her red curls bouncing, careless that her blue silk thin-soled slippers were soaking through to her white lisle stockings.

His hands on the knees of his cotton breeches, Benjamin had been watching a frog leap toward the muddy stream when he saw Jillian from the corner of his eye.

"Oh, no, Jilly!" he cried and took off, his strong little legs flying over the wet meadow grass.

Her big green eyes wide with fear, Jillian clung to a partially submerged log, close to the bank, where she had slipped into the deeper water.

Benjamin waded into the flowing river, almost up to his armpits.

"I got you, Jilly," he said and pulled the mite from the log and dragged her to the safety of the riverbank.

Jess and Bridget came running, the young servants' attention drawn by Benjamin's shouts. The shivering children were sprawled on the wet grass, chattering at each other . . . *Why did you . . . ? How did you . . . ?*

Bridget wailed like a banshee and crushed Jillian to her plump bosom.

"You are holding me too tight, Bridget," the squirming child protested, having recovered quickly as young children who were not really hurt were wont to do.

Jess had wrapped the goosefleshed Benjamin in his green and yellow coat, the livery of Whitlock House.

The footman kneeled in front of the boy, held the oversized coat tightly around his sturdy little body, and rubbed his back to warm him.

"You are a brave lad, Master Benjie. Sir Edmund and Lady Whitlock will be so proud of you." He turned to Bridget, who was wrapping Jillian in her coarse woolen shawl. "The lad deserves a medal."

Benjamin liked the sound of that and wondered if his medal would be like the one Bridget concealed beneath her clothes. Her talisman was silver and had a picture of a man with a halo whom she called St. Christopher.

But Bridget was having different thoughts from Jess's. She put her hands on Benjamin's small shoulders in the colorful coat that fell to his ankles. "You have been charged with a momentous obligation, Benjie," she said, her homey face solemn. "Tradition says that once you save someone's life, you are duty-bound to protect that person forever." She looked deep into his golden brown eyes. "From now on, Jilly is your responsibility."

Benjamin believed Bridget. Although he never got a

medal, his parents and the Blairs fussed over him. His mother called him her brave boy. Lady Blair said he was a little hero.

To the amusement of the Blairs and the Whitlocks, Benjamin took his commission from Bridget to heart. With his complete approval, Jillian became his shadow.

By the time Benjamin was mature enough to question Bridget's folklore, he and Jillian had already become fast friends.

Chapter 1

Hidden from view in the obscuring shadows of the birch trees, Jillian watched Benjamin. He had cast a fishing line into the river on this unseasonably warm day that her father called a false spring.

His white cotton shirt was rolled up to his elbows and hung untidily over his twill country trousers. His sun-lightened brown hair was mussed; his golden brown eyes were concentrated on a nibble.

Jillian felt a trickle of melancholy. Benjamin had been her confidant for most of her eighteen years. They were very close and told each other everything. But girls were meant to marry, leave home, and go to live with their husbands.

Tomorrow Jillian was taking a big step in that direction. In the days to come, she was to be launched into the fashionable world of London society.

The dry leaves beneath her old shoes alerted Benjamin to her presence when she stepped from the trees into the sunlight. He turned and smiled and lost his fish. Bending down, he pulled a worm from a tin bucket beside his timeworn boots, baited the hook, and recast his lure.

Jillian dropped down onto the grass and smoothed her plain white dress. She had joined Benjamin on the riverbank countless times when he fished. They would talk and talk or would just sit in silence with no need for words between them.

As usual, Jillian's red hair was drawn into a knot at the top of her head. To Benjamin she looked hardly old enough to be ripe for the marriage mart, her oval face small, her pert nose sprinkled with freckles like a schoolgirl's.

"Have you finished packing?" he asked her over his shoulder.

"Yes," she said. "How about you?"

"Perkins is handling my luggage. I would just be in the way if I tried to supervise a seasoned valet."

But Jillian had not sought out Benjamin for idle talk. Their mothers had leased a London house together for a month. It was no secret that he was going with them to make himself available as an escort for her and the ladies.

Jillian was reassured by this happenstance, for Benjamin was her best friend. But she also had qualms that his protectiveness might prove an obstruction to her freedom to choose her own husband.

Benjamin got a rise from a fish, but he made no attempt to land the trout.

Catching his eye, Jillian patted the ground beside her. "Benjamin, I want to talk with you."

"Certainly," he said, not the least bit vexed to have his angling interrupted, for he was not wholly absorbed in the sport. He reeled in his line, set aside the fishing rod, and sat down beside Jillian, his arm resting across one raised knee.

"I know you are supposed to look after me in London, but I trust you won't keep me on a short leash," she said, getting right to the point.

Benjamin looked amused. "You cannot expect to gad about by yourself as you do here at home where you have known everyone forever, Jilly. But I think what you fear is that I will be sitting in your pocket and, thus, discourage eligible young men from approaching you. I can promise you, my dear, that at social affairs where your mother and mine are present, I will keep at a distance."

"That sounds acceptable," Jillian said. "I want the leeway to pick my own husband. I will not be able to determine if a gentleman is suitable if you hover about and intimidate him and keep him from speaking freely to me."

Benjamin gave Jillian an agreeable grin meant to disarm her. She had no experience with gentlemen of the *ton*. He would not stand by and let an utter cad take advantage of her or break her heart into pieces. But he promised, "I shan't hover. Your choice of husband will be yours and yours alone."

He saw no point in adding the codicil. Jillian would be apt to tell him she preferred to make her own mistakes.

In fact, Benjamin had similar plans. He decided that this was a good time to share them with her.

"Remember a while back, Jilly," he said to that purpose, "when I went to London for several days to enact some business for my father?"

"Yes," she said, showing interest, for she sensed that he was going to tell her something important.

"A former Eton classmate invited me to a soirée where I met a young lady and stood up for two dances with her. I wrote to her and she has granted me permission to call on her during our sojourn in the City."

To Jillian, Benjamin in love seemed strange, yet wasn't that what she wanted, too, a love of her own?

"Who is she?" she asked.

"She is called Lady Anna and is the daughter of the Countess and Earl of Herridge. But don't say anything to anyone, Jilly. I don't want my parents to know until I have made more progress in gaining her favor and have reason to believe she might like me too."

Jillian promised, yet she could not imagine anyone not finding Benjamin perfectly wonderful. He had good height, an athletic build, a singularly attractive smile, and he always conversed intelligently.

"Is she beautiful?" Jillian felt compelled to ask.

"Very," Benjamin said and got up and emptied the contents of his bait bucket into the river.

Jillian was semiconscious of a funny feeling around her heart, but Benjamin was saying he was through fishing and would walk her home and the odd emotion vanished from her breast.

At Blair Hall, Lady Moira Whitlock gazed from the window of a spare bedchamber toward the parkland dotted with ornamental trees. Coming through the iron gate of the brick-walled estate were her son and the young woman who was as dear to her as a natural daughter would be.

She turned to Lady Delia Blair, who was sorting out the linens strewn across a four-poster bed.

"Benjamin is coming down the drivepath with Jillian," Moira said. "He must have seen my carriage."

Whitlock House, her own home, was a mile farther down the country lane.

Delia picked up some dish towels and put them into a spacious travel trunk. A Holland apron covered her sage green dress.

"You know, Moira," she said, cocking her red hair sprinkled with silver, "I seem to have a persistent sadness whenever I think of Jillian going off to be married. This house will seem desolate and empty without her."

Moira beckoned to Delia. "Come here for a moment." She was a tall woman, her neck long and stately, her light brown hair pulled into an elegant chignon. Delia, who was nearly a head shorter, went into the circle of the arm held out to her by her longtime friend with whom, like their children, she shared a wealth of memories.

"Look at Jilly and Ben, talking and laughing," Moira said, her face pressed close to the windowpane. "See how she tilts her head into his shoulder and how tenderly he touches her arm. Lud, Delia, even a casual observer can see that they take great pleasure in each other's company."

"What a handsome couple they make. If only they were in love."

"They are, but they just don't know it," Moira said, cutting to the heart of her reason for calling Delia to the window.

"Do you think so? I have often wondered, but put it down to wishful thinking."

Moira fingered a cameo pinned to the front of her gray heather day gown. "What would you say to helping me engage in a bit of selective managing to set them on the road to wedded bliss?"

Delia studied Moira's face. "Dare we interfere?"

"Dare we not?" Moira countered, holding Delia's unsure green eyes with her brown steadfast gaze. "Delia, marriage is too permanent for a tragic mistake."

"I agree, but, Moira, I must confess that I am at a loss as to how to convince Jillian and Benjamin that they should marry. Do you have a plan?"

"I know something of managing," Moira said confidently. "Careful planning is useless. People behave unpredictably. The trick is to seize an opportunity when it presents itself."

"Sounds sensible. Something unforeseen does always seem to crop up to put a spoke in one's schemes. Remember when we decided to set up tents for the annual church picnic in case of rain?"

"Exactly," Moira said. "The winds were so strong the shelters were useless against the storm. The flaps kept blowing up and exposing everyone to the elements."

Delia left the window and went back to packing the household goods to be transported to London.

Moira sat down on the edge of the bed. "I hear the downstairs door. Benjamin and Jillian are coming up. One thing more, not a word to Arthur. I shan't say anything to Edmund. He is bound to grouse that I have enough to do managing my own life without managing my son's."

"Gentlemen are so insensitive when it comes to affairs of the heart," Delia agreed. "Fortunately our husbands are to remain at home and will not be in London to voice their objections."

Sir Edmund Whitlock and Sir Arthur Blair were lifelong friends who had inherited adjoining estates and had been knighted years ago on the same day by King George, the Regent's father.

Moira put her finger to her lips in a sign of silence at the sound of their children's voices and the clatter of their footsteps on the stairs.

Benjamin followed Jillian through the door and greeted Lady Blair and said to his mother, "I saw your carriage from the road, Mama. Can I beg a ride home?"

"Of course, dear. Did you catch any fish?" She picked up a folded quilt and proceeded to arrange it on the top of the bed linens in a nearly full trunk. "I don't think it is going to fit," she said of the quilt.

Jillian went to help Lady Whitlock with the cumbersome bedcover. "Benjamin doesn't go fishing to catch fish," she said. "He likes the peacefulness of the sport. Your son, my lady, is the only angler I know who does not carry a creel."

With great difficulty, Moira finally mashed the quilt

down, but Jillian had to sit on the top of the trunk to close it completely.

Benjamin came over and secured the brass clasps with a businesslike snap. "I dislike the taste of fish," he said.

From her perch on the trunk, Jillian giggled. "Benjamin only eats the fish course at dinner parties so as not to insult the host's cook."

The twinkle in Moira's eyes embraced Jillian. "You know my son better than any of us do, Jilly. What will you do without Benjamin when you marry?"

For a moment, Jillian was bewildered by the odd question. "I suppose I shall cleave unto my husband as the Bible admonishes. But, then, perhaps I shan't even take."

Delia turned the key in the trunk's lock and rebuked her daughter. "Of course, you will take. Won't she, Benjamin?"

"If she gets rid of those awful freckles, she just might," Benjamin teased. Jillian made a face at him.

He laughed. "Silly goose, of course, you will take. Good day, Lady Blair, Jillian," he said. "Mama, I will meet you downstairs at the carriage."

Jillian left, too. Moira pressed her fellow conspirator's hand and smiled. "Mark my words, Delia, Benjamin will be popping the question before we return from London."

Delia wondered, *But to whom?* felt like a traitor, and because she wanted it to be so, she put her trust in Moira's expertise in meddling.

Chapter 2

Exploring the leased London house, Jillian followed the rich aroma of baking bread to the kitchen below stairs. The clatter of crockery and the banging of pots and pans and the chatter of the staff came to an abrupt halt when she went through the door into the noisy kitchen.

Jillian was made uneasy by the inhospitable glances turned on her, but forced a smile, which was not returned.

"Is there something you desire, miss?" the plump cook asked. Her fingers rested on the handle of a sharp cleaver with which she had been chopping carrots at the scarred wooden table that was used for preparing meals.

Had Jillian been in her own kitchen at Blair Hall, she would have been asked if she would like a cup of tea. She would have answered, "That would be kind, Cook," and she would have sat and gossiped comfortably with the kitchen help.

But here the scullery maid stared over her thin shoulder, her motionless hands immersed in the sink's soapy dishwater.

Another female domestic, covered from chin to ankle in a canvas apron, gawked, her appointed task at a standstill.

"Please, continue with your duties," Jillian said politely. "I was merely familiarizing myself with the house."

She backed out of the room under the blunt stares,

shook her head, and let out a sustained breath. Renters were apparently unwelcome in the kitchen.

She bypassed the butler's and housekeeper's private chambers and went up a short flight of steps into the sunny breakfast parlor and through it to the dining room and on to the drawing room where the family would receive visitors. The old-fashioned furniture in all of the public rooms was of good quality and had been well looked after, polished to a gleam, and smelled pleasantly of pine oil.

In the library, Jillian tried out one of the men's leather chairs and decided it would be comfortably conducive for an hour spent reading when she had the time.

Near the bay window was a well-appointed writing desk with a generous supply of stationery, ample ink, and a caddy of quills.

Climbing the carpeted stairs to the second floor, Jillian walked past her own bedroom, her mother's and Lady Whitlock's, paused before the door to Benjamin's chambers, and knocked.

"Come in," came his familiar voice, sounding uncharacteristically ruffled.

Jillian went inside, properly leaving the door open behind her.

"My, you look like a veritable pink of the *ton*," she said and proceeded to circle him for a complete examination of his new blue superfine coat and recently purchased beige gabardine pantaloons.

He nudged her aside and looked at his reflection in a cheval glass.

"Dash it all, Jilly, I cannot put a decent knot in my cravat."

"Where is your valet?" she asked, looking around the room, which was done in predominantly masculine browns.

"I sent him on an errand. In truth, he is not much good with neckcloths either," Benjamin grumbled.

"Why keep him, then? Surely the employment bureau can send a suitable replacement." The house came with the servants.

Benjamin waved a dismissive hand. "Alvin, that's his name, needs the work, I am sure. He is young, at least four years my junior, but he is an amiable fellow and tries hard to please."

Jillian had seen the youth. Alvin was as tall as Benjamin, but much slimmer, not yet having filled out to a man's body.

In the country Benjamin shared a valet with his father, but Perkins had remained behind to serve Sir Edmund.

"Let me have a go at it," Jillian said, examining the sadly mangled neckcloth.

Benjamin pulled the cravat from around his neck. "This one is beyond saving." He dropped it onto the other rejects at his feet and took a fresh white cloth from a neat stack on the cherry wood bureau and handed it to Jillian.

She stood in front of him and asked him to bend down a little to compensate for his much greater height.

She looped the endless material around his neck a number of times before settling on a plain fall. Standing back, she put a finger to her chin and admired her work.

"Quite respectable. Like Beau Brummell, I just might have created a new style." The arbiter of fashion was known for his inventiveness. "What do you think, Ben?"

Benjamin moved past her to gain access to the mirror. He smiled at his image. "I won't exactly cut a dash, but neither will I be shunned as a country bumpkin."

Jillian turned toward the door, interested, when Alvin came into the room, carrying a bouquet of early spring flowers, wrapped in green tissue paper.

The young valet's bow to Jillian was awkward. Tillie, the lady's maid who served her mother, Lady Whitlock, and her, was older but only slightly better trained.

"Put the flowers on the bureau, Alvin," Benjamin said.

"Yes, sir," the lad replied and did as he was bid. He went to where Benjamin stood before the looking glass and stooped down to gather up the neckcloths his employer had dropped onto the Persian rug at his feet.

"I'll take these to the washroom," he said.

"I am cow-handed when it comes to tying the things," Benjamin said in a sort of embarrassed apology.

Alvin smiled. "I see you got one right, though, Mr. Whitlock," he said as he backed out of the room with the soiled laundry.

Benjamin made a face when he was gone. "Alvin looked so pleased with me that I hate to disabuse him," he said to Jillian. "But if I don't, he will always expect me to wrestle with my neckcloths by myself."

Jillian laughed and stepped to the bureau and picked up the bouquet. "These pretty posies are for Lady Anna?"

Benjamin took the question as rhetorical and said, "What are your plans for the afternoon?"

"I am going shopping on Bond Street with our mamas," Jillian said. She glanced at the gilded brass clock on the mantel and put down the bouquet. "I had better step lively. Lady Whitlock fusses when I keep them waiting."

She turned back to face Benjamin when she reached the doorway. "You will remember not to hover over me at the Murchisons' soirée this evening, won't you, Ben?"

"You must take me for the veriest slow-top, Jillian. I have already promised you a dozen times in the last few days. I plan to keep my word," he said. "Now, close the door."

Satisfied, she did.

* * *

"Jilly," her mother called as she passed by Delia's bed-chamber. Jillian went back and walked through the open door into the bedroom, where Lady Whitlock stood behind Delia, who sat on the vanity bench, tying the ribbons on a gray bonnet trimmed in navy silk.

"Oh dear, I see you are ready to leave," Jillian said to the ladies, who were both dressed for the street. "I am sorry to keep you waiting, but Benjamin asked me to arrange his neckcloth for him."

A romantically agreeable picture formed in Moira's mind. She glanced at Delia. Such intimacy between their children boded well for their hopes for an early engagement between Jillian and Benjamin.

But to Moira's chagrin dear Delia seemed to have missed the import of Jillian's revelation.

"Shouldn't his valet be doing it?" she was saying to Jillian.

"Alvin is rather unskilled when it comes to cravats, but he was off running another errand. In any case, I did a beautiful job." She smiled smugly. "Ben was most anxious to look his best."

Moira took this in and wondered if she had jumped to a hasty conclusion concerning the neckcloths. So, Benjamin was being rather particular about his appearance. Why?

Jillian heard the butler on the stairs. "Barkley is coming. The carriage must be here. I must fetch my things."

She passed the butler as she left the room.

Moira let Barkley announce that the hired town carriage was at the front door before she asked him, "Do you know Mr. Whitlock's plans for this afternoon?"

Barkley believed that any butler worth his salt should know the whereabouts of every member of his household. Any lapse would be a dereliction of his duties.

"Mr. Whitlock has ordered the barouche to carry him

to the Countess of Herridge's. She receives visitors today," he said, his tone authoritative.

Moira was flabbergasted. "The Countess of Herridge's? Are you quite certain?"

Barkley looked down his rather long nose at her. He knew his duty. "Quite certain, madam. Alvin, Mr. Whitlock's valet, was sent to purchase a bouquet for the Lady Anna, the countess's youngest daughter."

Here Barkley had improvised. Alvin had reported that Mr. Whitlock wanted an arrangement suitable for a young lady. The resourceful butler had put two and two together and thought his assumption nicely rounded out his report.

Moira began to realize that Benjamin had been keeping secrets from her. It just wouldn't do. Acting quickly, she said, "Barkley, take a message to Mr. Whitlock. Say that I, too, wish to call on Lady Herridge and will accompany him to her house this afternoon instead of going to Bond Street with Lady Blair and Miss Blair."

Delia waited until Barkley left, and then she spoke candidly. "I had no notion that you knew the Countess of Herridge, Moira."

Moira pulled a wry face. "In truth, I have not seen the countess since our grass days when she was Cecily Tyler. Our paths never crossed again. She has never been at any of the few London entertainments you and I have attended over the years."

Delia tucked a gaily embroidered handkerchief into her fancy reticule and left the vanity. "I know it must be a shock to learn that Benjamin may have lost his heart to the countess's daughter."

Moira put a gloved hand on the sleeve of her friend's navy pelisse. "Don't even think that he has, Delia. Remember, I said from the start that managing successfully depends on seizing opportunities. This is one. Whatever happens, we must never despair. If we think positively and help Jillian and Benjamin to see the light, they, themselves, will come to the realization that they belong together."

Moira was so calm and in control that Delia had to believe her.

Chapter 3

Moira was far from calm and in control as the driver of the black-hooded barouche navigated the busy London streets. She was taking a risk. The former Cecily Tyler may not remember her and might take her for an encroaching mushroom who had fabricated a long-ago acquaintance to gain entry into her elite circle.

But she had to take a chance. Cecily had been a diamond of the first water. If Lady Anna was half as beautiful as her mother had been, Benjamin could lose his head and do something foolish before he realized that it was Jillian he loved.

In her nervous state, Moira knew she was talking too much, commenting on the passing scene as a city guide would do. She suspected from his curt responses that Benjamin was irritated with her for imposing herself on him.

There was that in Benjamin's attitude, but he really blamed Jillian. She must have let slip that he was calling on the Countess of Herridge's daughter. His mother recognized the name and decided to renew a friendship from donkey years ago.

He could hardly criticize Moira for wanting to see her old friend, although it baffled him. Moira Whitlock was not someone who was enamored of elevated society. Why Lady Herridge and why now?

The carriage turned into the drive leading up to the gleaming white stucco mansion.

"What a splendid house," Moira said, impressed.

Benjamin added his own acclamations to his mother's as the driver stopped the barouche at the marble steps of the porte cochere.

Moira was helped from the vehicle by a footman in a purple livery, trimmed in yards of gold braid.

Benjamin got down, carrying Lady Anna's bouquet in one hand, and offered his mother his free arm.

Inside he presented their gilt-edged calling cards to the butler, who escorted them to the drawing room where the countess was receiving her callers, ensconced like royalty on a high-backed red velvet chair.

Moira felt her knees go weak. The countess was nearly as beautiful as she had been when she was the reigning beauty during their Season some twenty-six years ago.

Lady Herridge glanced at the cards the butler handed her and said, "Mr. Whitlock, Lady Whitlock, how good of you to call."

Benjamin held up the flowers. "For Lady Anna," he said, his color rising.

"You will find her on the terrace," the countess said in a kind voice and turned to Moira.

"Pray do sit down, Lady Whitlock." Moira took the chair vacated moments earlier by a woman in a multicolored turban.

Moira watched Benjamin stride across the crowded room, wishing she had gone with him. Her heart was beating too fast. For a moment, she was certain that Lady Herridge did not remember her, but the countess smiled and said, "It has been ages since last we met during our debuts."

"I thought you would not remember me, my lady," Moira blurted out in her nervousness.

"Call me Cecily, Moira. Of course, I remember you." She laughed. "You were the tallest of us girls that Season."

Moira laughed, too. The two women fell into some comfortable chitchat until Cecily said, "Mr. Whitlock wrote to Anna after meeting her only once, begging to be allowed to call on her when next he came to the City."

Despite being caught by surprise, for she knew nothing of the letter, Moira kept her countenance. "Young people can be so impulsive," she said as though she and Cecily shared a secret.

Cecily agreed, then said, "I was impressed with Mr. Whitlock's restraint and propriety. Too many of Anna's admirers fill their billets-doux with encomiums to her lips and eyes and such foolishness."

Moira had mixed feelings. Motherly pride in a son with uncommon sense warred with a desire to crush any notions Lady Herridge had of an alliance between Benjamin and her daughter.

But Cecily's next words gave Moira hope that she and the countess might not be working at cross-purposes.

"Both of my older daughters made brilliant marriages, but live in the far North. The earl and I seldom see them. We want Anna to marry a gentleman who will be content to reside in London. But . . ." She shrugged a little. "Girls today have minds of their own.

It would have been impertinent for Moira to counter that Benjamin would never move to the City. She would be giving the impression that Benjamin was ready to propose to Lady Anna. She could not speak for her son. But she did know that Benjamin loved the country. He was active in running their estate, did all of the paperwork, and had assumed many of Sir Edmund's managerial duties. Yet, alas, boys also had minds of their own.

* * *

After a while Moira surrendered her place to another visitor and found her way to the terrace, where Lady Anna, a vision in pale pink, sat beside Benjamin, their garden chairs close together.

Benjamin seated his mother and made her known to Lady Anna. Moira could see why her son gazed at the beauty as if she were the sun and the moon rolled into one. The child was beautiful, her skin, satin smooth, her blond hair, perfect, her blue eyes, lovely. She said little, but smiled a lot, quite sweetly.

Instinctively Moira knew that Lady Anna was totally wrong for Benjamin. And it had nothing to do with Jillian. She had no conversation. He would be bored silly with the girl within a week of marrying her.

Suffused with the confidence that she had a right to nip this romance in the bud for Benjamin's good, Moira spun a bit of mischief.

"I really must tell you about Jillian Blair," she said as though she had just thought of something amusing to enliven their talk.

The girl with the face of an angel asked innocently, "Who is Jillian Blair?"

"It is such a sweet tale," Moira said, avoiding her son's eyes, knowing she was not going to like what she saw there. "Benjamin rescued Jillian from drowning when they were children. Jillian's nursemaid convinced him that since he saved her life, he must protect Jillian forever. He took the assignment seriously and has looked after Jillian ever since. Jillian Blair, my dear Lady Anna, is Benjamin's best friend."

"Now, Mama," Benjamin said, plainly disturbed, but he got no further.

Moira put up her hand and laughed. "It is all right, dear. I shan't go into detail about how you taught Jillian to be a bruising rider and to drive a curricle to the inch."

Lady Anna blinked. "Oh, my," she said. "Your best friend is a lady, Mr. Whitlock?"

Hurriedly, Benjamin got to his feet, his face a black cloud. "Why don't I call for the barouche to be brought around to take you home, Mama? Lord Collingswood goes my way. I shall beg a ride from him."

Benjamin appeared ready to strangle her. Accepting the inevitable, Moira decided not to demur. "Stay and visit with Lady Anna," she said. "I can find my way out." She smiled, but Lady Anna looked bewildered, and her son scowled.

Moira knew she shouldn't, but she could not resist saying, "Jillian made fine work of your neckcloth, Benjamin. No one would suspect she acted as your valet today. Such a sweet, helpful girl."

Benjamin gritted his teeth. His mother made her way to the terrace doors, nodding to several people as she passed before she vanished into the house. Why bring up that embarrassing story about him and Jillian? It didn't make any sense at all. His mother seemed to think the tale was cute, but it had put both him and Jillian in a bad light.

Although he had been caught off balance, Benjamin recovered quickly. "Let's take a turn around the garden, my lady," he said. "I assure you matters are not as improper as you might suppose from my mother's indiscreet disclosures."

Lady Anna rose, linked her arm through his, and said, "But a female tied your neckcloth."

Benjamin sighed at the rebuke.

"The bedroom door was left open," he said lamely as though that explained everything.

Lady Anna tittered nervously. "You have a very unusual household, Mr. Whitlock. I have never been in any gentleman's private rooms, not even my father's."

"I know on the surface it sounds scandalous, Lady Anna, but I assure you nothing is amiss where Jillian is concerned. The Whitlock and Blair estates march together, and our families have always been joined somehow. I have run tame at Blair Hall forever, and Miss Blair has run tame at Whitlock House."

"I see," Lady Anna said, a lift in her temperament. "Miss Blair is like an adopted sister to you, then." She seemed pleased with her deduction.

Benjamin had never thought of Jillian as a sister. She was more, much more, a beloved friend. But he let Lady Anna's conjecture pass.

The beauty thanked Benjamin for the flowers, which she had turned over earlier to a footman to be taken to her bedroom for display.

"Please see me inside, Mr. Whitlock," she said. She tapped the sleeve of his blue coat with her translucent fan in a flirtatious gesture. "I fear, sir, you have caused me to neglect my other callers." But her smile was warm and soft.

Benjamin's brown eyes, too, grew tender. "I relinquish your company with great reluctance," he said gallantly, content that he had undone the potential harm of his mother's inexplicable blathering.

Chapter 4

Jillian expected at least a mild scold from Lady Whitlock when she climbed into the leased carriage. But her mother was the sole occupant of the town coach.

Her anxiety lifting, she said "I thought I was late, but I see that Lady Whitlock is not here yet."

"Moira has changed her plans," Lady Blair said, volunteering no more information. "What held you up, dear?"

She turned sideways to face her daughter as the coachman drove the vehicle into the city traffic and rolled toward Bond Street.

Jillian looked down at the placket of her nut brown pelisse. "A button came loose and Tillie was all thumbs in sewing it back on."

She waited for her mother to start complaining about the staff, which Deilia did.

"It was a mistake not to bring our own people," she said. Jillian smiled at the familiar lament. She would not waste her breath going down that road again, defending her father's decision. Most of their competent staff were needed at home. Why pay double salaries when the house came with servants?

At least, her mother was pleased with the hired vehicles. The town coach and the barouche were well maintained and comfortable.

Jillian found it strange that her mother had not explained Lady Whitlock's sudden change of heart. Lady Whitlock had been the one who had been going on and on about the fine stores on Bond Street.

"Has Lady Whitlock developed a headache?" Jillian asked, fishing. "She is not going to miss the Murchisons' soirée this evening?" The soirée was the first important party to which they had all been invited.

"No, dear, Moira is fine," Delia said. "She has gone to call on Lady Herridge, an old acquaintance of hers."

"But Benjamin has spoken for the barouche," Jillian said. She immediately realized she had given away more than she had intended. Her mother would guess that she and Benjamin had discussed his destination.

"Yes," Delia said, not surprised that Benjamin had told Jillian about Lady Anna. The two had no secrets from each other. "How fortunate for Moira that she was able to get a ride with Benjamin to the Herridges'."

Just then the coach pulled up to the curb in front of the hat shop that Delia patronized, leaving Jillian with unanswered questions.

Inside the milliner's, the proprietress welcomed Delia warmly, asked about Lady Whitlock's health, was assured by Delia that she was not indisposed, and would be visiting the shop soon.

"I would like to see what you have in chip straw bonnets for both me and Miss Blair," Delia told her and was turned over to a favorite female clerk of Delia's who had served her on previous visits.

Jillian settled on the second bonnet she tried on, a yellow straw decorated with artificial daisies, but Delia could not make up her mind. She sat at a small table, looking glass in hand, rejecting hat after hat which the accommodating clerk showed her.

Besides the latest bonnets, the shop sold French

gloves and Belgium lace, colored ribbons, and all sorts of fancy fripperies to trim hats.

Jillian sorted through a box of faux jeweled hatpins. She could not help but conclude that Lady Whitlock's sudden desire to renew her acquaintance with the Countess of Herridge on the very day that Benjamin was calling on Lady Anna was not a mere coincidence. The only sensible reason that came to mind was that Lady Whitlock had learned that Benjamin was taking flowers to Lady Anna, a sign of more than a passing interest in the young lady, and wanted to get a look at a perspective daughter-in-law.

Jillian picked out an emerald, a pearl, and a ruby hatpin to buy and took her purchases to the counter. She smiled when she saw that her mama had bought the very first hat that she had tried on, a beige straw.

Delia felt a little foolish when she intercepted Jillian's smile. "I know; I know. I have already thanked Julia for being so patient."

Delia settled the bill and said to the clerk, "Please have the packages sent over this afternoon," and handed her a card with their London address.

Once back on the sidewalk, the ladies walked toward the cross street where the coachman had told Delia he would park.

Delia stopped at several of the windows of the smart shops to look at the German and Swiss clocks, fine jewelry, Sheffield cutlery, and other wonderful products made by skilled English and continental craftsmen.

Jillian's thoughts kept returning to the saga of Benjamin and his mother. She had figured out that Lady Whitlock must have learned that Benjamin was going to the Herridges from Bradley, who like all good butlers knew precisely where every one of his household was at any given time.

"I did not know that Lady Whitlock was acquainted with the Countess of Herridge," she said. Delia never answered, for at that moment an officious demand came from among the window-shopping pedestrians.

"Lady Blair, a word with you!"

A very tall, gaunt man of Delia's generation, dressed in deepest black stepped from the crowd and swaggered toward them.

Delia's heart lurched into her throat. *The Mad Baron.* The appellation sprang to her mind. What could he want with her? She had seen him perhaps twice, but had never exchanged a single word with him.

He navigated to her side. A chill went through Delia when she saw that his beady black eyes were on Jillian not on her. His expression was insolent as he looked her daughter up and down through his quizzing glass.

Delia knew his reputation for favoring nubile females. Had she been able to make her stiff limbs move beneath her long navy skirts, she would have pushed Jillian behind her. But she was frozen with fear.

"A word with me?" she asked, her voice shaky.

He never took his eyes from Jillian, but said harshly, "Did I not say as much? Make me known to your daughter, madam."

Delia thought she would faint. She had stepped into a nightmare. The Baron Lord Hoxbury was a lunatic. Good Lord, what was he doing now? Her eyes got big.

The baron pointed his gold-headed cane toward Jillian. "The chit looks healthy; cheeks kissed by the country sun. None of that pale, white countenance favored by society."

Delia did not know what to make of his rudeness or how to counter it. His familiarity was insulting.

He turned on Delia and shook his cane in her face. She cringed.

"Her name, woman!" he shouted. Passersby stared and gave him a wide berth.

Delia's heart was beating fiercely, but she found her voice and said, "My daughter Miss Jillian Blair. Jillian, Lord Hoxbury."

Lord Hoxbury made a leg in the old-fashioned manner; Jillian bobbed a curtsy.

"Now that was not so difficult, was it," he said, his baritone smarmy. "You may go on your way. I am done with you."

Delia snatched Jillian's hand and hurried down the sidewalk, never stopping until she came to the cross street, where their carriage was the first in a line of vehicles that stretched for blocks.

Delia sat back against the squabs, fanning herself with a handkerchief while she recovered her spinning senses.

Jillian was the first to speak. "Lud, Mama, who is that man and what did he want?"

"He is a raving lunatic, and I was just coerced into making you known to him," she wailed. "The last thing I should have done. I gave him the license to approach you with impunity at any social affair."

Jillian could not fault her gentle mother. She could hear in Delia's voice that she was ashamed that she had not stood up to the bully. But Jillian had seen that the odious man had taken her mother by surprise and overwhelmed her. Heavens, he had threatened to strike her down with his cane.

"Don't rake yourself over the coals, Mama. You are blameless," Jillian said, squeezing her hand.

But as Delia regained her composure, she knew she had to make Jillian understand just how dangerous the baron was.

The baron's first wife had been sixteen when he married her and he, already, was of an advanced age. The girl had died of a wasting disease. His second wife, who had been little more than a child herself, had died two years ago in chidbirth.

Delia suspected the baron's motive for gaining the introduction to Jillian was that he was thinking of marrying again and was looking for a third young wife. She and Arthur would never permit Lord Hoxbury to court Jillian, but she must be warned to have nothing to do with him.

Delia grasped her daughter's hand and looked into her green eyes. "Listen, my dear," she said. "Lord Hoxbury is deranged. He is exceedingly wealthy and carries a title which goes back to good Queen Bess's reign. Unfortunately, he is tolerated in some social circles because of his position in the aristocracy. You must promise me that you will avoid him."

"King George is locked up for his madness," Jillian said. "Why isn't Lord Hoxbury?"

Delia shrugged. "I can't answer that. It is one of the vagaries of the *ton*. Promise, Jilly."

"Of course," Jillian said. "He positively scares me."

Chapter 5

"You look nice, Jillian," Benjamin said, taking the green and gold shawl from her hand and draping it over her pretty shoulders.

In fact, he had to admit, she looked stunning in a jade silk gown that made her eyes radiate like green pools. Her hair shone like polished copper in the light from the hall chandelier. But he was still a little cross that she had not kept her word and had revealed his interest in Lady Anna to his mother.

"The lavish use of white beading on the skirt is a clever touch."

Jillian rolled her eyes at the meager praise. Something was bothering Benjamin. *Lavish use of white beading, indeed! How perfectly lame.*

Moira and Delia waited by the door in their evening wraps to be escorted to the coach which would take them to the Murchisons' soirée. "Really, Benjamin, such faint praise does not do Jillian justice. She looks like a princess," Moira chided.

She wanted to shake her son. He was miffed at her for interfering in his tête-à tête with Lady Anna, she was sure. But he shouldn't be taking out his pique on Jillian. If he would have brought up the incident, she would have apologized, although she was not really sorry, but he did not have to know that.

In the town coach Benjamin stared from the window as if there were something to see in the dark night other than flickering lights. Jillian sat beside him. Only recently had she come to see him as a strikingly handsome man. He looked fine in his new midnight blue evening coat and black satin breeches. She would tell him later when he came out of his sulks. For now she listened to Lady Whitlock and her mother going over a list of old friends who had been invited tonight. While smaller than a ball, the soirée would number close to a hundred.

Benjamin was still silent when the carriage pulled up to the Murchisons' splendid house and stopped. Moira leaned over and touched Benjamin's knee.

"Do not forget to take Jillian into the first set, Benjamin. You are considered her official escort tonight, you know."

Her son gave a theatrical sigh. "I know my duty, Mama. I am not a callow youth who needs instructions on how to go on in society."

All three ladies laughed.

"In high form tonight, ladies?" he said wryly. "Shall we disembark?" He released the inside latch to allow the Murchisons' footman to open the carriage door from the outside.

Even Benjamin's cool composure could not curb Jillian's happiness. She fairly bubbled as she took in the magnificence around her. The opulent room was peopled with elegantly garbed ladies and gentlemen in silks, brocades, satins, and swaths and swaths of the finest lace. Aristocratic throats, wrists, and ears blazed and twinkled with diamonds, rubies, emeralds, and pearls under the light from the myriad chandeliers.

Benjamin had been watching three gentlemen who

were at the far end of the ballroom where a five-piece orchestra played light opera music. The young dandies had been staring at Jillian and obviously commenting on the new face in the crowd behind their gloved hands.

Jillian touched Benjamin's arm with her gold fan, regaining his attention. Wide-eyed she admired the hundreds of fresh flowers in every imaginable color and hue. "Oh, Ben, the Murchisons' gardener must have stripped every single flower bed clean to fill the room."

Benjamin did not want to laugh, but he could not help it.

"Ninny," he said, aware she had deliberatedly goaded him. "More likely, a footman bought out the contents of all the carts in the local flower market early this morning. But you know it."

She grinned. "Of course, but now I have shaken you out of your doldrums. Why have you been starched up all evening? You might as well tell me, you know, for I do not have the least notion."

She looked so adorable that suddenly Benjamin's grudge ceased to exist. His eyes grew tender.

"Before I get into that," he said, "allow me to make amends for my earlier poor comportment. You are absolutely gorgeous tonight, Jilly. Fine as five pence and beyond."

Her expression became soft and dreamy for a moment before she said, "Thank you, Ben, but what put you in a bad mood?"

"I've been making a great dust over nothing," he said, truly contrite. "I did not like that you broke your promise to keep mum about me and Lady Anna."

"Not guilty, Ben," Jillian said. "The butler did it."

She chuckled. Benjamin grimaced. He had pouted like a badly behaved little boy. He should have known better. Jillian was true-blue. He should have guessed it was Bradley.

She was warmed by the apology he gave her and was as puzzled as he by Lady Whitlock's weird behavior when she met Lady Anna.

"You say she made much of our friendship?" she said, and when Benjamin repeated the cravat incident and their summer days when he came home from school and taught her to drive a chaise and ride like a man, she wondered if Lady Whitlock's purpose was to make Lady Anna jealous.

The thought was too silly to repeat to Benjamin. Lady Anna was beautiful, according to him. Why would she be jealous of a pixie with freckles and a mop of red hair?

"Finally, those three are making their move," Benjamin said, cutting off Jillian' s soul-searching. She followed his gaze to the fashionably dressed young men strolling toward them from where the orchestra was tuning up for the dancing.

Benjamin made the introductions. Lord Roderick Shelby was a good-looking gentleman, slightly above average in height with short dark hair.

"*Enchanté,*" he said, a twinkle in his fine brown eyes when he bent over Jillian's hand. She was immediately taken with him.

Mr. Robert Garfield was short and pudgy with hazel eyes while Sir George Pierce was of medium height with thinning blond hair.

To Benjamin's amazement Jillian, not only held her own in the social chitchat, but actually sparkled as if she had been in London society forever.

Other gentlemen came to be presented to her and sign her dance card before Lady Murchison signaled for the floor to be cleared for dancing.

Benjamin led Jillian to a favorable location on the

dance floor. She perused her dance card while she and Benjamin waited for the music to begin.

"See, I have but one space left," she said, a little excited.

Jillian had friends at home, mostly girls, but some boys whom she liked. Yet she would be with Benjamin for days and days without seeing anyone else. This newfound popularity was rather heady.

She looked up at Benjamin for his response, but he was staring over her head, his brown eyes bright and warm.

"Keep our place for a minute," he said and went to the side of a beautiful young woman, her blond curls and blue eyes the ideal of the *ton*.

This was Jillian's first glimpse of Lady Anna. Everything about her was perfection. No wonder Benjamin found her irresistible.

When he returned to her side, she said, "Lady Anna is truly lovely, Ben," and meant it. "I can understand why you are besotted."

"Not besotted, Jilly, just . . . interested," he hedged, but his eyes spoke differently.

Jillian would have argued, but just then the orchestra began a Mozart piece.

One advantage of the old-fashioned steps was that it was possible to carry on a conversation during the sedate music.

"Who are you standing up with next, Jilly," Benjamin asked.

"Mr. Garfield," she said and mentioned some of her other partners.

"I have you to thank for letting me get to Lady Anna before someone else petitioned her for the waltz," he said, sounding pleased with his coup.

Lord Roderick Shelby had written his name in for that popular dance on Jillian's card. She mentioned it to Benjamin and said, "He has a magnetic personality and a charming smile. Tell me more about him." She had been captivated by the gentleman on first sight, something which had never happened to her before.

Benjamin chuckled. "Handsome devil, isn't he? Rod's well liked in general, but he is sorely inept at gambling. No card sense at all."

"Really, Ben, that is hardly useful to me." Jillian rolled her eyes. "What about his family?"

Their clasped hands raised high, Benjamin took small steps around Jillian before he answered her.

"Lord Roderick's family is above reproach. He is the youngest of three sons. His brothers are established in life with lucrative estates and growing families. His father, though, suffers from a serious heart ailment."

Benjamin had broken his concentration during this discourse and missed some steps.

"Pay attention, Benjamin," Jillian scolded him, "or we will look like country dimwits."

"Your fault for distracting me," he countered unchivalrously, but cut his talk to keep from making a cake of himself on the dance floor.

Mr. Garfield was describing to Jillian a sporty curricle he intended buying when he was rudely pushed aside by a long, dark specter.

"I say," he protested, but his mouth snapped shut, cutting off any further objections. He stepped back and stared.

To her horror, Jillian saw the brash culprit was Lord Hoxbury, the so-called Mad Baron.

"I thought I would find you here tonight, Miss Blair," he said in the venomous voice she remembered from their Bond Street encounter. He bent toward her. "I shall claim this set."

Mr. Garfield looked petrified and had apparently lost his voice. Jillian lifted her chin in false bravado.

"This dance is already promised to Mr. Garfield, my lord," she said, determined not to be browbeaten.

He snorted. "Give me your dance card." The large hand he held out was ominous in a black glove.

Jillian lied. "My card is filled," she claimed.

"Really?" he sneered. "Show me."

Praying that he would not notice the single blank line, Jillian gave him the card and pencil. But she was not to be so fortunate.

He scribbled his name and handed the card back to her. "Lie to me again at your own peril, chit," he warned and walked off.

She did not have time to think too long about the threat, for Mr. Garfield found his voice.

"I could not have reasoned with Lord Hoxbury, Miss Blair. He is touched in the head, you know. The baron is rumored to have killed any number of men for crossing him over the smallest imagined slight. I did not dare challenge him."

Mr. Garfield was not even ashamed. Jillian bristled. She did not even try to disguise her disgust. Benjamin would not have quaked in his boots while a bounder insulted his dancing partner. Mr. Garfield's cowardice made mice feet of any intentions she might have had to consider him a friend.

Later in the evening, on the other side of the ballroom, Benjamin was having his own perturbations.

"Anna is overheated from the reel, Mr. Whitlock," Lady Herridge maintained. "I insist that she sit out the waltz. However, you may join her if you wish."

Seizing on the half a loaf, Benjamin took the empty

chair beside the beauty. If he couldn't hold her in his arms, he could at least ply her mind for her views on topics of current interest. She smiled and nodded, but he found himself filling in with his own observations since she seemed to have none of her own.

Benjamin was a man who thrived on give-and-take in conversations, not one who was in love with the sound of his own voice. He could always count on Jillian for a reasoned argument and strong opinions.

Lady Anna was content to let Benjamin talk. He finally decided she was so beautiful that it did not matter. It was reward enough to be allowed to gaze at the perfection of her face while the strains of a sweet, lilting waltz played romantically in the background.

Peripherally, he saw Jillian float by in Rod Shelby's arms, enjoying herself, just when Lady Anna was showing Benjamin her dance card. She found some bit of gossip to impart about each of her admirers until the waltz ended.

But through some fortuitous oversight she had not been promised to anyone for the next dance. It was not quite the thing to ask a young lady for two dances in a row. Benjamin decided to throw caution to the winds and do just that when Lady Blair plunged through a stream of people and stopped in front of him.

Benjamin leapt to his feet. "What is it, ma'am?" he asked anxiously, for she seemed beside herself.

"Benjamin, your mama and I require your immediate assistance," Delia cried, not even apologizing for interrupting his tête-a-tête with Lady Anna.

"Has something happened?" Benjamin asked, but she was abrupt and flustered.

"Come with me, please! Please!" she pleaded. She whirled around and fairly flew across the ballroom floor on her tiny slippered feet.

There was nothing for Benjamin to do but to make a hasty pardon to Lady Anna and follow Lady Blair.

Jillian sat beside Moira, her small oval face a thundercloud.

"Mama and Lady Whitlock are ripping up at me over something I could not help," she said to Benjamin, who suspected that she had committed some minor social impropriety that had the mamas upset.

Jillian looked defiant.

"What did you do?" he asked, acting on his assumption.

"Nothing," she said. "Lady Whitlock perused my card and saw that Lord Hoxbury had written in his name for a dance."

"Lord Hoxbury?" Benjamin said, puzzled. "The insane fellow?"

Lady Blair grasped that Benjamin was in the dark about Lord Hoxbury's forced introduction to Jillian on Bond Street. She explained and said, "But I warned Jilly not to encourage him."

"Mama, I did not. He behaved as odiously as he did when he stopped us on the street. Would you have rather I caused a scene? The Murchisons would never have forgiven me." Lady Whitlock looked determined. "We shall send the despicable creature away with a flea in his ear when he comes to claim Jilly."

"No, Mama," Benjamin said, shaking his head. "Refusing to honor Lord Hoxbury's request could push him into doing something extreme that would embarrass the Murchisons. Let me see your dance card," he said, holding out his hand to Jillian. She gave it to him. He looked over the names.

"Lord Hoxbury is signed up for a reel where one

switches partners a lot. You will be separated from him most of the time, Jilly. It shouldn't be too bad."

"I am glad it's not a waltz," she said, giggling. He smiled. "Good girl." Lord and Lady Murchison did not deserve to have their soirée turned into a brawl.

The mamas were not amused. Lady Whitlock demanded of her son, "Benjamin you are to be there at the conclusion of the dance to intercept Jillian. I do not trust Lord Hoxbury to bring her to Delia and me."

Benjamin promised.

Sir George Pierce came to take Jillian to the next dance, a quadrille, and Benjamin went to ask Lady Anna to join a square with him. But he was too late. She was already standing up with a young aristocrat of the dandy set.

Benjamin leaned against a Grecian column and watched them. Even without hearing the words that passed between them, he could see that the fellow was fawning over her with the exaggerated compliments and pretty lies that passed for witty conversation in the *ton* and which Benjamin abhorred. His heart sank to his toes. If Lady Anna's coquettish smiles were any indication, she was not only loving it, but was encouraging the fop.

Chapter 6

Moira entered the sunny breakfast parlor at ten o'clock to find Delia already there eating her breakfast. After wishing her friend a good morning, Moira went to the sideboard, filled a plate with coddled eggs and Thames salmon, pulled out a chair, and sat down beside Delia.

She poured coffee into a china cup from the pot on the table and added cream and sugar.

"Delia, after last night we need to talk," she said as she stirred her coffee. "It is apparent that Jillian is showing a partiality to Lord Roderick, and, sad to say, Benjamin still favors Lady Anna."

Delia looked thoughtful as she buttered a slice of toast. "Do you think the children are just following their hearts. Could we be wrong?"

"Wrong?" Moira said, a picture of indignation. "How could we be wrong? Would not Jillian's life be bleak without Benjamin in it? Wouldn't Benjamin be miserable if he had to cut his ties to Jillian?"

Delia did not cower under Moira's umbrage. She suggested quite calmly, "Perhaps Benjamin believes that he can maintain his friendship with Jillian even while wed to someone else, and Jillian might think it will be possible after she marries to remain close to Benjamin."

Moira gave an unladylike snort. "Really, Delia. No self-repecting wife would tolerate a husband who has another woman as his closest friend or vice versa. Such a relationship smacks too much of having a mistress or of being one."

"Yes, I see your point," Delia said and captured a scrap of fried egg on her gold-rimmed plate with a silver fork. "I would be frightfully suspicious if Arthur had a confidential alliance with another female."

"Any sensible woman would be," Moira said, moderating her tone. She sipped her coffee and looked over the rim of her cup at her friend.

As the silence between them stretched out, she warned, "If we begin to have doubts, Delia, all will be lost. Jillian and Benjamin are meant to be together."

Delia could not refute the assertion. "True," she said after a brief hesitation.

Moira bit into a crescent roll she had broken apart and smeared with raspberry jam. She chewed slowly and when she had swallowed the last delicious morsel of the freshly baked roll, she chuckled softly.

"What?" Delia asked, smiling faintly in reaction to the merry sound.

"Benjamin was so comical when he paced up and down the perimeter of the ballroom last night, determined to intercept Jillian before Lord Hoxbury walked off the floor with her."

Delia felt her own laughter bubbling up. "Plainly Benjamin had no earthly notion where to wait for the baron and Jilly as the reel progressed. The dancers skipped down the line of the dance from one side of the room to the other like schools of fish in a pond, back and forth, back and forth."

"But you must give my son his due," Moira said. "He played the watchdog to perfection and was in exactly the right spot to foil Lord Hoxbury at the end of the set."

"Bravo!" Delia applauded Benjamin verbally.

"Bravo?" echoed from the doorway as the unwitting hero entered the room. "Is that a shout of approval, Lady Blair," Benjamin asked, facetiously, "or are you referring to a villain? The word has dual meanings, you know?"

Jillian came in right behind him and sat down across the table from the ladies with a cheery, "Good morning."

Benjamin peeked beneath the covered dishes on the sideboard and filled a plate for Jillian without asking her preference, and laid it on the table in front of her. She had breakfasted on scrambled eggs and toast every morning since she was ten.

"Hmm, a bravo is also a villain," Delia repeated as Benjamin went to get his own breakfast. "Interesting."

Moira laid her knife and fork across her plate and poured herself a second cup of coffee. "Quite a coincidence," she said. "We were just speaking of a consummate villain, one Lord Hoxbury."

Benjamin speared a deviled kidney from the fare on the sideboard and added it to the food on his already groaning plate and sat down beside Jillian.

"You can rest easy on that score, ladies," he said. "I hurried Jillian from the baron's side without a word. Our quick exit was as good as a cut direct."

Delia pushed away her plate and folded her hands in front of her on the table. "Still, I wish Jillian had never come to Lord Hoxbury's notice," she repined. "He is a dangerous man."

Benjamin suspected that the tales about the Mad Baron were overblown. Lord Hoxbury may carry a pistol, but he was not likely to brandish it in anyone's drawing room. The man probably thrived on the myth that he slayed his foes. No corpses attributed to him had ever been found, nor murders proved.

With more insight than Benjamin would have credited her with, Jillian said, "I know that Lord Hoxbury is an old roué from whom no young female is safe. My appeal to him is that I am new to society, but the baron will lose interest in me once he sees that I take him in dislike."

Moira remained unconvinced and said, "He belongs in Bedlam."

"Hear, hear," Delia agreed.

But Benjamin was tiring of the topic and his thoughts turned to Lady Anna. He had learned that she took the air in the park at eleven in her father's open carriage. If all went well, he might see her there. He prayed that the opportunity would present itself when he went riding this morning.

He ate with a good appetite, then set his napkin beside his plate. "Excuse me, ladies," he said. "I am off for a gallop in the park."

He was dressed for riding in a hunter green coat, beige breeches, and dark brown leather boots.

His long-legged stride got him to the door before Moira's, "Wait, Benjamin," stopped him.

"Yes, Mama?" His jaw tightened. It seemed lately his mother was involving him in her life far more than she ever had before.

Moira ignored her son's obvious impatience. "Take Jillian with you," she proposed. "She has had no exercise since we came to Town. A horseback ride would be beneficial for bringing some color back into her cheeks."

The idea of a ride in the park appealed to Jillian, not that she was pale, if anything her skin was more tanned and freckled than was fashionable. But she missed the outdoors.

She fingered the white collar of her long-sleeved red plaid dress. "I would have to change, and Ben is in a hurry."

"Nonsense," Moira declared with a wave of her hand. "He can wait the few minutes it will take you to get ready." Benjamin saw no escape. "Just don't dawdle, Jillian," he commanded. "I ordered a horse to be readied by ten-thirty. I don't want it kept standing."

Jillian left the breakfast table, deciding to wear her new wood rose riding habit. The small matching hat had a jaunty pink feather stuck in the brim. The thrill of wearing the fashionable togs bought to make a splash in London society still had not worn off. She had never had so many new clothes at one time.

"Meet me at the mews," Benjamin called after her as she moved to the bottom of the stairs. "I will have a horse saddled for you."

When Benjamin's footsteps completely faded down the hall, Delia's face crept up into a smile. "That was a dandy move, Moira," she said with admiration. "I envy your quick mind."

"You are too kind, Delia dear," Moira said, beaming. "I had an inkling that Benjamin might have learned that Lady Anna would be driving in the park this morning."

"I guessed your motive. Benjamin cannot make headway in the pursuit of Lady Anna with Jillian by his side."

"Exactly," Moira said, and the ladies giggled.

The park, one of many in London, was close by the leased house. As Jillian and Benjamin approached the gates on their horses, which were beautifully trained to behave in city traffic, she asked, "Can I give my horse her head once we enter the park?" She rode a brown mare called Magic.

She was bored with the sedate pace she had been forced to maintain on the busy street.

"Not likely," Benjamin said from atop, Tor, his dappled gray gelding. "This isn't the country, Jillian. Bruising riders are not welcome in the park, too many other horse-men and carriages about."

"At least the cool air is invigorating after the stale rooms," she reflected. "Whenever I open my bedroom window, Tillie slams it shut. She says I let the smoke in."

"We are accustomed to the clean country air. I doubt either of us could be happy living in London for long."

One of the really nice things about Benjamin, Jillian thought, was that her feelings so often matched his. She could fully appreciate why their parents traveled to London only occasionally and put up at Grillon's, the family hotel which catered to families that came to the city for short stays.

Benjamin's thoughts paralleled Jillian's. Even in his sophomoric teens, a month in London had been enough for him. He hated to admit it, but he suspected that as he put on more years, like his father he would find it tiresome to leave Whitlock House and his country estate at all.

The weather was pleasant. The trees were greening with young leaves, bushes were budding in reds and yellows, and the call of songbirds could be heard over the distant city noises.

Jillian and Benjamin rode far into the park beneath the speckled sunlight coming from above through the branches of the lindens planted near the curbs.

Occasionally, carriages, coming and going, passed them. Benjamin examined the occupants of each vehicle. He had all but despaired of seeing Lady Anna when the Earl of Herridge's imported landau came into view traveling toward them. He brought it to Jillian's attention and said, "I want a word with Lady Anna," and rode across the road, positioning himself to be seen.

To his delight, he saw Lady Anna lean forward in her seat and speak to her driver, who brought the landau to a stop where Benjamin waited.

Removing his tall hat, he smiled at her. Beside her sat a dour-faced guardian dragon of a chaperon.

"May I present Miss Forsham, my companion," the beauty said in her musical voice. "Mr. Whitlock, Miss Forsham."

Benjamin acknowledged the middle-aged woman with a bob of his head and courteously repeated her name, adding, "Your servant."

He took a lesson from the fop at the soirée and admired Lady Anna's purple bonnet and the fair visage beneath it. She smiled coquettishly as she had at her admirer the previous night.

"You are such a flatterer, Mr. Whitlock," she said, but his practiced flirtation seemed to please her far more than his sensible conversation ever had.

But, alas, prolonged contact was not to be permitted, for Miss Forsham quickly intervened.

"We must go on, Lady Anna," she said, and not waiting for a reply, ordered their driver to spring the horses, and the carriage lurched forward, leaving Benjamin behind.

With a sigh, he replaced his hat on his head and rode across the road to where he had left Jillian. But she was nowhere in sight.

Benjamin was annoyed, even though he knew that she could not have gone far. He kicked Tor into motion. He had warned her about the dangers of a big city. Dandy knaves were known to accost young ladies who dared to venture forth alone and blister them with risque remarks.

By the time he came across Jillian sitting on Magic in one of the paved pull-overs where carriages could safely park and riders could visit with pedestrians who strolled by on the walks, he was in a fret. His mood was not improved when he found her talking and laughing with Lord Roderick Shelby and Sir George Pierce, who were on foot.

Jillian turned slightly in the saddle and said, "Here is Benjamin at last."

Benjamin brought Tor to a standstill beside Magic, Jillian's smile lost on him. "Dash it all, Jilly. Why did you take off like that?"

Jillian' s smile slipped a little. "I thought you wanted to speak with, ah, the lady, privately. I found this nearby pullover where I could wait for you safely without hovering."

Before Benjamin could say more, Lord Roderick interceded on Jillian's behalf. "Miss Blair was here when George and I came walking by. She told us you'd been delayed, Ben. She was in good hands with us."

It was his job to protect Jillian, not Rod's, but he had abandoned Jillian to gain Lady Anna's favor. Benjamin could not fault Rod, nor Jilly for that matter. He was to blame.

"No harm done," he said, feeling too guilty to scold. "Let's go home, Jilly."

She was perfectly amenable to his suggestion, but Rod had his hand on her saddle and was looking up at her. "If Lady Blair is receiving this afternoon, Miss Blair, I would like to call on you," he said.

"She is," Jillian told the charming young man. "My mama and Lady Whitlock will take callers from three to four o'clock."

Not to be outdone, Sir George Pierce said, "I shall be there as well, dear Miss Blair."

The smile she gave the dandy with the thinning hair was as sunny as the one she gave the young lord whom she favored. "I shall look forward to seeing you both," she said and joined Benjamin waiting for her in the road.

Low hedges bordered the path that Jillian and Benjamin took from the mews to the house.

"She was guarded by a chaperone called Miss Forsham, but I plan to see her again this afternoon," he said about his brief meeting with Lady Anna.

"Lady Whitlock expects you to be available to greet visitors at three," Jillian reminded him.

He made a bemoaning moue. "There's the rub," he contended. "The Countess of Herridge's at-home is at the same hour as ours. My mama will assume that I have fallen in with her wishes, so I plan to slip out of the house unnoticed."

"Not a very nice trick to play on your mama, Ben," she said, but her voice lacked the proper force of indignation for a serious condemnation. "Your secret is safe with me."

"I never doubted it, my dear," he said and brushed past her to open the side door beside a forsythia bush which bloomed in yellow profusion.

Jillian stopped him, her hand on his forearm.

"Ben, do you think freckles are awful?"

Benjamin scowled. "Where did you get that idea?"

"Tillie said that the gentlemen of the *ton* avoid young ladies with freckles. She has a recipe which she swears will get rid of mine."

"What sort of a recipe?"

"Well, one immerses grated horseradish in buttermilk and spreads the concoction on the spots."

"Horseradish?" Benjamin scoffed. "Lud, Jilly. Use your head! Your face will erupt in red blotches. How can you believe that twit?"

"Oh, I know it's tomfoolery, but I thought you might have heard of a formula that really works."

He saw that she was serious. His eyes dwelled appreciatively on her pretty face. He ran his fingertip across her pert little nose and smiled down at her. "I love your freckles, Jilly. I would truly miss them."

Jillian slapped his hand aside. "Don't fun with me, Ben." She turned from him and put her hand on the door latch.

Benjamin covered her hand with his.

"Listen to me. You have been attracting some of the worthiest gentlemen of the *ton*. None of them give a fig about a few freckles when a girl is as pretty as you are," he said.

Jillian saw the truth in his eyes. Benjamin really believed that she was pretty. She felt his words in her heart and never wondered why she cared more about his opinion than anyone else's, for it had always been so.

Chapter 7

By a quarter to three the drawing room of the leased house resembled a well-stocked florist shop. Jillian counted the bouquets sent to her and began to believe that Benjamin was right. She had acquired quite a few admirers.

For a second she buried her nose in the basket of fragrant red roses that Lord Roderick Shelby had sent her, lifted her head, sighed, and let her mind drift to last night's soirée. She had danced with the charming young lord twice and had had a witty and scintillating conversation with him when he invited her to take refreshments at a table for two while the musicians took a respite.

Jillian felt a small stirring of excitement somewhere in the pit of her stomach. Lord Roderick said he would call today, which meant she would see him sometime during the next hour. Though she cautioned herself not to rush into love, she could not help feeling that Lord Roderick just might be the gentleman to capture her heart.

Delia watched her daughter, lovely in a China blue silk dress, draw in the scent of Lord Roderick's roses, a sure sign that she was bemused by the young man. Delia frowned. Lord Roderick was well enough, but he wasn't Benjamin.

Moira sat beside her in a cane-seated chair like her own, waiting for the afternoon callers and gnashing her teeth over Benjamin's latest offenses. He had had the temerity to slip away to see Lady Anna against her wishes. There was more.

Moira swept the flower-bedecked room with an imperial hand. "I drew his attention to all these vivid blooms, believing Jillian's popularity would be a powerful motivator to make him jealous. 'Jilly, will soon be another man's wife,' I said."

Delia raised a blank countenance. "And?"

"And, the provoking creature had the audacity to say, 'I thought that was the whole point of this social exercise.'"

Delia almost said that it was the truth, which it was, but was saved from committing the heresy, and thus drawing Moira's ire, when the voices of visitors arriving came from the hall as the mantel clock struck three.

Jillian glanced toward the hall whenever someone new arrived while she conversed with Sir George Pierce and Mr. Garfield. Her vigil ended when Lord Roderick walked in the door, saw her, broke into an endearing grin, and came to her side.

She glowed when he looked at her with admiration and said, "You are a feast for the eyes, my dear Miss Blair," and lifted her hand to his lips.

To their mutual gratification, Sir George and Mr. Garfield stuck to protocol and left, for their minutes earmarked for a social call had expired.

The drawing room became crowded and Jillian and Lord Roderick found themselves squeezed into a corner. A big man bumped into Lord Roderick and knocked him against an enormous Japanese floor vase. The precious antique teetered, but the young lord got a handhold in the mouth of the vessel and righted it before it could fall to the rug.

Lord Roderick smiled sheepishly and turned up his palms in an I-couldn't-help-it gesture. Jillian breathed more easily after the near disaster was averted, but she boldly took his hand.

"Come," she said. "Allow me to remove us from this madness."

She bowled through the ladies and gentlemen in the latest mode of dress to a cozy nook on the other side of the room.

The settee she sought in a niche beside the cold fireplace was unclaimed. She sat down in a rustle of blue silk and patted the embroidered cushion beside her.

"Ah, this is splendid," Lord Roderick said as he happily joined her and stretched out his long legs. "Everyone seems to be congregated near to the door."

"Only because my mama and Lady Whitlock are seated there. Most of the callers are their friends."

He smiled his understanding and said, "It was difficult to carry on a conversation there. This is much more conducive."

She eyed him consideringly. "I want to know so much about you, my lord," Jillian said.

He looked amused, but pleased. "Fire away, my dear."

She thought a moment and broached a subject which he had mentioned casually the previous evening, but which Jillian sensed was important to him.

"Your interest in art," she said. "Tell me about it." He had said that he had once contemplated studying at the Royal Academy. Only a serious artist would have had such an ambition. He shrugged a little, seeming ill-at-ease. "I gave up those dreams."

Jillian should have accepted his demur gracefully and gone on to another topic, but her curiosity got the better of her.

She found herself blurting out, "Whyever would you do that? Weren't you good?"

He laughed. "In the danger of sounding immodest, I was talented enough to receive encouragement from Mr. Joseph Turner. He invited me to study with him at the Academy."

Jillian was incredulous. Joseph Turner was a respected artist. His paintings sold in all the best galleries. In fact, an oil that depicted sailing ships on the Thames at twilight hung in Benjamin's bedroom at Whitlock House.

"But . . ." she was at a loss for words.

Lord Roderick stepped into the breach. "Parental opposition, Miss Blair. My father considers painting an improper pursuit for a gentleman of my social standing."

With more spirit than tact, Jillian said, "What nonsense! Don't waste your gift. Rent a studio and paint anyway. Your parent will come around when you confront him with your dedication."

"That's a bit drastic, my little firebrand. I dare not defy my father. He would stop my allowance. Where would I be then?"

He gazed broodingly into space. There was nothing Jillian could say to that except, "I am sorry, my lord. That was bad of me."

"Not at all, but can we change the subject?"

The slight strain between them lasted until they began to laugh hilariously over a few of the ridiculous getups some of the younger dandies tried to pass off as high fashion.

Jillian had just wiped her streaming eyes dry with her handkerchief when her heart fell into her shoes.

Lord Hoxbury, the Mad Baron, was but a few yards from her perusing the callers as if he were looking for someone in particular.

She leaned against the back of the settee to make

herself small. She thought she heard Lord Roderick
utter a nasty word and took heart from his reaction.
He would be a bulwark against the baron.

But her enormous relief was short-lived.

Lord Roderick was on his feet. "Propriety demands
that I leave you now, Miss Blair, for I have overstayed my
allotted time."

Stunned by Lord Roderick's sudden departure, Jillian's gaze went back to the baron just as Lord Roderick
wordlessly passed by him, his eyes straight ahead. Her
stomach flipped over.

Lord Hoxbury had seen her and was coming right to
her secluded haven. Without invitation, he lowered his
tall frame onto the cushion Lord Roderick had vacated.

But Jillian did not accept the inevitable. The only thing
she could do was get up and leave. But she never made it.

The baron's long bony fingers were like a vise around
her small wrist. "None of that. Stay put."

Jillian froze. The private corner she had chosen for
her tête-à-tête with Lord Roderick worked to her disad-
vantage. The callers formed a human wall that screened
her and the baron from her mama's eyes.

Lord Hoxbury squeezed her wrist. His menacing voice
was low and did not carry beyond the nook when he
said, "Don't do anything foolish. You and young Whitlock are already in my black books, Miss Blair. I resent
him making game of me at the soirée last night. Some
dark night one of the cutthroats who roam the city
streets will get the credit for sending him to an early
grave if he doesn't mend his ways."

The threat to Benjamin sent a shudder through Jillian. Her mind refused to work sensibly. Although Lord
Hoxbury let go of her wrist, she was afraid to move.

Even seated, the baron towered over her, but he bent
his neck and shoulders to bring his head closer to her

face. The image of a cobra popped into Jillian's brain, but the words that came from his mouth were the ramblings of a madman.

"The latest medical information concludes that a dash of skin color is a sign of a salubrious constitution. The average gentleman's passion is for pale women, a serious mistake. I, myself, was at fault twice and married pasty-faced females who died on me. But I am wiser now."

Jillian wondered what he was nattering about in this queer soliloquy. "Sir?" she said.

"Obvious is it not?" He treated her single word as a complete question. "Your browned countenance indicates a healthy female. I think you will do very nicely as my wife."

Jillian's eyes widened with shock. "Your wife?" she sputtered. The man was a sheer horror. She could not imagine a worse fate.

He gave her a lunatic's grin. "I am confident that I can get a robust heir on you."

Jillian thought she would faint. "Lord Hoxbury, I find your speech vulgar and highly improper."

"Hang the proprieties. And don't put on that prissy face with me. If Lady Blair has not told you how a child is conceived, I shall have to show you."

Jillian, though flustered, felt she should say something to discourage him from this idea that he could marry her. The man belonged in a madhouse, but surely he would understand plain speaking.

She took a deep breath. "Frankly, my lord, I find our difference in ages offputting, and I have no tender feelings for you. You must look elsewhere for a compatible wife, for I shall not change my mind."

"You will marry me," he said quite calmly.

"You are demented if you think so."

She had made a terrible mistake. A hot flare of dangerous temper sprang into the baron's black eyes.

Against all reason, Jillian expected him to whip out a pistol and put a bullet into her heart.

She shut her eyes to ward off the image and suddenly everything changed. The room was a-buzz with normal conversation. She was in no danger. He would not dare to shoot her in her own drawing room.

Her foolish terror vanished in a flash. Jillian opened her eyes to a sane world of rational, right-minded ladies and gentlemen within ten feet of her that obliterated the fear of Lord Hoxbury's cold stare that still pinned her to this spot.

Full awareness of her silly paranoia brought on a laugh that came out sounding rather jolly.

Its effect on the baron was far from sanguine. He sprang to his feet in a cry of rage. "No one makes sport of Hoxbury. You will rue the day you laughed at me, you brazen chit."

Jillian sat for a long time on the cushioned settee, staring at her folded hands once the baron was gone. Her heart had regained its normal beat, but she could not dismiss Lord Hoxbury's threats. His senses were clearly disordered, making him a dangerous enemy. She had never felt so insecure in her life.

Benjamin had always protected her. But if she told him about Lord Hoxbury's bizzare proposal or of how risqué he had been or of how he had threatened to pay her back for the perceived insult, Benjamin would never let the matter drop, but would confront the baron. She did not want to pick up the *Times* some morning and find that Benjamin had been discovered in a dark alley with his throat slit. She would not be able to go on living if anything happened to him.

Chapter 8

Jillian's heart would beat faster whenever she went out socially. She dreaded that she would find Lord Hoxbury's black-suited figure among the assemblage. However, morning calls, Venetian breakfasts, parties, and routs came and went and Lord Hoxbury never appeared. Amazingly, the baron had completely dropped from sight.

Jillian stopped wondering why Lord Roderick had ignored Lord Hoxbury that horrible day, even though politeness alone would have demanded that he at least nod to the baron. But she was glad to put the incident behind her. The charming young lord was a constant among her admirers, and she liked him a lot.

Benjamin was having mixed feelings about Lady Anna and her habituallly shallow conversation. She had no discernible sense of humor, causing him to wonder if she would make a rather dull wife. But when she bent her exquisite face toward his to catch a soft word from him, he was lost. Inevitably, his eyes would drop to her mouth. Her rosy lips were so tempting that he longed to kiss her and drink in their promised sweetness.

Late one afternoon he sat behind a walnut desk in the library of the leased house, dreaming of this delectable prospect, neglected correspondence piled on the desktop waiting for his attention, when Jillian breezed through the door.

"Ben, you will never believe where Rod took me," she cried.

Removing her mulberry bonnet from her tousled red curls, she flung herself into a black leather man's chair.

Benjamin put down the quill pen with which he had been doodling while fantasizing about Lady Anna's luscious lips and raised an inquisitive brow. "When did Lord Roderick become simply Rod?"

Jillian wrinkled her pretty freckled nose at him. "Today, but forget that and listen." She made a show of pulling off her gloves and mashing them into her bonnet. "We went to Joseph Turner's studio!"

"The painter? How does Rod come to know Mr. Turner?"

"Lord Roderick wanted to be an artist, but his father objected, although Mr. Turner once urged Rod to study at the Royal Academy."

Showing no interest in Rod's talent, Benjamin said, "That so," and sat back in his desk chair, stretched out his long legs, and put his hands behind his head. But he was interested in the well-known artist.

"I bought one of Turner's paintings from Britton's Gallery, as you know, but I never met the man. What is he like?"

While Jillian considered her response, she leaned over and set her bonnet and reticule onto a small mahogany table with claw legs.

This done, she once again made herself comfortable in the nest of soft leather and said, "Well, Mr. Turner's countenance is rather spoiled by a prominent nose, but his eyes are intelligent. He made us free of his workroom, but did not ask us to stay. I'm afraid he was rather remote, and fiddled with mixing colors. We spent no more than ten minutes there."

Benjamin leaned partway across the desktop and asked, "Where is his house?"

Jillian brushed some powdery dust from the lapels of her mulberry wool carriage dress and frowned. "I am not certain, not being familiar with the area. We had rather a long ride along the Thames."

Benjamin gazed into space with an abstracted look before he said, "You know, Jilly, it is not at all the thing to go to a strange man's house escorted by a bachelor."

"In truth, Ben, I was surprised when Rod stopped at Mr. Turner's studio. He had hired a smart yellow curricle to take me for a drive. I was excited since I had never ridden in one before. Rod is quite a whip, almost as good as you. But I would be lying if I said I regretted meeting Joseph Turner. How often is that going to happen?" She smiled cheekily. "Admit it. You were impressed."

He chuckled. "Jealous is more like it," he said, nearly serious. "I never met a famous artist."

"You like Rod, don't you, Ben?"

Benjamin was caught off guard. "He's well enough," he said briskly, unsure of his opinion of Rod, if he even had a firm one. He did not know his London friends intimately, not like he knew his chums back in the country.

Jillian cocked her head to one side, like a crested cardinal. "Rod is a gentleman in the nicest sense," she said. "He is an able conversationalist, and never boring. He can be quite amusing, too."

"In a word, you like him," he said. "Since you spend so much time with him, I never thought otherwise. But is he *the* one, Jilly?"

Jillian looked through the bay window where she could see an elm tree coming into full leaf. "He might be," she said. "Do you think he will make a good husband?"

"How would I know?" Benjamin was aware he had snapped at her and was immediately sorry.

"You are a bright girl," he said, moderating his tone. "You can determine for yourself if he will suit you, Jilly. My opinion doesn't matter."

Jillian wanted to protest that, of course, it mattered, but she sensed that Benjamin wasn't going to be put in the middle on her love life, if that's what it was.

She moved to the door to go upstairs to change for dinner when Benjamin remembered the delivery from Madame Sofia's.

"Your gown for the Duchess of Maydown's ball came while you were out," he said. He had been there when Tillie unpacked the dress and had thought Jillian would look spectacular in that confection of light green organdy. She might even break a few hearts.

He would have said as much, but Jillian had been afraid the gown would not be finished in time and was anxious to see it and rushed off.

Benjamin sat for a long time staring at nothing before he pulled a blank sheet of paper toward him, picked up a pen and wrote: "Jillian and Rod. Anna and Benjamin." Like a romantic schoolboy, he thought, but he forebore sketching hearts around the names when he found himself wondering if Jillian was going to miss him as much as he was going to miss her.

The Duchess of Maydown's ball had been in progress for better than an hour when Moira spied Benjamin taking Lady Anna through the French doors onto the terrace.

"Look at that," she said, bringing the young people to Delia's notice.

"I don't wonder," Delia said, rapidly plying her Japanese

fan against the heat of the ballroom. "It is beastly hot in here."

"You are missing the point, dear," Moira said. "Remember our mission."

"Yes, I see what you mean. Sadly, Benjamin still favors Lady Anna."

The ladies' range of vision took in the steps going down into the grounds. Delia nudged Moira. "Look, Lord Roderick is taking Jilly into the garden," she said. "It seems she still favors him, as well. But Jilly will catch a chill out there in that thin dress. I better take her wrap."

She snatched up the Nile green shawl that Jillian had left in her care.

Moira stopped her with an imperative word. "Wait," she said. "Let Benjamin do it."

Delia frowned. "But, Moira dear, he is taking the air with Lady Anna."

"Exactly." Moira looked determined. "Remember what I said about seizing an opportunity."

"You want me to ask Benjamin to go after Jilly?" Delia was devoted to their cause, but there was a good deal of reluctance in her voice, and Moira heard it.

"Not in this instance, dear," she said, diplomatically. "This bit of managing is better left to me."

Delia relinquished the shawl, happy to be liberated from the reponsibility.

The haven at the end of the dark terrace to which Benjamin led Lady Anna was behind a giant potted plant.

Violin music floated through the tall windows. He looked down into the perfect face gazing up at him and searched for a romantic phrase. But devising fresh compliments was becoming tedious. He stared at her in the dim light, doing his best to compose a paean to her beauty.

Suddenly, Benjamin blinked, blinked again, and smiled slyly. Damned if Lady Anna hadn't closed her eyes, puckered up, and was inviting him to kiss her.

Benjamin was no slow-top. He brought his lips down onto hers and groaned, but, alas, not from passion. He had heard his mother calling his name.

He peered over Lady Anna's blond head through a break in the tropical foliage as large as elephant's ears to see the shadowy figure of his tall parent coming in their direction.

Benjamin stepped around the concealing plant to intercept her. "What is it, Mama?" He decided it might be prudent to keep his tone tepid.

Flushed from her mad dash, Moira said, "Jillian catches a chill so quickly. She is overheated and has gone into the garden with Lord Roderick. You must take her shawl."

To Moira's surprise Lady Anna moved into view, looking hostile. "I felt faint and Mr. Whitlock brought me out for a breath of air," she said, her chin rising a notch as if she were daring Moira to accuse her of an impropriety.

Moira clucked her tongue. The lady doth protest too much. Obviously, Lady Anna was guilty of an indiscretion, but did the child think she was intent on soiling her reputation and ruining her? Moira was not so small-minded. All she wanted to do was to separate Lady Anna from Benjamin.

Benjamin was paying no attention to Lady Anna. He was seriously disturbed that Jillian was in the dark garden with Rod Shelby. She was an innocent. Rod was experienced with women.

Could she handle him if he became amorous?

Moira saw the dismay on Benjamin's face and was reassured. He cared deeply for Jillian. Finding her in

Lord Roderick's arms could not fail to bring him to his senses.

"I will see Lady Anna safely to the countess and explain that she needed some reviving air," she said to her son and pushed the shawl into his hand.

Jillian sat beside Rod on a wrought-iron bench, gazing at the silver stars in a dark blue sky. She had been chatting with him easily while they strolled down the brick path, but now he was quiet, as if something weighty was on his mind. Jillian smiled a little. He was plucking up his courage to ask for permission to court her.

The moon came from behind a cloud and bathed the garden in light. Rod reached for Jillian's hand. "You must have guessed that I have formed a *tendre* for you, my dear."

Jillian immediately lost interest in the stars. "Yes," she said, seeing no point in being coy.

Rod stared down at their entwined hands and sighed dramatically. "If my state of affairs were different, I would not hesitate to press my suit, but I am all but *point non-plus.*"

Jillian felt as if someone had dumped a bucket of ice water over her. *Point non-plus.* She knew what that meant. Rod was bankrupt. He owed far more money than he had and had run out of credit with the merchants of London.

"The quarterly allowance I get from my father doesn't begin to put a dent in my debts. Lord Hoxbury is my largest creditor."

Jillian gasped at the dreaded name, but was too flabbergasted to speak.

"I am ashamed to admit that the baron holds a staggering number of my gambling vowels," Rod went on, "a sum large enough to land me in debtors' prison. It's the reason I fear getting on his wrong side. My father suffers from a weak heart, you see. The shock of my imprisonment would kill him."

Jillian had liked Rod enormously, but he was not the man she had thought he was. She could not remember when she had felt so let down. So disillusioned. He had played ducks and drakes with his patrimony. Now he lived in fear that Lord Hoxbury would expose his foolishness. It explained, but hardly excused, Roderick's quick exit the day he left her to the baron's mercy in the drawing room of the leased house.

Despite her disenchantment with him, Jillian took pity on Rod, although she removed her hand from his. She could not verbally trample the man when he was already so far down.

"Well, my lord, it seems you are deep in the suds."

"I knew you would understand," Rod said, mistaking her sympathetic tone for true compassion. His voice became animated with hope.

"I do love you, Jillian. If you would consent to be my wife, we could use your dowry to clear up my gambling debts. I could take up painting again, my dear. I know you would make a new man of me."

From the darkness came Benjamin's voice. "Jillian, where the devil are you?"

"Here, Ben," she called into the night.

She rose slowly to her feet and looked down at Lord Roderick. "I don't think it would work, Rod," she said. "I am not cut out for martyrdom."

Benjamin stepped from the shadows and took in Rod seated and Jillian standing. "Is anything wrong?"

With a ghost of a smile, Jillian shook her head.

Benjamin gave Rod a suspicious look, but wordlessly placed the shawl around Jillian's shoulders.

"Let's go back inside, Benjamin."

Neither of them looked back, and so they did not see

Rod staring despondently at the ground, his large hands loose between his knees.

"Trouble in paradise?" Benjamin wondered. He couldn't keep himself from asking, "Did Rod make improper advances?"

Jillian made a self-abasing sound. "No, he simply gave me a hard lesson on how London dandies get themselves out of financial ruin."

Chapter 9

Benjamin drove past the park in a one-horse hired chaise on his way to Lady Anna's house. He spotted Jillian on Magic, riding through the entrance gate with Rod Shelby. She saw him, too, and waved, and he waved back before he tooled around a slow-moving delivery wagon and left her behind.

Benjamin had been shocked by Rod's ramshackle proposal and his smoky association with Lord Hoxbury. Rod was an inept card player, he knew, but that knowledge had come from low stakes gaming in the drawing rooms of the *ton*, not from the gambling hells of London which were alien to Benjamin except by reputation.

Rod had salvaged his friendship with Jillian in spite of the lethal blow to his marriage plans. But Benjamin was satisfied. Jilly tended to be the forgiving sort, but Rod did not have a prayer of reviving his aspirations as a suitor.

Benjamin drove onto the street of beautiful, costly homes. As he neared the Herridge mansion, he recalled last night's kiss. Against his high hopes, Lady Anna's lips had not exactly set his senses on fire. Yet he had invested so much energy in his courtship, he hated giving up without one last attempt to determine if Lady Anna had anything besides her beauty to recommend her as a wife.

* * *

"It's Benjamin," Jillian said as she lowered her gloved hand. Rod turned to look, but Benjamin was already lost in traffic.

"Where is Ben going?" he asked. Rod was mounted on a gray stallion called General.

"To Lady Anna's," Jillian said. "He is driving here in the park with her at four o'clock."

The breeze was mild and soft clouds floated overhead, a decidedly pleasant day. Side by side, Jillian and Lord Roderick rode in silence. There was no longer a chance of their forming a lasting attachment, so neither of them felt inclined to talk much.

Since her heart was not broken, in fact, it was barely bruised, she had forgiven him. In truth, she was grateful to him for not lying to her. Without his candid confession, she might have married him only to find out too late that she had made a terrible mistake. Under the circumstances, it was easy not to stay angry.

The paved road came to an end and Jillian was about to turn Magic around when Rod said, "Not many people know about it yet, but beyond those trees is a meadow which will be opened to the public in a month or two. I know the path that the workers doing the clearing use to access it. Would you like to see the field in its natural state?"

No other riders were in the vicinity.

"Yes," Jillian said, always ready for a little adventure.

Rod led her through a grove of trees onto a trail that opened onto the flower-filled meadow. Wildflowers in riotous colors grew among the tall grasses. Jillian was enchanted. The fields were alive with flitting yellow butterflies, all sorts of birds, and chirping insects. Nearby the foresters had culled some trees and stacked the branches and trunks into a towering pile.

Absent was the rumble of traffic. The park meadow was as peaceful as the country.

"This reminds me of home," Jillian said, in a wave of nostalgia. The field stretched far into the distance to a knoll.

"Let's race the horses to that ridge." Ever since she had come to London she had longed to take Magic for a real gallop.

Rod shook his head. "I don't think that would be wise until the grass is mowed. Our city horses are not accustomed to wildlife and might unseat us if we inadvertently flushed out a quail or hare."

Jillian was disappointed, but Rod said, "We could get down and walk around." His offer appeased her. He dismounted and went to help her down, but she slid from her horse before he could reach her.

She examined a wildflower growing where she had stepped down onto the ground. "Look, Rod, these cornflowers are the exact shade of my riding habit."

Rod stood tall beside her. "Indeed they are and a very pretty blue habit it is, too." Days ago, his smile and compliment would have charmed Jillian, but she felt nothing special today.

When she and Benjamin had been children, her governess and his tutor had them memorize the names of the wildflowers that grew in the country fields. *Daisy, bluebell, foxglove, clementis,* went through her head. Benjamin had hated the exercise, calling it "girl stuff." She was thinking about this when she was jolted from her reverie by the pounding of a horse's hooves coming through the trail at great speed.

"What the devil!" Rod cried, jumping back. The horseman burst past them into the meadow.

Jillian's heart pounded and her hand shook. The rider was Lord Hoxbury. The devil incarnate!

The baron turned the coal black stallion around, trotted back, reined in, and quickly dismounted.

Although Rod was tall, the black-suited baron eclipsed him. Rod had to look up at him. "My lord, how do you happen to be here?"

Lord Hoxbury glanced at him sharply. "By design, Rod, not by accident, I have been shadowing you and Miss Blair since you came into the park."

Rod frowned at him. Jillian knew the young lord was bewildered, but she was mindful of her past dealings with Lord Hoxbury and knew instinctively that she was the one who was in danger.

"The baron is here because of me, Rod," she said, hating that her voice trembled. "He means to take revenge on me for an imagined slight he suffered at my hands. You see, he took offense when I refused to accept his marriage proposal."

"She laughed at me," Lord Hoxbury said. "No one laughs at me."

Rod seemed to be struck dumb. He stared from one to the other. He opened his mouth a number of times, but no sound came out.

"Don't tax your poor brains, Rod," the baron said, sneering. "I have stalked Miss Blair for weeks, but never could get her alone, even though I dropped from society to give her a false sense of security. By an amazing stroke of luck, you played into my hands and brought her to this isolated meadow far from prying eyes."

Lord Hoxbury opened the folds of his coat and checked the pistol tucked into the waistband of his black breeches.

Rod gasped. "Surely, you are not threatening us with violence."

"Well, dear boy, it is not kindness that drives me," the baron said, laughing. "But your fate and Miss Blair's, for that matter, is in your hands."

"What do you mean?"

Alice Holden

"Leave now with Miss Blair and within the hour I shall have you arrested for nonpayment of your debts. You will rot in a rat-infested jail until restitution is made. But surely your father will bail you out, if you beg him for help." He paused pregnantly. "Or not, but I can tell you how to avoid prison."

Jillian listened, her spirits sinking with each word. The baron would pay Rod's passage to France, where he was to remain in exchange for the canceling of his debts. To ensure that Rod kept his part of the bargain, Lord Hoxbury had henchmen on call, who were prepared to kill Rod, his father, and his brothers if Rod revealed that the baron had abducted Jillian.

Rod looked miserable as he stared at the ground. He finally raised his head and stepped toward General. The horse paced sideways. Rod brought him to a standstill and sprang up onto the gray's back.

"You win, my lord," he said, sounding defeated.

Evidently content with his capitulation, Lord Hoxbury tossed Rod a leather pouch, which he caught in midair.

"Money for your passage," the baron said. "Remember, no heroics. My cohorts will take care of you and your family if I am arrested for kidnapping Miss Blair."

Rod stowed the bribe in an inside pocket of his riding coat, rode General slowly to the trail, and was gone at a canter.

Abandoned, Jillian felt genuine alarm at her precarious position.

"Not so amused now, are you, Miss Blair?"

Her temper flared at the taunt. From some hidden reserve, Jillian brought to bear a measure of pride. "How do you intend to punish me, my lord? A sound beating? Slow torture? Ravishment?"

"You have read too many Gothic novels, my dear," he

jeered. "I am a gentleman of refinement. I have only marriage in mind."

"Marriage?" Jillian was astonished. "How idiotish! No clergyman will wed us without my consent."

"Fustian!" If his overconfident demeanor had not warned Jillian that she was assuming too much, his next words convinced her. "Money speaks even with some so-called men of God." He tapped his breast pocket. "I control the living of more than one impoverished cleric who will honor the special license I carry without responses from you." He stepped toward her.

Jillian took a step back and said, "My parents will never believe that I married you of my own accord."

But her hopes all but ebbed away when he said, "I will stash you in one of my lesser estates in the North Country, incognita and under guard. Society loves a scandal and will conclude that you eloped to the Continent with Lord Roderick Shelby. Neither your parents, nor Mr. Whitlock, your sometime protector, will ever know of your true fate."

Jillian's throat went dry and tears welled up in her eyes, despite her intention to stay brave. To have Benjamin believe that she had run off with Rod was too painful to imagine. Here at this low moment it became clear to her. Benjamin was part of her, heart and soul. He meant everything to her. She loved him. Really loved him. Not as a friend, but as a woman loves a man.

But she did not have the luxury of indulging in self-pity, for Lord Hoxbury said, "Mount up, Miss Blair."

He looked across the meadow. The field made a gradual rise to the knoll, which was forested with trees like the ones that had been felled, but not yet carted away.

"We will leave in that direction," he said. "The park backs up to a little-used street where we are unlikely to meet other riders or pedestrians. I own a house close by where we will remain until morning before we begin our trip north."

"Wait," Jillian said, not with any plan in mind, but to gain time. Lord Hoxbury was a man without a conscience. She knew that if he succeeded in abducting her, she would never see Benjamin and her family again.

But the baron was having none of her stalling. "It will do you no good to grovel. Come here."

Jillian kept backing away from him until she lost her balance and fell against a woodpile which the workmen had sawed into practical lengths for easy hauling.

Lord Hoxbury made a sound of exasperation and came toward her with long strides. Jillian's hand rested on a short limb which had been stripped clean of branches. Her fingers curled around the makeshift club.

"Willful female, I shall soon tame you," Lord Hoxbury muttered, bending over to pull her to her feet.

Violence born of self-preservation stormed through Jillian. She lifted her cudgel, smashed her foe below his ear, and sent him to his knees. With all her might, she brought down the club onto his skull. The baron's eyes rolled back into his head, and he crumpled onto the grass.

Rod had never intended to abandon Jillian. To put Lord Hoxbury off guard, he had pretended to go along with the baron's despicable scheme. He was breathing hard as he searched every path and road throughout the park searching for Benjamin Whitlock. After less than ten minutes, to his profound relief, he saw him. Benjamin was handing down Lady Anna from a chaise parked in a cul-de-sac, the carriage horse tied to a hitching post.

"Ben, I need your help," Rod cried as he rode up to Benjamin. "It's Jillian."

Benjamin's face became grim. He let go of Lady Anna's gloved hand. "What about Jillian?"

Rod's lips trembled and his heart pounded as his words tumbled out. Benjamin's face turned pale and horror filled his eyes.

Lady Anna made small disparaging noises and shook the creases from her canary carriage dress. She looked up at the sky and reached back onto the seat and removed her yellow-fringed parasol.

Benjamin could hardly breathe. His alarm and fear increased in intensity. In a swift motion, he reached up and summarily hauled Lord Roderick from General's back.

Rod protested. "No, Ben. I mean to confront the baron with you after you get your own horse."

But Benjamin had already taken Rod's place in the saddle and kicked his boots into the stirrups.

"No time to lose. Rod, you see Lady Anna home and leave the carriage at my mews. You can collect your horse there later. I am going after Jilly right now."

Rod watched meek little Lady Anna turn into a termagant. She shook her parasol at Benjamin. "Mr. Whitlock, this is the outside of enough. Your duty is to me, not to Miss Blair."

Ignoring her, Benjamin spurred General onto the road and took off like a shot.

"Come back here this instant," Lady Anna cried, forgetting her consequence. "You are no gentleman!" But Benjamin was long gone.

"Hush, my lady. People are staring," Roderick cautioned, his voice discreetly low. He took her arm to help her up onto the seat of the chaise. She shook him off, her eyes shards of blue ice and climbed up by herself, something he knew she would never have done in a million years had she not been all worked up.

Rod freed the horse and picked up the reins. He settled himself beside Lady Anna, whose bosom heaved with righteous indignation.

"Mr. Whitlock is nothing but a vulgar gapeseed straight from the country. Lord Roderick, you are never to breathe a word of this day to anyone, do you hear? I will not have it said that I was belittled and humiliated by such a boorish nobody."

Rod relaxed. Jillian would be safe from gossip. "My word as a gentleman, Lady Anna," he promised, only too ready to agree to her demand.

Benjamin rode neck-or-nothing, scattering any of the park's equestrian population who got in his way. He was immune to their curses. He could think of nothing but Jillian in Lord Hoxbury's clutches. Never had he been so frightened in his life.

He had to find her. Jillian was his life, his all. Panic gripped him when the road ended, but then over to the left he saw the trees and the trail that Rod had described to him.

The big horse crashed through the bushes, exploded into the meadow, and reared up onto its hind legs. Benjamin lost his hold on the reins and jumped from the saddle before he was thrown. Immediately he saw Jillian, her mouth open in surprise, standing beside Lord Hoxbury's still body near a pile of cut-down trees.

Benjamin sang out Jillian's name and she ran into the safety of his arms. He rained kisses onto her face.

"Jilly, my beloved, I love you; I love you." He couldn't stop saying it. His lips came down on hers, and she kissed him back as only a woman in love would do.

He held her tight until she turned her head and

looked at General. "Rod's horse?" The questioning rise in her voice begged an explanation.

"Rod fooled the baron," Benjamin said. "He saw Hoxbury's gun and came to me for help." He told her the rest. "I don't like it by half, Jilly, that you never mentioned that Hoxbury proposed to you."

Jillian stepped from Ben's arms. "I thought the baron's threats were all bluster when he dropped from sight. Not in my wildest nightmares did I believe that he would stalk me and kidnap me and try to force me to marry him."

Her nightmares had been steeped in fears that Lord Hoxbury would ambush Benjamin some dark night. But she could never tell this dear man that she remained silent to protect him. His pride would be shattered in guilt.

Lord Hoxbury began to moan, bringing them back to the moment. Benjamin held Jillian's hand and walked back with her to stand over the wounded baron. "What happened to him?" he asked.

Jillian blushed and told him.

"You struck him with that branch?" he said with some amazement.

"I guess I could have killed him, but I used it as a club without an ounce of compunction," she admitted. "I threw his gun into that patch of bluebells."

The anguish that Benjamin had felt as he had ridden to Jillian's rescue had eased, but he doubted that if he lived to be a hundred he would ever forget how scared he had been.

Lord Hoxbury's lashes fluttered and his eyes opened. He attempted to sit up, but fell back onto his elbows. Making no overt mention of Benjamin's presence, he mumbled, "Seems Rod found his backbone. What are you going to do with me?"

"Kidnapping is a hanging offense," Benjamin said, "but Miss Blair must decide your fate. She is the injured party."

Lord Hoxbury snorted. "My bursting skull disputes your contention."

"Jilly?"

She stared down at the injured man at her feet. "I do not relish a sensational trial, but I do not want to have to remain on guard against another attempted abduction."

Lord Hoxbury sniffed. "Your wits have gone begging, Miss Blair, if you think I want anything more to do with you. Had I married you, I fear you would have poisoned my morning coffee or smothered me with a pillow in my bed while I lay sleeping."

Persuaded that the mad baron was no longer a danger to her, Jillian tented her fingers beneath her chin.

"One more thing, my lord," she said. "You are to forgive Lord Roderick's gambling debts and promise not to hurt his family."

"Are you dicked in the knob, woman!" The injudicious squawk caused the baron to clutch his aching head.

"I am owed that money fair and square," he said with less heat. "I did not cheat Rod Shelby. He just happens to be the worst card player in the kingdom."

Jillian's expression remained rock hard.

"All right," he said, finally.

Benjamin stood by with his arms crossed over his chest. He shook his head in wonder as Jillian bested the evil baron. He must have lost his wits to want Lady Anna when his brave, sweet, wonderful Jillian had always been there.

"I feel like I have stepped into a hornet's nest," Lord Hoxbury muttered when Benjamin helped him to his horse and gave him a hand up into the saddle. "You, Miss Blair, are a dangerous woman."

Had Jillian not known better, she would have sworn that he said it with admiration. But that idea was as insane as he was.

The baron chose to leave the park by the meadow, walking the black horse all the way to the knoll until he was swallowed up by the woods at the top.

Benjamin found Lord Hoxbury's gun in the clump of bluebells and examined the weapon. "The damned thing isn't even loaded," he said before he dropped the pistol into his pocket.

Jillian stroked Magic's soft muzzle. "Lord Hoxbury probably never shot anyone, but simply used the pistol to intimidate." To Benjamin she sounded distracted.

He slipped his arm around her waist from behind and rested his chin on her head. "What troubles you, sweeting?"

Jillian leaned into him. "Am I a coward for not taking the baron to court?"

"No, not at all," Benjamin assured her. "Any woman involved in a public trial is fodder for the gossip mills. Lord Hoxbury is a wealthy peer of the realm, Jilly. He can afford clever lawyers who can twist the testimony to make it seem as if it were your fault that the lunatic abducted you. I would not have you go through the mental anguish only to have him released from custody with no more than a slap on the wrist."

Jillian turned around and slipped her arms around Benjamin's middle and held on to him as if her life depended on it, her heart filled with love. She took comfort from his protectiveness.

"I want us to marry as soon as possible," Benjamin said, thankful to have Jillian secure in his arms. "Fifteen years is quite long enough for a courtship, don't you think?"

"Yes," she said, "by anyone's reckoning."

Epilogue

Benjamin shepherded Jillian down the hall toward the drawing room where Bradley had informed them that Lady Blair and Lady Whitlock had requested that Benjamin and Jillian were to be sent the moment either of them came home.

Informing the mamas of their marriage plans had been a first priority with the young couple, so the summons worked in perfectly with their wishes.

On the ride from the park, Jillian and Benjamin had made a pact to relegate her attempted abduction by Lord Hoxbury to the archives of untold tales.

"There is nothing to be gained by disturbing our parents' peace over something that is resolved. It will only take away from their happiness over our forthcoming wedding," Benjamin had said.

Neither said as much, but both realized that Jillian's plight, however horrible, had caused them to recognize the true nature of their love for one another.

"I think Lady Whitlock and Mama will be in transports of delight that we are to marry," Jillian said. "You know, I believe they have been meddling in our lives to that purpose."

Benjamin agreed. But at this point they were too light-hearted and happy to be out of charity with their mamas.

They had barely passed through the drawing room

door when Moira commanded from the chair where she sat, "Don't say a word, Benjamin."

She had been flipping through the pages of *La Belle Assemblée*, but she put the periodical aside and stood up, looking imperial in a royal blue gown.

"I am glad that you and Jillian have come in together," she said. "It will save Delia and me from repeating ourselves."

Delia had been leaning against the jamb of the French doors, gazing into the walled garden, but she left her post and hastened forward to stand in solidarity beside Moira.

"We have your best interests at heart," she said, her voice soft, but determined. She appeared less imposing than Moira, in a simple dark brown muslin gown, but every bit as resolute.

Shimmering with happiness, Jillian looked at Benjamin, taking her cue from him.

"Mama," he said, but Moira put up a ring-bedecked finger.

"Hush, dear," she said, "just listen. Delia and I have decided that the time has come for some honesty."

Jillian and Benjamin stood side by side. She moved her head sideways to glance at him. He shrugged and waited.

Moira took a deep breath and said, "You are committing a tragic error in courting Lady Anna, and Jillian will never be content with Lord Roderick."

"Jillian is the one you should marry, Benjamin," Delia put in. "Lord Roderick is not right for her."

Not a second passed before Moira said, "Delia and I are in perfect accord that you should take Jillian to wife."

She nodded toward Delia, who bobbed her red curls in return.

Benjamin spent only a moment taking this in, then said, "You know I will do anything to oblige you, Mama."

Moira narrowed her eyes. "But?" she asked, foreseeing his objection.

Jillian bit her lower lip to keep from giggling when Benjamin assumed a pained expression and said, "You wrong me, Mama. Have I not always been a dutiful son? If you insist, I will take Jilly to wife."

But Jillian could not stand it. She succumbed to the laughter percolating inside her breast.

"Lady Whitlock, Ben is funning you," she blurted out. "We are in love and want to marry as soon as we return home."

Delia let out a whoop of joy, and Jillian flew into her mother's outstretched arms.

But Moira's expression became stony. "You are a shameless scapegrace, Benjamin, to play such a mean prank on your mama. Why did you not speak up when you came into the room?"

Laughing, Benjamin put his strong arms around her tall, unyielding body and held her close. "Why, Mama, you bid me not to speak. I did not dare to interrupt you."

"For the first time in your life you chose to obey me without an argument, did you, you cheeky boy?" she scolded, but her voice was filled with maternal love.

Later Jillian gave herself up to Benjamin's deep kisses under the sheltering branches of a linden tree. Twilight cast romantic shadows on the small garden. Jillian could not get enough of Ben's kisses and the sweet words he whispered in her ear. It was wonderful to be wildly, passionately in love, and she kissed him back with full measure.

But after a long time he sighed and lifted his mouth from hers and glanced toward the house where the windows on the garden side were thrown open to catch the cool night air.

"Let's sit down for a moment, sweeting," he said and led her to a marble bench, "or we shall find ourselves anticipating our wedding night in the bushes."

At this point, Jillian did not think that would be such a bad idea, but Delia's gay laugh came from the drawing room, bringing a breath of sanity to her wayward thoughts. Benjamin held her hand to his lips as Moira's chuckle came from the house.

"You know they are in there planning every detail of our wedding," he said, but he did not sound too critical.

Jillian laughed. "And the number of our children and the order in which they are to be born."

And, indeed, at that moment, Moira was pouring sherry from a decanter on the sideboard into two crystal glasses and handing one to Delia.

"When a man and woman are in love, the saying goes that they smell of April and May. We are too late for an April wedding, but May will be perfect," she said.

Delia concurred and raised her glass in a toast. "To nuptials in May, then."

Moira, too, lifted her glass. "And to the grandchildren in our future, a boy first, then, a girl, and, after that, we will let Ben and Jilly determine for themselves the subsequent children's gender and order of birth."

This settled, their mood decidely ebullient, the managing mamas giggled happily and drank their wine.

Too Many Mothers

Julia Parks

"Your Grace! Are you all right? Oh, dear!" exclaimed the pretty blonde as she slipped from her horse and knelt beside the still figure. "Your Grace!" A moan escaped the injured rider, and Harrietta Tate heaved a sigh of relief.

"Can you speak?" she whispered. He only moaned again, but his blue eyes popped open. "Pray, do not move. Let me check you for injuries first."

Harrietta proceeded to feel his arms and his legs, then lifted his head ever so cautiously.

"Any pain, Your Grace?"

He shook his head and smiled at her.

Sitting back on her booted heels, Harrietta frowned at the Duke of Fairhaven, saying, "Whatever were you thinking, trying to jump that fence with your pony? You could have been killed."

The duke's lower lip protruded, and he raised himself on one elbow. Harrietta leaned forward to help him sit up.

Glancing over his shoulder at the patient pony, she added more sternly, "What is worse, you might have injured your pony."

"Is he all right?" asked His Grace.

"I'll check him, if you like," said Harrietta. Rising, she walked over to the pony and began to run her hand down each leg, grunting with satisfaction as she straightened.

"Well?" came the anxious query.

"He seems to be fine except for a bit of swelling on the left hock, Your Grace. You really should not ride him until your groom has checked him over."

"But how will I get home? It must be miles and miles to Fairhaven."

"You will come home with me. I live at Rosemary Cottage. It's not far at all. You may ride in back of me on my gelding."

"On Charger?" he breathed, leaping to his feet.

Harrietta grinned. "You know my horse, then?"

"Everyone knows Charger and Miss Harrie Tate."

She laughed and picked up the big gelding's reins before mounting. The duke handed her his pony's reins. Then he reached up, and she grabbed his hand and pulled him onto the horse's back, behind her sidesaddle.

"Put your arms around me and hang on. I don't want you to take another spill."

"Yes, Miss Tate," he said obediently.

"Now, tell me why on earth you did such a foolish thing as to try and follow the hunt on your pony."

"Trojan and I have been practicing that jump all week. He hasn't had any trouble before."

Harrietta could hear the petulance in the boy's voice, but she commented kindly, "Yes, but was Trojan galloping then like he was today when you took the jump?"

"Oh, I hadn't thought of that. How did you happen to see us, Miss Tate?"

"Call me Miss Harrie, Your Grace."

"Then you must call me Will," he replied formally.

"Thank you. And I saw you because I had fallen behind to wait for my friend whose horse, unfortunately, had pulled up lame. When he realized it, he waved me on to rejoin the hunt. Then I saw you and your Trojan trying to take that fence."

"Do you really think he will be all right?" asked the young duke.

She glanced over her shoulder, watching the pony's even gait for a moment before responding. "He should be fine. And here we are at Rosemary Cottage." In truth, the cottage was a rambling house of three stories with an ivy-covered portico.

Harrietta dismounted and reached up to help the boy down.

"Come into the house, Will. We will send for your groom, but while we wait, I'm sure my cousin will have something to tempt your appetite."

"I do not like very many foods, Miss Harrie."

She raised a brow, but refrained from comment. The boy was a duke after all, and one did not instruct someone of his rank on polite behavior. She wondered what her very exacting cousin would do when Will related his opinion to her.

Harrietta's lips twitched, and she said, "Margaret will no doubt be interested to hear your opinions, Will."

He nodded and waited for her to open the front door for him.

"Well, who do we have here?" asked a gray-haired man as they entered the neat drawing room.

"This is Will, Papa, the Duke of Fairhaven. He had a bit of a tumble, and since our house was closer, I brought him here."

The older man sketched a slight bow, and the boy responded with a regal nod.

"How do you do?" he asked.

"Very well, thank you, Your Grace. I am Clarence Tate, the vicar of Fairhaven Church."

"Oh yes, my tutor has mentioned you, I think. I do not attend services in the village. We have our own chapel at the manor, of course."

The vicar and his daughter exchanged amused glances before Mr. Tate said, "Will you be seated, Your Grace?"

"Thank you," he said, taking the best seat in the spacious drawing room.

"If you will excuse me a moment, Papa, I will tell Margaret we are in need of some refreshments and ask Ben to take a message to the manor."

"An excellent idea. I will stay and keep our young guest company."

A few minutes later, another young lady entered the drawing room. She was blond like her sister and every bit as pretty.

"Honoria, this is Will, the Duke of Fairhaven. Your Grace, this is my older daughter Honoria."

Will rose and bowed over her hand while Honoria smiled and curtsied in reply.

"Harrietta has gone to get some refreshments for us."

"Then I will certainly stay because Margaret was preparing her cherry tarts when I went through the kitchen earlier. I don't want to miss those."

The vicar winked at the boy and said, "We shall have to be fast, Your Grace, or Honoria will eat them all up before either of us have a chance to taste even one."

The boy flashed the vicar an uncertain smile.

"Papa is only teasing, Your Grace. Besides, our cousin always makes plenty."

The boy smiled and sat back in his chair, kicking his short legs back and forth.

Honoria settled her skirts about her and asked, "What brings you to Rosemary Cottage, Your Grace?"

"Will," he said with a shy smile. "You must all call me Will."

"Very well, Will," said Honoria, favoring him with her pretty smile.

"I fell from my pony, and your sister brought me here. It was closer than the manor."

"Are you all right? Has anyone sent for the doctor?" asked the kindhearted Honoria.

"I am fine, but Miss Harrie thought there might be some swelling in my pony's hock so I didn't want to ride him."

"I should say not," replied Honoria, her green eyes twinkling. "I remember hearing once about a gentleman who took a nasty fall, just like you. Why, he got back on his horse and rode him the rest of the hunt. When he finally reached home and dismounted, that horse shoved him to the ground and sat on him, refusing to get off until the man was flat as a fritter."

"You're making that up," said Will, a fierce frown wrinkling his brow.

"I vow that I speak the truth. The man finally relented, of course, and apologized to his horse. From that day forward, the man led his horse everywhere they went together."

"Then why bother having a horse?" asked the boy, drawn in by her merry grin.

"Oh, he bought another horse to ride. It would be a silly story if he never rode a horse again."

The duke cocked his head to one side and then joined his hostess in merry laughter.

"Good afternoon, Your Grace," said the diminutive Miss Margaret Tate as she entered the room with a tray of tempting cherry tarts. Behind her, a maid followed with a silver tray loaded with cups and a teapot.

"He is Will to all of us," said Honoria, putting an arm around the boy and giving his shoulder a squeeze.

"Will, this is my niece, Margaret, who takes care of all of us here at Rosemary Cottage," said the vicar, making room by his side for the plain young woman.

"How do you do?" said Will, rising and bowing to her.

"I am very well, thank you," she replied, nodding to him before sitting down and beginning to pour tea into the delicate flowery cups.

"Don't burden Will with one of those," said Harrietta, returning to the room and placing a small tankard of cold cider before the boy. She gave another one to her father and added, "Men much prefer cider to tea, especially after a grueling day on the hunting field. Isn't that so, Will?"

"I certainly do," he replied, lifting the tankard to his lips.

"And so do I," said the vicar, taking a sip of his own.

Margaret gave the duke a delicate plate with one of her famous cherry tarts. He took a bite, made a happy sound, and began to eat with relish.

"Here now, save some for us," said Honoria, setting her cup down and devouring her own cherry tart.

Will laughed and continued eating. Margaret placed a second tart on his plate before serving herself.

Smiling, Margaret said, "I don't think I have ever seen anyone enjoy my cherry tarts quite so much—except Honoria, of course."

When the young duke had sated his appetite and wiped his mouth, Honoria said, "Why don't we play Spillikin while we are waiting for your servant to arrive?"

"What is spillikin?" asked Will.

"You have never played spillikin?" asked the incredulous Honoria, who lived for games.

"Honoria, pray do not be rude," said Margaret.

"I beg your pardon, Will, but I thought everyone had played spillikin."

"No, there is no one to play games with at the manor. Nurse is too old and Mr. Right, my tutor, is too stuffy."

"But surely . . ." Honoria was silenced by a gentle hand from her older cousin.

The knock on the door heralded the entrance of a nervous gray-haired man who afforded only a sketchy bow to the ladies before frowning at Will.

"Your Grace, you were to be back from your ride at ten o'clock for your mathematics lesson."

"I'm sorry, Mr. Right. I didn't mean to fall off."

"Very well. I am sorry my pupil has been so much trouble, Mr. uh, Tate, is it not?"

"Yes, and you are Mr. . . . ?"

"Right. I am the duke's tutor, and I do apologize for discommoding you, sir."

"Not at all," protested the vicar. "We have been very entertained by Will. He is a delightful boy."

"It is good of you to say so, Mr. Tate," said the tutor, his tone doubtful.

"May I present my niece, Miss Tate? And my daughters, Honoria and Harrietta."

"Delighted. Now come along, Your Grace."

"No! I am going to play spillikin with Honoria and Harrietta."

The tutor turned scarlet, and his hand formed a fist. Will ducked his head. "There is no time for that, Your Grace. You have missed your lesson, and you have imposed on these good people long enough."

Margaret Tate looked regal when she rose, despite her height of only five foot three. Placing a hand on Will's shoulder, she said softly, "As my uncle said, the duke has been nothing but a pleasure to entertain. We were glad to have him. We were also glad to know that he came to no harm from his fall." Her declaration made the tutor turn scarlet.

"Madam, I am certain you are too kind to say otherwise, but it is time I take my charge in hand." The tutor placed a heavy hand on Will's shoulder.

Will twisted away and would have hidden behind

Margaret's skirts, but she knelt to his level and said quietly, "You must run along now, dear, but you may come back tomorrow, after your lessons. We will have more cherry tarts, and we will all play at spillikin. I promise."

He smiled and nodded, going willingly with his tutor after giving each of the Tates a grave handshake and bow.

When he was gone, Honoria and Harrietta drifted away. Margaret, however, followed her uncle into his study, where he was working on Sunday's sermon.

"That poor child. Is there no one at the Manor to . . . to care for him?"

"No, as I understand it, upon his father's death, his uncle, who is in Spain, was named guardian, along with a solicitor from London. When his mother passed away last year, there was no one else to look after the boy."

"But surely the uncle has had time to get home by now. It has been almost a year since the duchess died."

"I believe he has no plans to come home."

"But that is intolerable!" declared Margaret. "A little boy of seven being raised by servants and a tutor who . . ."

"Now, Margaret, we do not know that the tutor and the other servants do not care for the boy."

"It is not the same as parents or an uncle. Do you know the uncle's name?"

"I believe it is Ash. That was Will's mother's family name, as I recall. He is a major with Wellesley."

"Someone should tell him that his obligation to his young ward outweighs his duty to his country."

"There are those who would argue that point. I understand your empathy with the boy, my dear girl, but it is not our place to interfere in the matter," said her uncle, his smile vague as he returned to his notes.

With a thoughtful frown, Margaret returned to the small room from which she ran the Tate household with quiet efficiency. Placing her spectacles on her nose, she repaired the point on her pen and dipped it into the inkwell.

"Dear Major Ash," she began.

The month that followed saw a change in the quiet Tate household as the little duke became a constant visitor. He and Honoria would while away an afternoon in the garden, trying to top each other making up their outrageous stories. Other visits, he would enlist Harrietta to accompany him on a ride, either to the village for a sweet or across the countryside.

On rainy days, Will would sit in the kitchen, chatting with Margaret and the cook while they made biscuits or baked bread. He was always happy to sample and praise their efforts.

One afternoon, when Margaret was busy mending the household linens, Will wandered into the drawing room and sat down, watching her hands move the needle in and out of the fabric.

After several minutes of companionable silence, Margaret said, "You are very quiet today, Will. Is something troubling you?"

"No," he said, looking out the window and surreptitiously wiping away a tear. "Mama used to do that. I would sit beside her, and she would work for hours, telling me about Papa and . . ."

"And how proud he would be of you," murmured Margaret, continuing her work, but more slowly as her heart melted for this child.

"How did you know?"

"My mother passed away when I was very little. I don't even remember her, but my father would sit and play patience—that's a card game—and he would tell me about my mother and how much she loved both of us."

Will nodded, his chin trembling. Margaret set aside her mending and put an arm around his shoulder, hugging him to her.

"We are very glad you have become a part of our family, Will. You know that, don't you?"

Leaning back in the circle of her arm, he said, "I am part of your family?"

"You most certainly are! Why, Honoria and Harrie consider you their little brother, and uncle is so fond of you he talks about you all the time. How dull things were before you came to us."

His smile faded, and he looked into her eyes and asked, "What about you, Miss Margaret?"

"Well, I suppose you are too young to be my brother. I am seven-and-twenty, you know. Actually, I am old enough to be your mother," she added with a gentle laugh.

He snuggled against her and murmured, "That's okay. You may not be as young as Miss Honoria or Miss Harrie, but you are just as pretty, and you can cook, even better than Mrs. Argyle at the manor."

"High praise indeed," said Margaret, kissing the top of his head.

That night, Margaret climbed the stairs to her neat bedroom. She was tired and looked forward to settling into the bed. Sitting at her dressing table, she removed her lacey cap and took the pins out of her hair. A nondescript sandy brown, it fell down her back and across her shoulders in thick, luxurious waves. Picking up the brush, she ran it through twenty times, but she did not plait it. When she slept, she preferred having it loose and unrestricted.

Margaret looked at the image in the glass and made a face. When was the last time anyone had told her she was pretty? It had probably been her dissolute father before he lost all their money. How long had it been since . . . her eyes filled with tears, tears for the loving man who had missed his wife so much, he had never recovered from his grief. His grief had turned him into a reckless gambler, and she had been forced to make her home with Uncle Clarence. Oh, it had been a happy union, and she still missed her father.

At seventeen years old, she had taken on the role of aunt or older sister to eleven-year-old Honoria and nine-year-old Harrietta. Her uncle, long a widower, had been only too happy to have her take over the household.

It had been a quiet household until Will had adopted them. Margaret smiled at her image, rendering it almost pretty. Will's advent into their little family had changed everything for the better. With the boy's cheerful presence, all of them had more to smile about . . . especially her.

Margaret rose with a sigh and slipped into bed. She had resigned herself long ago that she would have no children of her own. It wasn't that she had never received an offer. Twice, she had attracted the attentions of good, stable men—gentlemen farmers who would have been good husbands. Margaret, however, had felt no flicker of love, and both times she had refused.

Though she looked forward to Will's visits, being with the engaging little duke pulled at her heartstrings, and her anger at his unfeeling uncle grew. Her letter had gone unanswered. Not that she had really expected a reply. A man who would choose the army over his lonely nephew had to be a cold sort. In the meantime, she and her cousins would continue to serve as family to the poor little duke.

* * *

"Bloody hell! What the devil did you do with my boots, Daschell?"

"'Ere they are, Major. You didn't think I'd be letting you return home with scuffed boots, now did you? Whoever 'eard o' such?" grumbled the grizzled batman, entering the tiny room they had shared the previous night at the inn in Portsmouth.

"Well, give them to me," replied the frowning major, taking the boots from his man and putting them on.

"Wot's more, Major," said the batman, stooping and helping his master, "they're gonna think yer an odd sort, always wanting t' dress yerself. You ought to let me do that."

"I'll be dashed if I will. I'm not some helpless babe. You can take 'em off, but I'll put them on."

The batman struggled to his feet, his knees creaking though he kept the moan to himself. Aiden Ash looked up at the servant and grinned.

"Sorry to be such a bear, Daschell. You know how I am when traveling."

"Aye, an' right glad I'll be when we finally reach this Fairhaven of Miss Belinda's."

"Of her son, you mean," corrected Aiden.

"Aye, of the young duke," said the batman, turning to gather up their belongings, stowing them in two valises.

Aiden's morning scowl returned, and he pulled a worn envelope from the pocket of his scarlet coat.

"Demmed female," he muttered as he read again the words Miss Margaret Tate had written to him almost four months earlier. "Unfit guardian . . . unconscionable neglect . . . unfeeling . . ."

"That's everything, sir, and the carriage is waiting in the street."

The old man waited patiently by the door, his eyes twinkling as he watched his master put away the letter that had brought them from Spain, all the way home to England.

Aiden ran a hand through his thick blond hair and grumbled, "We might as well get the journey over and done."

"Aye, Major," said the batman, following with the cases.

"Miss Margaret! Miss Margaret! He's coming! He's finally coming!"

Margaret caught the speeding figure in her arms as Will flew into the drawing room the next afternoon.

His face bright, and his eyes shining, he gave her cheek an impetuous kiss.

"Who is coming?" she asked, laughter in her voice.

"Uncle Aiden, of course. He sent my tutor a letter, and Mr. Right told me this morning. I came to tell you as soon as I finished my lessons."

Margaret glanced at the clock hanging on the wall and shot him a doubtful glance. Will hung his head.

"Well, I was very nearly finished," he muttered.

"So we can expect to find Mr. Right on our doorstep at any moment. Will, I have told you several times that you must put your lessons first."

"I know, but I really wanted to tell you, all of you."

"Very well," she replied, putting a hand on his shoulder. "Come into the kitchen. I think Cook has some biscuits for tea. Are you hungry?"

"I am always hungry," said the boy.

They entered the kitchen to find Cook still working on the biscuits.

"I am that sorry, Yer Grace," said the cook. "I didn't expect to see you this early, and I made my bread this morning instead of the biscuits."

"Shall we help, Will?" asked Margaret. "They'll be done that much sooner."

Will nodded and went to the basin to wash his hands. Sitting down at the large table, he took a ball of dough, scattered a handful of flour, and began rolling it out. Margaret took a glass and began cutting the dough into round disks.

"A little thinner, Your Grace," said the cook.

"Yes, Cook," he replied politely.

Margaret smiled. The little duke's manners had improved since he began frequenting Rosemary Cottage. She could tell there was a difference in the way he addressed the servants. There was a new respect for them in his mien.

"Tell me about your uncle, Will," said Margaret.

"Uncle Aiden wears a red coat because he is in the army," said the boy proudly.

"When was the last time you saw him?"

"I don't know. I think I was five years old. Mama used to talk about him all the time, almost as much as she talked about Papa."

Margaret and Cook exchanged pitying glances.

"He must be very brave."

"Oh, he is. And he rides a big black charger. Oh, I forgot. I brought a miniature of him." He fished in his coat pocket and produced a tiny oil painting, handing it to Margaret. "Mama used to have it in her room. I took it to my room. That's not stealing, is it?"

"No, of course not. It is yours now," said Margaret, staring at one of the most handsome men she had ever seen. "You take after him, I see."

"Hm? I suppose. My hair is the same color, and I have blue eyes, but so did Mama."

"Yes, I remember," murmured Margaret. She returned the painting to Will and said briskly, "Come along. If we're going to get to sample these biscuits before Mr. Right comes looking for you, we had best not dawdle."

Half an hour later, they were settled on the sofa in the drawing room, a tray of biscuits beside them with two glasses of cold milk on the table.

Will's shirtfront was littered with crumbs and flour, but he was not concerned about his appearance as he ate his biscuits and listened to the tale of knightly adventures which Margaret was reading aloud.

A rap on the front door brought the maid to answer it. Margaret closed the book and leaned close to Will, whispering, "I believe our time is coming to a close."

"I know," he grumbled.

Flushed and breathless, the maid entered the drawing room and said, "Miss Tate, a Mr. uh . . ."

"Major," corrected the figure in the doorway, looking over the maid's shoulder with ease from his vantage point of six feet tall. "Major Ash," he supplied.

Margaret uttered a little, "Oh," and rose halfway out of her seat. Recalling herself, she resumed her seat and sent the maid away with a nod.

"How do you do, sir?" she said, striving for a firm tone.

"In truth, I am quite weary from traveling, Miss . . . ?"

"Miss Tate, Margaret Tate."

"Ah," he murmured, looking down at her from his great height.

Not to be intimidated, Margaret pursed her lips and stared back. Remembering her spectacles, she whisked them off her face and hoped she had wiped away all the flour.

"Won't you be seated, Major?"

"Thank you." He sat down, but his new position opposite her and face-to-face did nothing to restore her shattered equilibrium.

With a nod to the boy, the major said, "You must be

Will. I hardly recognize you. You have grown so since I was last here."

"Say hello to your uncle, Will."

"Hello."

"Your tutor told me I could probably find you here. He also told me you were absent without leave."

Will frowned at this, and the major explained, "You left without finishing your lessons, didn't you? You must always place duty before pleasure, Will."

"He wanted to tell us that you were coming home, Major," said Margaret.

"It could have waited until he finished his lessons," said the major.

Her eyes hardened, but she smiled sweetly and said, "But he was excited."

"I didn't know you were coming today," mumbled Will, ducking behind Margaret as best he could.

"Yes, I quite surprised everyone. Mr. Right told me my letter only arrived a day or two ago. I almost beat it home."

"Mr. Right received your letter a day or two ago? Then how is it Will only learned of your visit today?"

"I assume, Miss Tate, that his tutor did not want him distracted by the news and decided to withhold that information. He is, after all, in charge of my nephew in my absence. And now, Will, I think we should be going. Take your leave of Miss Tate."

The boy clung to her hand, and Margaret leaned forward to give his cheek a kiss of encouragement.

"Don't be shy, Will. You and your uncle will get on famously."

Will glanced at his tall uncle doubtfully.

"Come along, Will," said the major, holding out his hand. "While I am here, you and your family shan't be put out with his frequent visits, Miss Tate."

Will looked over his shoulder, his blue eyes wide with dread.

"I assure you, Major Ash, that your nephew's visits are ever a welcome diversion. Indeed, we have all of us come to think of him as family."

"So I gathered from the letter you sent me," came the dry reply. The major looked at his nephew closely and wiped a smudge of flour from one rosy cheek.

"What have you been doing, boy?"

"Baking biscuits."

"Baking . . . well, at least you have been earning your keep around here. Good day, Miss Tate."

Then he was gone. Margaret could not refrain from rushing to the window to watch their retreat. Harrie, who was returning from her ride, blocked the narrow drive. It was obvious that the major was more pleased to meet the pretty woman on horseback than he had been to meet her—a spectacled spinster with a waspish tongue and pen. Margaret let the curtain drop and turned away.

She did not care in the least what the major thought of her. Being so handsome, he was probably vain and self-centered. Poor Will. He had so been looking forward to his uncle's visit.

Well, the major had best behave around Will. That was all Margaret had to say. If he did not, the major would be receiving the full force of her waspish tongue!

"The most charming man," decreed Harrietta at dinner that evening. "He asked me very prettily if I might show him the countryside—along with Will, of course, Papa."

"I think that is a fine idea. If he is to be our neighbor, we should strive to be on good terms with him," said the vicar.

"I am so sorry that I had gone to town. Describe him, Harrietta," said Honoria.

"Blond hair, very thick and wavy. Tall and with wide shoulders. He is very commanding, just like a soldier should be."

"His face, Harrie. What about his face?" asked Honoria.

"He is so very handsome. He has lovely blue eyes and a strong jaw."

"Stubborn," muttered Margaret.

"I daresay he might be," said Harrietta. "I only spoke to him for a minute or two. But one can forgive such a trait coming from such a handsome man."

"I don't know. I am waiting to see how he treats our Will."

"Now, Margaret. The little duke is not really ours," said her uncle.

"I know that, Uncle Clarence, but I do hope he will try to befriend Will. Surely that is only Christian of us to hope that Will's uncle is a man of compassion and honor."

"An odd choice of words, Margaret. Honor, I mean," said Honoria.

"And he must be honorable," said Harrietta. "He is an officer and a gentleman, is he not?"

"One does not necessarily guarantee the other," said Margaret, her lips pursing again.

Why was it every time she thought of the maddening major she felt defensive? It was ridiculous. She hardly knew the man. She had no reason to suspect him of being dishonorable. It was most vexing to have her emotions running so high. She wished she could chalk it up to a woman's intuition, but she had never believed in such folderol.

No, she had taken the man in dislike the moment she had set eyes on him. Only time would tell if he could be trusted to put Will's best interests at heart.

And if the handsome major did not, then he would have to answer to her!

It was just as the major had said. They saw nothing of Will or his uncle in the days that followed. Then on Sunday, Clarence Tate was gratified to see the Duke of Fairhaven's pew was occupied for the first time in years. Will grinned at him and waved, causing the boy's uncle to nudge him.

After services, under the shade of the oak trees that surrounded the old church, Will dragged his uncle up to Clarence Tate and proudly introduced him.

"Good morning, Major Ash. I must tell you and Will that it was a pleasant surprise to see the Fairhaven pew occupied again."

The major frowned and said, "Do you mean my sister never attended services here?"

"On occasion, but there is a chapel at the manor, I believe, and the old duke's brother was used to conducting a service there on Sundays for the family."

"I told you, Uncle Aiden," said Will.

"But he drowned with Will's . . . that is, with my brother-in-law over three years ago. Will, have you not been attending church?"

Will's face scrunched up at the reproof in his uncle's tone, and he shuffled his feet guiltily.

Margaret said, "I believe, Major, that this matter would best be taken up with Mr. Right, the man to whom you have given the care of Will since his father's passing. Will told me that he is the one who conducts the services at the manor now."

"Of course," he said with a nod.

The peacemaker, Clarence Tate, beamed his approval

of this scheme and said, "We would be honored if you and Will would join us for dinner this evening."

The major hesitated, and Margaret found she was holding her breath.

Harrietta touched his arm and added, "Oh, please do come, Major. We would love to get to know you better."

Honoria chimed in, "Yes, do come. We have been missing our Will so."

The major returned their smiles and acquiesced. What else could he do, being cajoled so prettily by the two beauties? Will took Margaret's hand and gave it a squeeze.

"Good afternoon, Your Grace," said Mrs. Hatcher, the squire's wife. She glanced expectantly at the major.

Will made a polite greeting, but Margaret took over, introducing the major to the matron and then to her numerous offspring, including two daughters of marriageable age. The entire village seemed to have gathered for an introduction to the handsome major, and after watching the neighboring females gush over him for twenty minutes, Margaret slipped away.

She found peace in the quiet of the kitchen garden, hidden away in a small arbor, surrounded by the fragrant smell of the herbs.

Stripping off her gloves, she pinched off a mint leaf and brought it to her nose. The fresh smell helped to clear her senses. She found herself fighting the overwhelming desire to burst into tears. How unlike her! She was not some schoolroom miss. She had long since realized that she was not a beautiful princess waiting for her handsome prince to come and sweep her away.

With a snort of derision at such absurdity, Margaret took hold of herself. She would not allow herself to become maudlin over the handsome Major Ash. He could and should admire her cousins. They were not only beautiful, but they were sweet as well. As for her, she had no need of his admiration or approval, and so she would tell him if he asked. He was much too rigid and unfeeling, just as she had suspected when he never answered her letter.

A contrary little voice whispered inside that his visit itself was an answer to her letter.

Good! she told herself. At least her letter had sparked him to do his duty by his nephew. For that she would be thankful.

As for the way his presence had upset her serenity, she fully intended to ignore him and thereby keep her usual poise intact!

Margaret rose, smoothed the skirt of her pea green gown, squared her shoulders, and marched toward the house.

Glancing down, she wondered what had ever possessed her to have a gown made up in such an unflattering hue. She must look an absolute fright.

"Drat the man!" she whispered.

Dinner that evening was torture, or it would have been if Margaret had not managed to keep her head on straight. Harrietta and Honoria kept the major thoroughly entertained with their charming chatter. Will, allowed to join them since they were practically eating *en famille*, watched the proceedings, but said little. Indeed, thought Margaret, the boy was looking a bit anxious. She would take him to one side when they retired to the drawing room and find out what was bothering the boy.

"And you, Miss Tate, what is your passion?"

Taken unaware, Margaret could only stare.

The major's lips twitched suspiciously as he added, "Miss Harrietta has her horses, and Miss Honoria has her gardening and fashion. What passion occupies your every waking moment?"

Blushing uncomfortably, Margaret said, "I have many interests, sir."

"Ah, such as letter writing?" he teased.

Margaret met his eyes squarely and added with a slight smile, "And dragon slaying."

With a tug on her sleeve, Will whispered, "There are no dragons in Fairhaven, Miss Margaret."

The major continued to spear her with his deep blue eyes as he smiled and replied, "You are correct, Will. I believe most of the dragons are fighting the French in Spain."

Margaret could not help but chuckle. The others at the table endured a moment of confused silence before Harrietta returned the conversation to more sane topics.

Margaret rose after the last course to signal an end to the meal. Taking Will's hand, she led the way to the drawing room while her uncle offered the major a glass of port.

As they entered the elegant drawing room, Margaret said, "Honoria, why don't you play that new piece you have been practicing?"

"Very well, but I have not quite perfected it so do forgive me if I stumble," said Honoria, settling herself at the pianoforte.

"I will turn the pages for you," said Harrietta, joining her sister.

Margaret led Will to the sofa across the room. He stifled a yawn as he took the seat by her side, and Margaret put an arm around him.

"Is something the matter, Will? You were rather quiet at dinner."

"Nothing," he mumbled, but she could see that he was troubled.

"That's good, because if something was the matter, you know I would be happy to help."

"Uh huh," he replied, looking thoughtful for a moment before glancing up at her and adding, "he is not going to stay."

"He? Oh, you mean your uncle." She could not help the wave of relief that rolled over her at this news, but she felt immediately contrite when she saw the pain in Will's eyes—eyes that were the same color as his handsome uncle's. "I suppose he feels his duty is with the army."

"I guess, but he told Mr. Right he wouldn't be needing his . . . uh, services anymore."

"Why ever not?"

"He's going to send me away to school. I am old enough, you know," added Will bravely, though his misgivings were plain to see by the way his chin quivered.

"Perhaps, but is that what you want, Will?"

Will frowned and shook his head. "I want to stay here, with you." Brightening, he added, "You could be my teacher, Miss Margaret. You know just about everything!"

Margaret chuckled and shook her head. "I know quite a bit, but not the sorts of things a young man must know for school . . . when he is ready to go to school. Why don't I speak to your guardian for you? Perhaps I can persuade him to put school off for a while."

"Would you?"

"I would be only too happy to do so," said Margaret.

"To do what, Miss Tate?" asked the major, looming over her suddenly.

"I did not hear you come in," she said, looking past him for the comforting presence of her uncle.

Reading her thoughts, the major grinned and said, "The vicar was called away. Someone was ill and . . ."

"I must see if he needs my help." Rising and hurrying

to the door, Margaret added a quick, "If you will excuse me."

"But, Miss Margaret," began Will.

"Miss Tate must attend to her duties, Will. Can I help?"

The boy sat back on the sofa and swung his feet back and forth. "No, it has to be Miss Margaret," he mumbled.

"Very well, but please remember that, as a guest in someone's home, it is impolite to pout." Ignoring the lower lip that poked out suddenly, the major strolled toward the two young ladies.

"I'm afraid we must be going, ladies."

"Oh, surely not so soon, Major."

"Alas, I fear it would be improper of two gentlemen to remain when your chaperones are gone away."

Harrietta gurgled with laughter and said, "This is the country, Major. We do not abide by such strict rules here. I mean, if you wanted to ravish us, you would find it difficult with your nephew in the room and a legion of servants within a scream's reach."

"Harrietta! You must forgive my little sister, Major. She is so uncouth at times. I think it comes from spending too much time in the stables."

"I think she is refreshingly honest," said the major, taking Harrietta's hand and lifting it to his lips. "That reminds me, Miss Harrietta, you promised to show me the countryside—and Will, of course. Are you free tomorrow morning?"

"Yes, that would be delightful. Will, do you think Mr. Right will allow you to join us tomorrow morning?"

"Mr. Right is going away tomorrow," said Will.

"Oh?" asked Honoria, turning away from the instrument where she had been picking out a tune.

"Yes, I have decided it is time for Will to go to school."

"But where?" asked Harrietta. "There is not a school for miles around."

"To Harrow. That is where I went, and his father, too. He'll be happier there with playmates. He'll learn a great deal more, I wager."

"I don't want to go!" said Will, leaping up and throwing out his chest.

"Will, you mustn't speak to your uncle like that," said Honoria.

"I will take care of this, Miss Honoria. Come along, Will. We have stayed long enough. You should be in your bed. Make your apologies for your unruly behavior, and let us go."

Will looked around for an ally, but his only possible ally had already abandoned him. Shuffling his feet, he made a bow and said a grudging, "I'm sorry."

Harrietta gave him a hug, which made him feel much better.

Miss Honoria leaned over and kissed his cheek, whispering to him, "It will all work out for the best, Will. I'm sure of it."

"Good evening, ladies. Thank you for the delightful meal and company. We shall call for you at nine o'clock, Miss Harrietta."

"It's Miss Harrie," said Will.

"Is it indeed?"

"That is what most of my friends call me, I'm afraid." She bestowed a merry smile on the major which made Will frown slightly. "I am looking forward to our ride. Good night."

"Night," said Will, grabbing his uncle's hand and practically dragging him from the room.

When they were settled in the curricle his uncle had borrowed from the stables at the manor, Will said, "Miss Harrie is a great gun."

"Is she indeed?"

"Oh, yes, she is the one who saved me when I fell from Trojan's back in the hunt."

"You rode your pony in the hunt?" asked his uncle.

"Yes, well, only a little way. But she made sure Trojan was not harmed or anything."

"And you?"

"I was fine," he replied. After a moment, he reiterated, "Yes, Miss Harrie is a great gun."

"That is good to know, but perhaps it would be best not to refer to such a pretty young lady as a gun, Will, even a great one."

"Really? Oh, all right. So you think she is pretty?" asked the little duke, his mind turning over this revelation.

"Very pretty. As is her sister."

"And Miss Margaret is pretty, too, isn't she?"

"Well, I would not place Miss Margaret in the same category as her cousins. Miss Margaret is more . . . unique."

"Miss Margaret is a wonderful lady," said Will. He was not certain that his uncle had insulted his friend, but he would defend her just in case.

"I am sure Miss Margaret is quite wonderful. She is also a woman of great conviction," said his uncle. Will swung around to look up at him, and he explained, "She says what she thinks."

Will smiled. Yes, he thought, she certainly did, and he was glad to know his uncle's opinion of Miss Margaret was just as high as his own.

"Do you have a wife?" he asked suddenly.

His uncle gasped and almost dropped the ribbons. Clearing his throat, he said, "No, Will, I do not. If I did, you would have an Aunt Something-or-Other."

"That's true. I could have an aunt." On this happy thought, Will fell silent, his mind whirring away, filled with new possibilities.

* * *

Major Aiden Ash fell onto the bed fully clothed. Rubbing his eyes, he sat up when the door to the adjoining sitting room opened and his batman trundled in.

"I told you not to bother waiting up on me, Daschell."

"Aye, Major, but I didn't pay that no mind," said the older man, kneeling down to remove his master's shoes.

Too weary to argue, Aiden permitted him to remove them. Help getting undressed, however, he would not allow, and he put up his hands to ward off the servant's ministrations. The batman took this in good form, simply taking the shoes and carrying them through the door to the dressing room.

"The Tates are very kind people," said Aiden.

"And some of them are very pretty, too," said the servant.

Aiden chuckled and shook his head. "Yes, two of them are quite beautiful, I would say, but they cannot be much older than twenty, if that. Much too innocent and . . . inexperienced—for my taste, that is."

"And the third Miss Tate?" asked the servant.

Aiden was not fooled by his batman's seeming disinterest. Daschell had been with him for a donkey's years, having served as Aiden's valet when he was a mere stripling. Becoming his batman had been a matter of course when Aiden joined the army. The old man didn't like army life, and he made no secret of the fact that he would enjoy settling down to life back home, but he would not hear of being replaced by a younger man.

"The third Miss Tate is a bit of an antidote," said Aiden.

"Is she so old?"

"Not so old, but very definite in her opinions. She is the one, you know, who wrote to me."

"Ah, I knew I liked her," said Daschell, gathering up

the discarded evening clothes and carrying them into the dressing room, too.

"Yes, you probably would. Will certainly thinks highly of her."

The servant returned and said, "Can't blame the boy. Being without a father was bad enough, but to lose his mother, too . . ."

"Yes, I know, and that is why he should go away to school. He'll have plenty of company there."

"Company is not the same as family, sir."

"And what would you have me do? Stay here for the rest of my life playing mother and father to him? I am hardly trained for such a task. He'll be much better off at school with teachers who know what to expect, know what to do for the boy."

"If you say so," said the batman. "Will there be anything else, sir?"

"No, go to bed like you should have done hours ago," grumbled Aiden.

When he was alone, he thought back to each and every encounter he had had with Miss Tate . . . Miss Margaret, as Will called her. The name suited the lady. It was rather formal, rather daunting, and that is how he felt when he was in her company. Oh, he had held his own with her. Dragon slayer, indeed. He smiled, recalling how her gray eyes had flashed with silver when she dared him to argue—and then how her freckled nose had wrinkled when she laughed at his admission of guilt.

If he was a dragon, then Margaret Tate would be the perfect dragon slayer.

Rising, Aiden shook off such nonsensical thoughts as he straightened the coverlet. He then climbed into the large bed and pulled the covers up, the soft sheets caressing his naked body.

The trouble was, he had no desire to be slain. Will's

question about him having a wife had sent his thoughts in entirely the wrong direction. He was a happy man— happy in the army and in life. He neither needed nor wanted a wife. Nor did he wish to play father to his young nephew. School was the answer for Will, and returning to Spain was the place for this dragon.

Resolutely, he turned on his side and fell asleep, dreaming of dragons and the short, smiling creature who slew them without so much as a sword.

Will's Grand
Scheme

"Do you hunt in Spain, Major Ash?" asked Harrietta, bringing Charger close to Aiden's mount as they reached a clearing.

"If you can call it that. We sometimes have informal hunts, though often it is for hares. Colonel Spivey keeps a pack of dogs."

"How intriguing," said Harrietta. "That does not exactly fit the picture of army life I had."

"We only hunt when we are not occupied fighting the French, of course," he said with an indulgent chuckle. Twisting in the saddle, he called, "Will, come along! Leave that poor turtle in peace."

"He is always finding things that interest him," said Harrietta. "He is such a charming child. I don't understand how you . . ."

"You are wondering how I can bear to abandon him," said Aiden. Her shocked expression was all the confirmation he needed, and he smiled. "I thought Will had probably told you all about my dastardly plan."

"No, he only told Margaret. She told the rest of us."

"With her own embellishments, no doubt," he said. "Miss Harrie, you must believe that I think school is the best place for my nephew. I went to school at nine. I know he is only seven now, but there will be other boys his age, and it will be good for him."

"I suppose," she replied slowly. "Besides, you certainly don't have to explain your decision to any of us, Major. Papa said we should accept it and be done with . . . it."

"With me, you mean. And what does your cousin say?" The young lady blushed a rosy red, and Aiden observed, "Your cousin does not have a very high opinion of me, I think."

"It is just that Margaret is so very fond of Will. We all are, truly, but Margaret and Will have a very special bond," she explained.

"Yes, I am coming to realize that, but as his guardian, I must do what I feel is best for the boy. You would not have him living in that big manor house with only servants for company, would you?"

"No, I suppose not." A question in her voice, she said, "And you must return to Spain?"

"Yes, I must," he said firmly.

"Then it is like Papa said. We must resign ourselves to it."

"Thank you, Miss Harrie. I am glad to know I have your support." Will's pony trotted up, and Aiden frowned at the turtle he clutched in one hand.

"He followed me, Uncle, and I just had to bring him along. I can keep him in a box in the kitchen."

"It won't hurt, I suppose, until you go to school. However, I think it would be best to keep him in the kitchen garden. That way he will have plenty to eat."

Will looked skeptical and asked quickly, "But what about the cook? She sometimes makes turtle soup. I don't want her cooking Tabby."

"Tabby, eh? Well, we shall have to let her know that Tabby is your pet and not supper."

Will nodded gravely and turned to Harrietta. "Is he not a splendid turtle, Miss Harrie?"

Over a quiet dinner that evening, Will broached the topic of Miss Harrie with his uncle. He had been gratified by the laughter they had shared, and he thought his plan was going very well. It took only a little probing, however, to discover that his uncle was not quite convinced.

"Did you enjoy seeing the countryside with Miss Harrie today?" asked the little duke.

"It was very enjoyable. Miss Harrie is an excellent guide."

"And she has the fastest horse in the whole parish," said Will, putting down his fork and wiping his mouth.

"Oh? How do you know that?"

"When we had our fair last month, she and Charger won the race with ease."

"I am surprised her father allowed her to enter."

"Oh, everyone entered. Trojan and I came in second in the pony race."

"That's very respectable."

"Yes, but it was Miss Harrie who won the big race, against all the men, too. I think she is wonderful."

"I'm sure you do, Will."

"Do you think she is wonderful?"

"She is . . . nice. I hardly know her, nor am I likely to know her better in the short time I will be in England. Here now, what is this all about?"

"About? Oh, nothing."

"Then eat your green beans and quit dawdling."

"Yes, sir."

So much for Miss Harrie becoming his aunt. Well, he would have to see if his uncle preferred Miss Honoria. She was a jolly good storyteller. Perhaps that would impress his uncle.

He knew that Miss Honoria usually worked with some of the ladies on Wednesdays, cleaning the church. He would have to ask his uncle to go for a ride with him and then they could visit the church when Miss Honoria was finishing up.

Watching his quiet uncle eat his own green beans, Will realized that Miss Honoria was much more suitable for him. Miss Harrie was too lively, but Miss Honoria was quiet and loved to simply sit around and talk, telling her stories. Yes, she was the most likely one to become his uncle's wife. Someone had even mentioned that she was a good dancer. He studied his uncle again.

"What is it, Will?" asked the major.

"Do you like to dance, sir?"

"What on earth makes you ask such a question?"

"Oh, I, uh, heard Miss Honoria talking about the assembly that they hold once a month at the squire's house. I thought you might like to go."

"Perhaps. If I am still here."

"I think it is this Friday."

"Then I might attend. Now do stop wasting time and eat."

"Yes, sir," said the boy, stuffing his mouth with green beans.

Wednesday dawned cool and dreary, nothing like the spring weather they had been enjoying. Will paced the breakfast room, stopping by the window and staring as if this would make the sun magically appear.

Smiling at his nephew's restlessness, Aiden said, "That's not going to help. You might as well settle in for the day with a book or a puzzle, my boy."

"I don't feel like doing a puzzle. We were supposed to go riding this afternoon."

"Perhaps we will if it does not start raining."

"You don't think it will, do you?"

"I have no idea, Will. I have to go over the books with the steward this morning. Would you like to listen in?" he asked. It was never too early to begin instilling in the lad the sense of the amount of work the large estate required.

"I guess so," said Will.

Aiden shoved away from the table and rose. "We'll ask Cook to send us some chocolate and tarts in the library."

"They are not as good as Miss Margaret's."

"Not having had Miss Margaret's tarts, I couldn't say," replied Aiden, trying not to laugh. Something about the words "tart" and "Margaret" in the same sentence struck him as hilarious, but he couldn't say this to the boy, of course.

"Miss Margaret's tarts melt in your mouth."

"Well, perhaps we can ask Miss Margaret to make some for us the next time we visit."

"This afternoon?"

"If the weather holds," tempered Aiden.

As he sat down behind the big desk, he felt his spirits climbing at the idea of visiting the vicarage that afternoon. And why not? he demanded of himself. The Tates were a delightful family, every one of them. If one of them was perhaps a little prickly, albeit in a charming way, then that only added to his anticipation. One never knew what Miss Margaret might say.

Aiden smiled. He wondered if Miss Margaret knew herself. He had the distinct feeling that she was not quite as demure and sensible as she painted herself.

"Uncle, may I have some paper?"

Aiden stared into his nephew's upturned face a moment before coming to his senses and opening the drawer he had been blocking. The boy shot him a quizzical glance and reached inside for some paper.

"I am going to draw you a picture," he announced.

"Oh? What are you going to draw?" asked Aiden.

"You'll see when I'm finished."

Aiden sincerely hoped he would be able to identify whatever it was the boy drew. He would hate to disappoint the child and be forced to answer to Miss Margaret.

"Do you like to draw?"

"Uh-huh," said the boy, thoroughly engrossed in his efforts.

"Do you draw for Miss Margaret?"

"Sometimes. She's not very good at guessing what it is though." Will looked up with a frown and added, "Once I drew an owl, and she thought it was a cat."

"How very obtuse of her," murmured Aiden, storing away this bit of intelligence for later use.

The steward entered the room with his ledger books and pulled up a chair. Duty called, and Aiden responded, putting aside his ideas of torturing Saint Margaret with this tidbit of information. That particular pleasure would have to wait.

The afternoon was still chilly, but the sky cleared. Aiden met the restless Will at the stables at three o'clock for their ride. Although the boy professed that he had no destination in mind, it was obvious that he had made plans to ride to the vicarage. When they passed the house and continued on to the church, Aiden was surprised.

"Look, there's Miss Honoria," said Will, pointing to the doorway of the church where Honoria Tate was sweeping the stone steps.

Aiden almost didn't recognize her with her blond hair

hidden by a large cap and a serviceable apron covering her gown. Nevertheless, she waved at the boy's greeting.

"Good afternoon, Will, Major. What a pleasant surprise."

"Surprise?" said Aiden. "Yes, we will call it that, will we not, Will?" His nephew ducked his head.

"We were just finishing with the cleaning," she continued.

Aiden greeted the other ladies as they left the church behind. They dismounted, and Aiden offered his arm to Honoria.

"If you are finished, may we escort you back to the vicarage?"

"That would be lovely," she replied, removing the large cap and smiling up at him. She tucked the cap into a pocket on her apron and took his arm.

"Do you do this every week?" he asked, gesturing back at the church.

"Oh yes. It is a rather large parish. This is my way of helping Papa with the parish duties. Harrie delivers food baskets to the destitute, and Margaret always tends to the sick. We try to do what we can to help."

Bored by this talk, Will injected, "Has Cook made any tarts today?"

"I am not sure, but I would be happy to help you find out," she said with a laugh. "If you will excuse us, Major?" Picking up her skirts, she chased the boy down the road into the vicarage yard, and around the house.

Aiden followed more leisurely and was rewarded by the sight of a well-turned ankle clad in serviceable cotton stockings when he reached the front yard of the vicarage.

"Good afternoon, Miss Margaret," he intoned.

"What? Oh, blast," she muttered.

"I beg your pardon?"

"I said good afternoon, Major."

"May I be of assistance?"

"I doubt it," came the pert reply. "Oh, drat that cat! Very well, just stay up there, you silly thing!"

As she stepped down, he put his hands around her waist and set her lightly on the ground.

"It is a cat stuck in the tree, I assume," he said, gazing into her frank gray eyes.

"A very recalcitrant cat," she replied with a smile that lit up her eyes. "Every time I reach for him, he skitters just out of my grasp. Then, when I tell him he is on his own and start for the house, he lets loose the most mournful meow."

"Meeooooooow."

"There, you see," she said, putting her hands on her hips and glaring at the tree.

"May I try? I have a way with felines."

"Try if you must, but I don't think . . . you will meet . . . with any . . . well, I am surprised," she said, taking the small bundle of gray fur from his hands.

Aiden hopped off the stool and grinned at her. His hand over hers to pet the frightened kitten, he said softly, "I told you I had a way with felines. Other things, too."

The cat chose that moment to jump down and run away. Margaret smiled after him and then invited Aiden to follow her inside.

"Thank you, I will. My nephew, along with your cousin Honoria, is already investigating what the kitchen holds." He caught her up in two strides and offered his arm.

Placing her hand on his sleeve, Margaret said, "They each have a very large sweet tooth."

"And what about you, Miss Margaret?" he asked, placing his hand over hers as they crossed the threshold.

Looking at his hand, she shivered slightly before shaking her head. "No, Major, I do not have much of a sweet tooth. I prefer sensible meals."

"To be sure, sensible meals for the sensible Miss Margaret."

She withdrew her hand and frowned up at him, saying, "I have not given you leave to use my given name, sir."

"I do hope you will forgive my forwardness. It is just that Will peppers his speech with Miss Margaret this and Miss Margaret that. I have fallen into the habit of thinking of you in those terms." He bent his head close to hers, smiling at her and wondering what her reaction to his nearness would be. She did not disappoint.

Jerking her head back, she pursed that rosebud mouth and said sternly, "I think you must try harder to remember to use the proper form of address, Major. I am not accustomed to such familiarity from a gentleman I have only just met." Spinning on her heel, she turned and retreated to the drawing room.

Following her more leisurely, Aiden was smiling when he entered the room. She had not used the proper strategy if she wished to keep him at arm's length. She had foolishly chosen the sofa. He could hear his nephew and Honoria's approach. There would be no time for her to switch.

Taking the spot by her side, he said, "A gentleman you have only just met, but one you decided to take in dislike before ever having met him."

She gasped at his accusation, but she did not deny it. If he knew Miss Margaret Tate, she prided herself on her good manners. Given such a challenge, he could count on her bending over backward to show him that she had not hastily formed such an unfavorable opinion of him. Aiden grinned and greeted not only his nephew and Honoria, but the vicar as well.

Aiden proceeded to ignore Margaret and concentrate on entertaining Will and Honoria, regaling them with tales of knightly daring on the battlefield. Every once in a while, his hand brushed Margaret's fingertips or the edge of her skirt, causing her to stiffen once again.

He was not going to make it easy for her to pretend that she had not taken him in dislike, to pretend that she did like him. Especially since he was finding it so amusing to annoy her.

He was not quite sure why he was expending so much time and energy on the nondescript Miss Tate. Perhaps it was because he knew she did not care for him. Or perhaps it was because there was a spark between them that needed fanning—just to see where it would lead, he told himself.

"Major, are you planning to attend the assembly on Friday evening?" asked Honoria.

"I'm afraid not. Will mentioned it to me. He said it was at the squire's house, but I have not received an invitation."

"It is not at all that sort of affair," said the beauty. "The squire has a large conservatory where it is held, but everyone pays a subscription just like a regular assembly. It used to be held at the inn, but the public rooms there were really too small. Do say you will come as our guest."

"Then I certainly shall, Miss Honoria. On one condition. You must promise to save your first dance for me."

She gave a trill of laughter and said, "Gladly. It can do a girl no harm to be partnered with the most handsome man at the assembly."

"Now you are putting me to the blush," he protested.

"I am only speaking the truth. You will wear your regimentals, will you not?"

"Honoria!" gasped Margaret. The blond beauty shrugged and rolled her eyes.

"And will you grant me the second dance, Miss Margaret?" asked Aiden with honeyed tones.

"I do not dance," she said.

"Margaret, what a whisker!" said Honoria.

"That is, I do not plan to dance this Friday."

Her uncle and cousin objected, but Margaret steadfastly refused to explain.

Aiden tried to appear solicitous as he said, "I do hope it is not something I have said or done that has brought you to such a pass, just to avoid dancing with me."

"Certainly not," she said, staring straight ahead to avoid his eyes. With a grimace, she finally relented. "Oh, very well. I shall dance, and you may have the second set, sir."

"How gracious of you, Miss Margaret."

She shifted to face him, but her eyes turned icy when she realized he was barely containing his laughter. She gave him her profile again.

No one noticed this exchange. Will and Honoria were bickering over the last tart, and the vicar finally settled matters by taking a knife and cutting the tart in half.

The diversion gave Margaret the opportunity to turn and say through gritted teeth, "Devil."

His eyes wide, Aiden replied, "I thought I was a dragon."

She opened her mouth to speak, then closed it again, trying not to smile. Humor won the day, and her nose wrinkled delightfully as she smiled and whispered, "You are both, sir, and well you know it."

"Only when a certain lady is involved," replied Aiden, his blue eyes drinking in every inch of her face. She blushed under this intense scrutiny and rose.

"We need more tea," she said, taking up the china teapot.

"Will and I really should be going," said Aiden, rising, too. He took the pot from her and returned it to the silver tray. "Thank you for your hospitality, Mr. Tate, ladies."

Honoria remained seated but offered him her hand

to bow over. "I am so looking forward to the assembly on Friday. The other girls will all be so jealous."

Harrietta walked in at that moment and asked, "Jealous of what?"

"The major has agreed to attend the assembly with us on Friday, and Margaret and I are to partner him for the first two dances. Priscilla Hatcher will be absolutely green."

"Then may I have the third?" asked Harrietta, earning a protest from her father and her cousin. "Oh, pish-tush. The major thinks nothing of it. Do you?"

"Not at all. I find your suggestion utterly charming, Miss Harrie. What time shall I call for you?"

The girls exchanged glances and nodded as if they had spoken. Honoria said, "Half past seven should put us there after everyone else has arrived." With a bright smile, she added, "It will be perfect for our grand entrance."

Aiden gave a general bow to the ladies and said, "Until then. Come along, Will."

"Uncle Aiden."

Aiden moaned and turned over. Something was disturbing his sleep. A flash of lightning. Ah, it was just a storm.

With a boom, thunder rattled the leaded windowpanes.

"Uncle Aiden!" said that voice again, this time accompanied by a small, warm body throwing itself against him.

"Will, what are you doing in here?" he asked, rising on one elbow and looking down at the boy, who had buried his head in the pillow when the lightning flashed again. He pried him loose from the pillow. The boy's eyes were like saucers. Another clap of thunder, and the child threw himself against Aiden's broad chest.

"It's only a storm," whispered Aiden, putting one arm around the boy to pull him close. He pulled the covers over them both and settled against the pillow again. "Don't worry. You can stay here with me as long as it lasts."

After a while, the small body relaxed, and Aiden settled him more comfortably by his side. He smoothed the tousled blond curls. Leaning over, he kissed the boy's brow before settling down to sleep again.

Unbidden, another small face came to mind. The freckled nose was not wrinkled with amusement, and the gray eyes were frosty with disdain.

"Blast," he whispered, glancing at the sleeping figure by his side. "All right, all right. Perhaps he is too young to go away to school. But what would you have me do? I cannot leave him here in this house with only servants."

The Major's Grand Scheme

"Good evening, Major. Do come in. The girls are not quite ready yet. But then, when were ladies ever on time?" added the vicar. "Would you like something to drink?"

"No, thank you," said Aiden.

"Mind you, Margaret usually is."

"Is?"

"Oh, on time. She is usually here waiting before I come down."

"How long has your niece lived with you?"

"Years and years. She was seventeen when her father died."

"Illness?"

"No, no. A tragedy, really. After Margaret's mother died, my brother became addicted to gambling. When he lost everything, he ended his life. Margaret was away at school, about to finish there and make her bow in Society. Robert's death put an end to all that."

"So she was never presented?"

"No. I do not aspire to such heights. We live very comfortably here, but I married my childhood sweetheart—a country girl. Margaret's mother was a different story. A wonderful wife and mother, to be sure, but her father was an earl. She preferred London to the country and so did

my brother. I often thought that if Robert had been
content to come and live nearby . . . but there, one cannot
turn back the clock."

"Certainly not. It explains a great deal," said Aiden.

"Does it?" asked the vicar.

"Yes, it explains why your niece is so voluble about
family."

The vicar still looked puzzled, and Aiden continued.
"You knew she wrote to me in Spain, didn't you?"

"No, did she? Well, I am not surprised. She thinks very
highly of your nephew. We all do. We hated to see him
stuck at the manor with no one but that cold fish, Mr.
Right, for company. I do hope she was not rude."

Recalling the letter, Aiden grinned. "Just very em-
phatic. And she was right. I did need to come home and
make certain Will was being cared for properly."

"Do you plan to stay then?" asked Margaret from the
doorway.

She wore a gray gown shot through with silver threads.
It was cut in simple lines and hugged her petite frame
like a glove, skimming the hips and then flaring wider to
swish seductively as she walked across the room. Aiden
shook himself.

"Margaret, you mustn't question the major like that,"
the vicar was saying. "It is his decision. He is Will's
guardian, after all."

"Yes, and he is also the only family Will has. So are you
going to stay?"

"No, I have to go back to my regiment soon. But I have
another idea . . ."

"Hurry, everybody. We don't want to be too late for
our entrance!" Honoria linked arms with her sister as
they reached the foot of the stairs, and together, they
sailed through the front door to the Fairhaven carriage
waiting outside.

* * *

Margaret moved her skirts to one side as Aiden slipped into the carriage, taking the empty space beside her. The girls and her uncle sat in the forward-facing seat of the spacious vehicle.

"Are you sure you wouldn't prefer this seat, Margaret?" asked her uncle. "I'm certain I would be fine sitting backward on such a short journey."

"There is no need for it, Uncle. You know I don't mind riding backward," said Margaret.

Besides, she thought, in such a large carriage surely the major would have no need to crowd her. And sitting by his side, she would not be forced to look at his handsome face.

It was a face that haunted her dreams and most of her waking moments. She did not know why this particular man had taken hold of her senses with such tenacity, but she felt like she was being sucked into a whirlpool, drowning with emotions she neither wanted nor understood.

His shoulder touched hers as he entered the carriage and sat down. She moved her skirts, but he still sat so close she thought she could feel the heat of his leg against hers. Nonsense, she told herself. It was just her imagination.

"I am counting on all of you to help me with names," said the major. "I met most of the people after church services last week, but I will never be able to put faces and names together."

"We will be happy to help, Major," said Honoria.

"And if you get stuck, and you're addressing a young person, just call them Mr. Hatcher or Miss Hatcher." Harrietta giggled and explained, "That's the squire's name, and since he has six children between the ages of seventeen and twenty-four, you will probably be safe."

"Harrietta, that is not true," said her father, his tone

reproving. Then he smiled and added, "There are seven of them now, and the eldest, John Hatcher, is five-and-twenty—still three years older than you, Honoria."

They all laughed, and then Aiden turned to Margaret and asked, "And do you have any advice for me, Miss Margaret?"

"Only that you behave yourself," she replied, wishing her voice did not sound quite so shrewish.

Well, that did it, she thought, as a shocked silence descended on the occupants of the carriage.

"I shall try to follow your wise counsel," he replied finally.

Margaret wanted to crawl under the seat. Whatever had possessed her to say such a rude thing? She felt unaccustomed tears spring to her eyes, and she turned to stare out the window into the gathering gloom for the remainder of the short journey.

Aiden jumped down when they arrived and turned to help all of them descend from the carriage. Margaret was last, and he kept her hand, tucking it into the crook of his arm to follow the others inside.

Leaning close, he asked, "Have I done something new to earn your disapproval?"

Margaret shook her head. Refusing to be a coward, she looked up into the face that tormented her.

Years of training stood her in good stead as she said evenly, "No, Major, you have done nothing, and I hope you will forgive my unruly tongue."

"Gladly, if we can be friends again."

Margaret frowned and said, "Are we friends?"

"I would like to think so. You know, I never thanked you for your letter. You were quite right about my coming home. Will was not being properly cared for—except by you and your family—and I needed to be made aware of that. So I thank you for that."

Surprised, Margaret stuttered, "You—you're welcome."

"And I have something I wish to ask of you. I have come up with a plan and I need your opinion . . ."

"Certainly, I . . ."

"Come in, come in, Miss Tate. And I am delighted you thought to bring Major Ash with you," said the squire, a tall, distinguished man of some fifty years. "My daughters have asked me time and again if you were coming tonight, Major. Welcome."

"Thank you, Mr. Hatcher," said Aiden, sharing a smile with Margaret. "I believe I met your charming wife last Sunday. Good evening, Mrs. Hatcher."

And so the social whirl began, leaving Margaret to wonder in silence what plan the major had come up with and why he thought he needed her opinion.

At eight o'clock sharp, the musicians struck up the first tune, called "Bath Carnival." Honoria and Aiden lined up with all the other couples, the ladies on one side and the gentlemen on the other. Each couple then proceeded to go down the line, their steps perfectly attuned. The dance, which lasted twenty minutes, afforded Margaret the chance to study the major without anyone noticing, not even the perceptive major himself.

He was graceful, just as she had expected. He was also entertaining, for he had Honoria giggling with glee. When her cousin missed her step, he had no difficulty righting her before she could fall. He was the perfect partner.

Margaret turned away from the dancers. It was impossible to continue watching and not feel the tug on her heartstrings. How could he think that she did not care for him at all? She cared for him all too much—like some sort of schoolgirl fancy. This infatuation was completely out of character. It frightened her by its intensity. Aiden—when had she started thinking of him by his given name?—had said he would be returning to Spain soon. For her peace of mind, it could not be soon enough!

She accepted a cup of punch from Mrs. Hatcher with a word of thanks. Drinking the liquid, she wished she could add a dash of something like the squire's son, who was opening his flask and pouring its contents into his cup. Would he be too shocked if she held out her cup? The red-haired young man glanced up to see her watching him and winked. With a glance at his mother's back, he raised his flask in suggestion. She hesitated, then shook her head. With a shrug, he turned away. Margaret watched as he secreted the flask in the potted fern near the window.

Moments later, when no one noticed, Margaret slipped over to the fern. Her back to the crowd, she poured a good measure into her cup of punch. It might only give her Dutch courage, but it should help her through her dance with the major. After that dance, she would be able to relax and enjoy the evening.

Turning, Margaret watched the dancers for a moment. Honoria and Aiden were moving down the line, and her cousin waved to her. Lifting her cup in salute, Margaret drank deeply, her eyes watering as the liquid burned its way down her throat. She was left with a warmth in the pit of her stomach, but she was glad she didn't need to speak at that moment. She doubted she had a voice left.

Just then the music came to an end. Aiden led Honoria to her side, leaving her there to go and fetch them both some punch.

"Did you see everyone staring at us? He is the most handsome man in the room, don't you agree?" said Honoria.

"I suppose so."

Margaret's voice was raspy, and her cousin asked, "Are

you all right, dear? You have not contracted a cold, have you?"

"No, no. I am perfectly fine."

Aiden returned just then with two cups of the innocuous punch. He handed one to Honoria before draining his own.

"Dancing always makes me thirsty. One cup is never enough. Shall I refill yours, Miss Margaret?"

"Yes, thank you," she said. Anything to take him away again.

When he returned with her cup, his expression was quizzical. Margaret had the horrible presentiment that he had guessed what she had done. It was not that women did not drink, but to add spirits to her punch at a country assembly smacked of intemperance. He was so close. Could he smell the spirits on her breath?

The music for the second set began. With an alien giggle, Margaret thrust her cup into Honoria's grasp. Aiden set his on a nearby table and took her arm.

"No rest for the weary," she said, leading him onto the dance floor.

"You are very eager," he commented.

"Perhaps I want to hear my opinion . . . that is, perhaps I want to hear what it is that you want my opinion about." Having found her tongue, Margaret smiled proudly at him.

The steps of the quadrille separated them. She passed by each of the other gentlemen in the square before returning to Aiden's strong arms. The movements made her dizzy, and she leaned on him heavily.

"Margaret, are you all right?" he asked, that puzzled expression on his brow once more.

She wanted to smooth his brow, but she was not so light-headed that she succumbed to this odd impulse. Instead, she smiled at him again.

"You seem very . . . happy tonight," he said, his eyes glowing with amusement.

"Do I?" she asked, missing her step as she was passed to the next gentleman before returning to the major.

"Back again," she said when she took his hand.

"Miss Margaret," he said, leaning close to her ear, "have you been drinking?"

She gave him that same smile and was gone again. The room seemed to be turning with the music. Or perhaps it was the floor that was twisting round and round. Margaret felt her cheeks becoming flushed. The temperature of the room rose until she wanted to wipe her brow. Still the music continued.

She stumbled, and he caught her in his arms.

"My dear, are you all right?"

"It is the heat," she whispered, clinging to him.

Finally, the music stopped, and Aiden led her off the floor and out through the garden doors.

"Where are you taking me?"

"Outside for some air," he replied as he slipped one arm around her waist.

In the cool evening air, Margaret revived and wriggled out of his grasp.

"Not yet," he said, pulling her close again. "I will let you go when you are seated. There, we'll sit down on that stone bench."

"Really, Aiden, I should go back."

"You need air first, and a few minutes to get your bearings."

"What do you mean by that?" she snapped.

"I mean, my dear Margaret, that you have imbibed too freely and need a chance to recover before you return to the assembly."

"How dare you, sir!"

"I dare because it is the truth. What's more, you know it

is the truth." By this time, they were seated, and Margaret began to feel more the thing.

"I must protest, Major."

He chuckled and said, "You called me Aiden a moment ago. Perhaps I should discover where you keep your flask and pour you some more." He reached for her reticule, and she slapped his hand away.

"I don't have a flask."

"No? Well, I know the bowl was not spiked so where did you get the . . ." He sniffed and said, "Whiskey, or I miss my bet."

"Oh, very well. I saw where John Hatcher hid his flask, and I thought, why not?"

"Are you in the habit . . . no, I can see you are not."

"It was just a whim. What are you laughing about?" she demanded, glaring at him.

After straightening his face, he said, "I am sorry, Margaret. I have no right to interrogate you on this or any other matter. It is patently obvious that you are not in the habit of imbibing more than a glass or two of wine with your dinner. We will say no more about it."

"Thank you," said Margaret, staring into the shadows and wishing she could disappear. Such wishes were impossible, of course, and she said, "We really should return to the conservatory. You are promised to Harrie, you know, when they strike up the third dance."

"Yes, I suppose we should go inside." He took her hands and pulled her to her feet. Margaret peered up at him through the gloom. The stillness of the night enveloped them, and Aiden bent his head, his lips brushing hers ever so slightly. He pulled away, and Margaret rose on tiptoe to reach those lips again.

"The music is starting," he whispered, taking her hand and placing it on his arm.

On the threshold, Margaret looked up and said softly, "Thank you for rescuing me, Major."

"You are very welcome, Miss Margaret." He lifted her hand to his lips, placing a chaste kiss on the back of it.

"There you are!" exclaimed Harrie.

"What was it like?" demanded Will the next morning when he entered his uncle's room and bounded onto the bed.

Aiden groaned and turned away from the bundle of energy, but he was not to be denied.

"Did you dance with Miss Honoria? Isn't she pretty? I think she is. She's funny, too."

"Miss Honoria is a delight, just like her sister. Now, do go away, Will, and let me sleep."

"But, Uncle, it is already nine o'clock. You promised to teach me . . ."

"Will, if you do not go away this instant, you will learn what it is to be on the receiving end of my temper. I will see you at breakfast later!"

Will sighed and retreated. As the door opened, Aiden called, "Much later!"

Quiet at last, thought Aiden, sinking back onto his pillow. A few moments later, he sat up. It was no good. Once he was awake, he could never get back to sleep. He threw off the covers and swung his legs over the side of the bed, stretching his arms and rotating his head in a circle.

He padded to the window to see the bright sunshine. Smiling, his mind returned to the assembly and Margaret Tate's impetuosity. He wondered what could have led her to do such a thing.

No one else had guessed. He felt certain of that. For the remainder of the evening, he had watched her closely, and she had behaved in the most proper fashion—as was her custom. She had danced with the squire once and with her uncle. Other than that, she had sat with the matrons, wasting away.

Aiden frowned. Now what had made him think that? Margaret Tate, except for her unmarried state, was of an age with many of the matrons. It was hardly a waste.

"Bah! You spend entirely too much time thinking about Margaret Tate," he told his image in the cheval glass.

He rang for Daschell, who brought hot water and a razor. Shaving was one task Aiden left to Daschell. The man was quick and efficient at the task. When he was done, Aiden dressed quickly.

"I will be gone most of the day. The steward is going to take me around to the tenant farms. Would you see to it that Will behaves himself?"

"His Grace told me you were teaching him to fence today, Major," said the batman.

"Did he? Well, I shall try to return in time to do so. He will understand."

In the breakfast room, Aiden took little note of his nephew as he filled his plate. When he was seated, he said, "Will, I won't be able to teach you about fencing until this afternoon. I'm sorry, but I promised Williams that I would ride out with him this morning."

"Why?"

"Because I want to make certain the tenants' farms are being tended to as they should be. You want your tenants to be happy, don't you? Perhaps you should come along."

"No, I'll go another day. I want to go over to the vicarage this morning. Wouldn't you rather do that? You can go around with Mr. Williams any time."

"No, I must attend to my duty first," said Aiden, taking a sip of his coffee. "Besides, I will not be here much longer, and there is much to do before I return to Spain."

"Spain!" said Will, climbing out of his chair and going

to stand in front of his uncle. "But what about Miss Honoria?"

"What about her?" asked Aiden, completely perplexed by the boy's agitation.

"Aren't you going to marry her and make her my aunt?"

The major gave a snort of amusement and asked, "Where did you get that notion? I never had any intention of wedding Honoria Tate!"

"Then what about Miss Harrie? She loves horses like you do, and she's as pretty as Miss Honoria."

Aiden took the boy's shoulders, and said firmly, "Will, I have no intention of marrying either of the Tate sisters, not even to give you an aunt. I am sorry to disappoint you, but I simply don't love either one of them."

"But . . . but . . ."

Will tore away from him and ran out the door. Aiden half rose to go after him, then shook his head, resuming his seat. He should have guessed what Will was thinking when the boy kept singing the praises of the Tate sisters.

The boy would feel better if the vicar agreed to his scheme. He really needed to speak to Margaret about that as soon as possible. He hoped she would help him persuade her uncle to allow Will to live at the vicarage for a year or two, until he was truly ready for school.

Aiden finished his breakfast quickly. The sooner he and Williams finished, the sooner he could speak to Margaret.

Morning brought a harsh light to Margaret. As she went about her morning routines, she berated herself for acting like such a ninnyhammer. She had never, in the whole of her life, behaved in such a fashion. Considering her infatuation with the major, she should never have gone to the assembly. But to go and then act in such a foolish manner . . . to jeopardize her reputation like that! What had she been thinking?

There was nothing for it. She had to avoid being in company with Aiden Ash for the remainder of his visit.

A timid voice inside her heart protested, but she thrust it ruthlessly downward, drowning it in her pool of self-loathing. Nothing could make her see him again!

"Miss Margaret, may I speak to you?"

She turned to find big blue eyes staring at her—eyes that were bright with tears. She opened her arms, and Will flew to her embrace.

"There, there," she murmured, raining kisses onto his golden curls. "It will be all right. Just wait and see."

When he had recovered, she drew back and asked, "What is it, darling?"

"It is Uncle Aiden. He is going back to Spain again. I don't want him to go!"

"But, Will, your uncle is a soldier. He never promised to stay here forever."

"But he could marry Miss Honoria or Miss Harrie, and then he would have a reason to stay."

Margaret's breath caught in her throat, but she managed to say, "Has your uncle expressed an interest in marrying either of them?"

Will shook his head and mumbled, "He said he doesn't love them." His tone showed he did not hold a high opinion of love.

"So you are the one who wanted him to marry Honoria or Harrie." He nodded, and Margaret squeezed his shoulder. "Love is not something that can be ordered about, Will. It is very complicated. I know you don't wish to be sent away to school, but if your uncle is going back to Spain, perhaps it would be for the best."

"But I want to stay here, at Fairhaven Manor. It is where I belong," he asserted, his childish voice taking on an air of authority before he ruined the effect by wiping his nose on his sleeve.

"I know, darling, but sometimes we cannot do what we want. Sometimes we must do what we must. Now, I shall speak to your uncle . . . not about marrying my cousins, but about your situation. Perhaps he and I can hit upon some other solution. Until then, why don't you go out to the kitchen and help Cook with her baking? I know she will appreciate your help."

He hopped down and shuffled out of the room. Margaret climbed the stairs to change her morning gown for a carriage dress. She would go to Fairhaven Manor and speak to the major immediately.

She hesitated only a second at the thought of facing him, alone. No, Will needed her, and as she told him, sometimes a person must simply do what she must.

Margaret was disappointed to learn that the major was out for the morning. She glanced at the small watch pinned to her bosom.

"It is already eleven o'clock. Would you mind if I wait for him?"

"Certainly, miss. Come this way. There is a fire in the smaller drawing room. I think you will be more comfortable there," said the old butler. "Would you care for some tea and refreshments?"

"No, thank you, Edwards."

"Very good, miss."

Left alone in the small room, Margaret chose the chair closest to the fire. The early morning sun had given way to clouds and a stiff wind. After services in the morning, she knew everyone would be discussing whether summer would ever arrive.

Margaret's eyes closed, and she shifted in her chair,

trying to ward off her fatigue. She rose and took a turn around the room.

She should not be sleepy, she reasoned. Instead, she should be on pins and needles, wondering what she would say to the major. He had been very gracious the previous evening, thanking her for that very blunt letter she had sent him in Spain, but she did not think he would welcome her interference now—especially since she did not have a viable alternative to sending Will away to school.

Margaret sat down again, staring into the hypnotic flames until sleep overtook her.

"Where is she?" asked Aiden, striding past the butler and into the small drawing room.

He didn't see her at first, curled up in the big chair near the fire.

Peering over the major's shoulder, the butler asked, "Shall I send for Mrs. Gibson, Major?"

Aiden shook his head and said softly, "No, I will wake her."

He crossed the room and put a gentle hand on her shoulder. When she still didn't stir, he shook her slightly.

"What? Oh, where am I?" Her eyes flew open as she recalled exactly where she was. Jerking away from his touch, she breathed, "It's you!"

"I'm sorry, Margaret. I did not wish to startle you."

"You didn't. That is, you did, but that is all right. I didn't mean to fall asleep."

"You must be a very sound sleeper," he said, turning away to give her time to straighten her gown and the small lace fichu that was meant to cover the expanse of milky skin exposed by her fashionable gown. "I'll tell Edwards to bring a tray. I am starving. What about you?"

"Yes, that would be fine," she said.

Out of the corner of his eye, he saw her rise and tuck in the lace neckerchief. She was her usual composed self when he returned to her side.

"Shall we sit down on the sofa?" he said. When they were comfortable, he asked, "What did you wish to talk to me about?"

"Will."

She related his visit earlier that morning, and Aiden shook his head. "I don't understand how he came up with such an absurd plan."

"He is only a child. He thought you could marry one of the girls and give him an aunt and a home. It's understandable. It would have solved everything, in Will's eyes."

"Yes, but . . . well, never mind. That brings me to the topic I have been wanting to discuss with you."

The butler entered with a large silver tray, placing it on the low table in front of them.

For the butler's benefit, Aiden asked very properly, "Will you pour, Miss Tate?"

"I would be happy to do so, Major." The butler left them alone, though he didn't close the door.

Aiden grinned and whispered, "He's still not sure about me. He's afraid I will try to seduce you."

"Trying is not succeeding," she replied. "But please, tell me what you have been wanting to discuss with me."

"It is a scheme I hope you will endorse. I have not mentioned it to Will, of course, in case you and your family cannot agree. What would you think about letting Will live at the vicarage for a year or two until he is ready to go to school?"

"Why, I think that is a wonderful idea!" exclaimed Margaret. "It would solve everything!"

"Not everything, but I think Will would benefit from

it, and I hope he would not prove too troublesome for the household."

"He is never any trouble." She returned his smile and said, "That is, he is rarely any trouble."

"Do you think your uncle will agree?"

"Oh, yes. He positively dotes on Will, and he is always saying there are too many females around the house."

"Then you will broach the matter with him?"

"I would be delighted," she said, sitting back against the high back of the sofa. A frown creased her brow, and she said, "How will you decide when it is time to send him to school?"

"You will write and tell me. I'll come home to visit in a year or so, but I will rely on you to make that decision. You and your uncle."

Margaret clapped her hands and said, "I cannot wait to tell Will!"

"Nor can I, but we must wait until we have your uncle's consent," said Aiden, sitting back with a smile as he watched her animated face.

Suddenly, she rose and said, "I must go home right now!"

"Not now, my dear. It is raining cats and dogs outside."

"Oh, I had no idea." She sat down again, but her agitation didn't allow her to sit still.

After a moment, Aiden laughed and suggested, "Why don't I send to the stable for the landau. I can take you home in that."

"Oh, yes, please!"

Twenty minutes later, the butler announced that the carriage was waiting in the drive. Aiden held his greatcoat over her head, and they hurried out the door and into the snug carriage. The coachman had thoughtfully provided hot bricks for their feet and a warm rug for their knees.

Margaret hummed a tune under her breath. After a

moment, Aiden joined in until they were both singing, grinning at each other like idiots.

The short ride over, Margaret said, "Uncle Clarence will be in his study working on his message for tomorrow. I will go in there while you remain in the drawing room. Will is already there, of course, and I'm sure the girls will be, too."

A worried frown on his face, Aiden said, "Good. I want you to be able to speak to your uncle first."

Margaret patted his hand as the coachman swung open the carriage door. "Don't worry. Uncle Clarence will agree with your scheme wholeheartedly."

Inside the house, they were met with the news that the vicar had been called away to the deathbed of one of his parishioners. Aiden and Margaret shared a disappointed sigh, but set this aside to join Will and the girls in a rousing game of spillikin.

The afternoon whizzed past, and Aiden finally rose and motioned to Will to do the same. "We really should be going, Will." With a quick farewell, Will bounded outside.

Margaret followed Aiden to the door and whispered, "I'm sorry. If the opportunity presents itself tonight, I will speak to my uncle. We will speak after morning services."

"Thank you, Margaret. Good-bye," he said, bowing over her hand and giving her a warm smile.

"Are you coming, Uncle Aiden?" called Will from the carriage.

"I'm coming," he replied, winking at her before hurrying through the rain and climbing inside.

Best Laid
Plans . . .

It was all arranged. Everyone was satisfied to have arrived at such an excellent solution to the problem of the little duke and his living arrangements. The Tate household was only too happy to include Will in their family, and for Will, it was a dream come true. Even Aiden was pleased, when he was not becoming morose over leaving England.

It was not, he assured himself, that he was tired of being a soldier. Instead, he was simply growing soft and complacent. And who would not? Each time he met anyone in the Tate household, they treated him like he was part of the family, too. They exuded a warmth which he had not experienced since his own childhood, when he and his sister had been the darlings of their household.

Time did not wait on him to sort out his feelings about the matter, and the day of his departure was rapidly approaching. Aiden and Will had decided to end his stay with a picnic at the manor for the Tate family. Summer had finally arrived, and the day was clear and warm.

Honoria and Harrietta wore sprigged muslin gowns, their blond hair tied up with simple bows. Margaret wore a cotton gown in willow green. The color suited her complexion, and the gown's simple style was flattering to her petite figure.

"Good afternoon, Miss Margaret," said Will, bowing over her hand, just as he had over the two sisters'.

"Good afternoon, Your Grace," she replied with appropriate formality. Then they giggled, spoiling the effect completely.

"Shall I bow over your hand, Miss Margaret?" asked the major.

"You, sir, may lead me to the closest glass of water," she replied. "This weather is wonderful, but I am unreasonably thirsty today."

"Right this way," he said, leading her across the lawn to the tables which were covered with crisp white cloths that waved in the gentle breeze.

"We could not have asked for a better day for our picnic," she said, looking about her at the idyllic scene.

"We are going for a boat ride," called Will, Honoria on one side and Harrietta on the other.

"I wonder if they know what a close call they had," commented Aiden.

"What do you mean?"

"You know. Will had one of them wed to me without their even knowing it."

"Now you are being absurd." Margaret accepted the glass of water and sipped it thoughtfully. "Still, it could have been worse, you know."

"And how is that?"

"It could have been me."

She put the glass down on the table and strolled away. Aiden caught her up and fell into step by her side.

After a moment, he said, "I wonder why he didn't think of you."

Margaret stopped in her tracks and frowned up at him. "I would think it is quite obvious." At his blank stare, she added, "Only look at my cousins. They are young and pretty and a great deal more fun than I am. Why would Will want me for his aunt when he could have one of the girls?"

"I don't see it," he persisted. "You are every bit as pretty as they are." At her look of incredulity, he continued. "I know you are not twenty years old, and your hair is not blond, and your eyes are not blue . . ."

"Thank you, sir, you have just made my case complete."

"No, no, I didn't mean that, Margaret."

"Did you not? Aiden Ash, I know very well that I do not measure up to my cousins. I do not aspire to their heights, but I don't think I am a complete ogre." She turned on her heel and headed for the small lake.

Throwing up his hands, Aiden called, "I never said that you were!" He rolled his eyes and grunted in frustration.

The vicar, seated beneath a tree with an unattended book in his lap, said sympathetically, "You will never win an argument with Margaret, young man. She can argue circles around anybody."

"I hardly expect to win when she will not even let me get a word in edgewise. Look at her! She's getting into that boat and trying to row it by herself."

"Nothing for it then. You had best go after her, or you will surely find yourself in the basket."

Aiden hurried down to the lake as Margaret pushed the boat away from shore. Unfortunately, she had forgotten to untie it, and he hauled it back, climbing in despite her protests.

Once seated, he tried to wrest the oars from her, but she would have none of it.

"I'll have you know, I am quite capable of rowing a boat."

"Go right ahead," he said. He shrugged and leaned back, resting his elbows on the seat behind him.

Margaret had no difficulty at first, but the small boat, resting lower with the weight of two people, soon proved too much for her. Her face red with exertion, she put the oars down and leaned back, imitating her passenger.

With an infuriating grin, he observed, "We seem to be drifting."

"So we are."

"The others have already returned to shore," he added.

"Yes, I believe they have."

"Do you want me to row us back?"

"Not if you don't want to."

"Very well, then we will just drift."

They floated there, in the middle of the small lake, with the soft breeze bathing their faces, ignoring each other.

"You know, Margaret, I was not implying that you were unattractive."

"Please, Aiden, you need not explain."

"Yes, yes, I need must, I'm afraid. The truth is, you may see yourself as too old and plain." He paused when she sat up to glare at him. "I, on the other hand, think you are the perfect age, and with those expressive gray eyes and that dusting of freckles across your nose, you are certainly pretty enough to please the most discriminating beau."

He paused again, to gauge her reaction to his words. He did not wish to lead her on, but he wanted her to know that she was every bit as desirable, as marriageable, as her prettier cousins.

When she didn't speak, he added, "Honoria and Harrietta are pretty young ladies, but their beauty is rather ordinary. Your beauty comes with knowing you, with . . . caring for you."

Aiden hesitated again, but this time it was his own confusion that made him pause. What was he saying to her? If he was trying to trap himself in parson's mouse-trap, he was doing a very good job of it. What was worse, though, was that he was leading Margaret on. She didn't deserve that. He was going back to Spain in the morning. He wasn't interested in marrying her or anyone.

"So why are you talking about caring for her?" asked a persistent voice inside his head.

Margaret was sitting up now, facing him. Her color was high again, but it wasn't from exertion. That rosebud mouth was pursed, too, and she looked vexed, if not outright annoyed.

After a moment, she asked quietly, "Are you leaving for Spain tomorrow?" He nodded. "Then, Aiden, I think you should pick up those oars and row us back to shore and sanity."

He swallowed hard and obeyed, neither of them saying a word until they were out of the boat and with the others.

The picnic was a huge success with Will. He ate very little as he hopped from one blanket to the next, chattering happily to the three ladies and then back to the one occupied by his uncle and the vicar.

"You know, Will, you will have to study very hard if you are to be ready for school. I will be your teacher now, and I have very high expectations for you. Was Mr. Right teaching you Latin?" asked the vicar.

"No, he said I would do better to learn English first."

"Correct, but you must also learn the classics. I think we will begin Latin in the fall."

"Is it very hard?" asked the boy.

"It is difficult, but nothing you cannot achieve. What do you think, Major?"

"I found it rather easy, but then, I always liked memorizing things. If you work hard at it, Will, you will do fine."

Will sat back on his haunches and grinned. "I can't believe I am going to be living at the vicarage with all of you."

The Tates returned his smile indulgently.

After their dinner, they all played blindman's buff. When the vicar took his turn with the blindfold, he became so disoriented, he fell down and rolled halfway to the lake, laughing all the while.

When they tired of this game, a servant was sent to the nursery to find an old wooden frame with its ball and ninepins. Will, who had never played skittles before, was soon frustrated by his uncle's expertise. Losing interest, he wandered over to the tree where Margaret was pretending to snooze.

"Are you asleep?" he asked, flopping down beside her.

Honoria cheered as she knocked down all the pins at once, and Margaret said, "Not now. Why aren't you playing?"

"I'm not very good at that game."

"It just takes practice. If you practice, you'll be as good as they are in no time."

"Do you really think so, Miss Margaret?"

"I know so. You have that natural ability at games. I, on the other hand, do not. I prefer to sit quietly with a book or my needlework."

"Or your sketchpad," he said. "Did you bring it today?"

"No, I did not."

"I could go inside and get us some paper and pencils," said the boy.

"A splendid idea. I will go with you."

Margaret rose and took his hand for the short walk to the house. He led her to the library and opened one drawer to find the required supplies.

"I have not been in this room before," said Margaret, staring at the huge bookcases that lined the walls.

"My mother used to sit in here at night and read. The nurse would bring me down, and Mama would tell me a story, or read me a book."

"You miss her very much, don't you?"

"Yes. That is why I thought Miss Honoria might be a good aunt for me. At first, I wanted Miss Harrie. She is such a bruising rider, but then I realized that she and Uncle Aiden were just friends."

"You gave a great deal of thought to all this. I'm sorry it did not work out."

"Uncle Aiden says it is for the best. At least I am going to move into the vicarage. It will be almost like having three aunts, won't it?"

"Yes, dear, and we all love you very much," said Margaret, giving him a quick hug. "Now, shall we take our drawing supplies and rejoin the others?"

Outside again, they settled under the oak tree, chatting amiably while they drew their pictures.

"Let me see," said Will, leaning over her paper. "That's me," he crowed. "Look, Uncle Aiden, Miss Margaret drew a picture of me!"

Aiden strolled over to the blanket and watched as Margaret put the final touches on the sketch.

"That's very good."

"Thank you. I thought you might like to have it, to take with you to Spain."

"May I?"

She handed it to him, and he studied it for a moment before tousling Will's blond curls.

"When I am missing you, I will take this out and study it. Then when I return next year, we'll compare you to the picture and see how much you have changed." He appeared moved by a powerful emotion and said hoarsely, "Thank you, Margaret. You couldn't have given me anything better."

Margaret found her own voice had fled, so she merely nodded.

"May I show it to the girls?" Aiden handed it to him, and he sped away.

Kneeling down on the blanket, Aiden said, "It is not going to be easy, leaving."

"Good."

"It's not just Will either."

Her eyes flew to his, but again, she couldn't muster a reply. Will came skipping back to them, sliding into the blanket and making a mess of the papers. Straightening them, Aiden came across Will's drawing and held it up.

"This is quite good, my boy," he said. His lips twitched and his eyes sparkled as he added, "Why don't you see what Miss Margaret thinks of it?"

Will grinned and handed it to her.

"This is very good," she said. He turned it right side up.

"There, you know what it is, don't you?"

"Well, it is definitely not an owl or a cat," she said. Tilting her head to one side, she continued, "Why, it's a picture of . . . of you and your pony."

Will giggled and shook his head. "No it isn't. It's a picture of Patrick, the stable boy, and his new dog."

"I saw that immediately," said Aiden. "Of course, I had the advantage of seeing the real thing in the stable yard earlier this morning. Why don't you show it to Honoria and Harrie?" The boy trotted away.

"You cheated," said Margaret.

"Let us say, I was forewarned," he replied. "For somebody who draws so well, you certainly need practice with Will. As a child, I was never any good at drawing. One thing always looked like the next, but I remember my mother would always say, 'Tell me about your picture,' saving her from a colossal blunder."

"I shall have to remember that." Will returned and Margaret said, "Will, why don't we give your uncle some paper and let him draw something?"

"Wretch," he murmured, taking the paper and pencil offered.

He gazed at her a moment and then began to draw in strong, swift strokes. Glancing up from time to time, he continued with Will hanging over his back, watching his progress with wide eyes.

"Jiminy!" said Will. "I didn't know you could draw. May I show it to her?"

"If you like," said Aiden.

Margaret took the sketch, turning pink as she studied it. It was obviously her in the picture, sitting under the oak tree, her face open and wide-eyed. She had never looked so pretty, but there were the freckles. It had to be her.

"Very flattering," she said, returning the paper to Will.

"You should give your drawing to Miss Margaret like she gave you the one that she did of me."

Aiden took the sketch, paired it with the one of Will and folded them together, putting them in the pocket of his coat.

"I think I'll take both of them with me if Miss Margaret doesn't mind."

"No, I don't mind," she whispered, her color deepening.

"Why don't we have that special treat now?" he announced. "Will, run and tell the cook we're ready."

"Ice cream!" squealed the boy as he headed for the house.

"So much for the surprise," said Aiden, rising and helping Margaret to her feet.

The rest of the picnic passed without any personal exchanges between Margaret and Aiden. He felt a cad for his behavior. He had acted like a man courting a woman, and he certainly did not wish to lead Margaret on. She might be nearing thirty, but she was still an innocent in so many ways. He had behaved like so many soldiers when they are going off to war, but he had no intention of following up with an honorable proposal—or any other sort, considering Margaret's high moral standards.

He would write to her when he arrived in Spain. Perhaps he would even send his sketch of her in the letter. That would let her know that he was not interested in pursuing her.

With this little problem settled in his mind, he pulled off his boots, setting them aside with the clothes he would wear the next day. Daschell had packed everything. There was nothing else to do.

Putting on his dressing gown, Aiden trudged down the hall to Will's room to check on him. There were bandboxes in this room, too, waiting for the move to the vicarage the next day after he and Daschell left.

Aiden sat down on the side of the bed and stared at his nephew. He looked positively angelic in his sleep. Aiden kissed those golden curls and stroked the boy's smooth cheek.

Closing his eyes, he recalled his arrival at the vicarage that first day. Was it only a few short weeks ago?

Will had hidden behind Margaret, peeking out to study him, his eyes wide with excitement and apprehension. Margaret had reassured him, had known just what to say when Aiden, a virtual stranger to the boy, had called him to his side to leave.

At the time, he had not appreciated what a gem she was. He had thought her plain and drab, and most of all, meddlesome.

Aiden smiled. Margaret had certainly proven him wrong on all accounts. Frowning, he returned to his room and took out the two drawings he had tucked inside his coat. Smoothing them out on the dressing table, he sat down and stared at his sketch of Margaret, leaning against the oak tree, her eyes wide with . . . longing.

He shook his head and studied it again, moving the candle closer to see her face. She was so petite, so perfectly formed, but it was the expression on that dear face that he had captured—without even realizing it—the expression of love as she watched him.

"Blast!" he said, shooting to his feet. He paced the room, returning each time to pick up the sketch and stare at it. With another muttered curse, he set off again.

Daschell appeared in the doorway, scratching his head and frowning. "Is something the matter, Major?"

Carrying the paper with him, he crossed the room and thrust it under his batman's nose.

"Do you see it? Do you see it, too?"

"See what?"

"The . . . the . . . oh, blast! I'll ask Will. He'll be able to see it!"

Flying down the corridor this time, he threw open Will's door, causing the little boy to sit up with a squeak of fright.

"I'm sorry, Will. I didn't mean to frighten you, but I wanted you to look at something."

Rubbing his eyes, Will said, "What?"

Again Aiden thrust the picture forward. Will looked at it in bewilderment.

"Do you see it?" demanded Aiden.

"See what? I see Miss Margaret."

Aiden sat down by his side and took a deep breath before trying again. "Yes, of course, but what do you see in her face, my boy? What do you see in her expression?"

He shrugged and studied it more closely. "I don't know. Love?"

"I knew it! And she was looking at me!"

Aiden leapt to his feet, grabbing the boy and whirling

him around and around. Laughing, they tumbled onto the bed.

"Get dressed, Will. We have to pay a call!"

"Where?"

"On Miss Margaret Tate, my boy. We have to find out if this picture is telling the truth. We have to ask her to marry us!"

Aiden strode out of the room, calling for Daschell, who had already laid out his riding gear.

Fifteen minutes later, the two were mounted, riding with maddening sluggishness down the dark drive and onto the road. Too nervous to speak, Aiden remained silent all the way to the darkened vicarage.

"They're all asleep," whispered Will.

"Then they will have to get up. Or at least, Miss Margaret will have to." Glancing at the tall facade, he said, "I don't suppose you know which one is her bedchamber?"

"It's in the back," he replied, dismounting and following Aiden around the house.

Will pointed out the correct window, and Aiden picked up a handful of pebbles. One at a time, the pebbles found their way to the window.

"I do wish she were not such a sound sleeper," Aiden grumbled. "I'm going to need something bigger."

Will bent down and picked up a rock. "What about this? This should do the trick."

Aiden hefted the rock in his hand. "It may do more than that," he said, raring back and letting it fly.

Still, no result.

"Something a little bigger," he told Will.

With a chuckle, Aiden again tested the weight of the rock before sending it to its target.

The shattering glass produced the result they were looking for. A minute passed and candlelight appeared in the broken window as well as in two others.

"You've done it now, Uncle," said Will, backing away and tugging at his uncle's sleeve.

"Now is not the time to retreat," said Aiden, shaking off the boy. "Margaret Tate!" he called.

The two windows opened on either side of Margaret's room and blond heads appeared. Another candle flickered at the back door as it opened, and Clarence Tate stepped into the garden.

"Who's there?" called the vicar.

"It's only me and Uncle Aiden, Vicar," said Will.

"Oh? Oh, I see," said the older man, chuckling now.

"Margaret Tate!" called Aiden, his voice more demanding.

She thrust her candle out the jagged window and said firmly, "I am here. What do you mean, waking up the entire household and breaking my window?"

"Waking the entire household was not part of my plan. Neither was breaking your window. If you were not such a sound sleeper, I would only have roused you, my dear girl."

"I am not your 'dear girl.'" As an afterthought, she said, "And what is Will doing here? He should be asleep at this hour."

"He was, but I woke him up to come with me."

"Are you mad?"

Aiden shook his head, glancing at the vicar, who was grinning widely.

"No, I think I have finally come to my senses."

"You have an odd way of showing it," she said.

"Will you come down and speak to me?"

"No, I most certainly will not!" She pulled the candle inside.

"Then I shall simply have to shout my proposal." The candle reappeared, and Aiden grinned.

"Your . . . your . . .pro . . . wait, I'll be right there."

Clarence Tate motioned to them, saying, "Come in, gentlemen, come inside. No need to be standing about in the garden. Will, why don't you help me in the kitchen? I believe there is a bottle of French champagne somewhere in the cellar. I think your uncle and Margaret can take things from here. Major, go right on in to the drawing room."

Aiden took a deep breath and proceeded on his way.

Covered in a lacey wrapper with her hair tumbling around her shoulders, Margaret appeared in the doorway.

Now that he had come to a decision, Aiden wasted no time. "Margaret, will you? Will you make me the happiest of men?"

He opened his arms in supplication, and she tripped across the room and threw herself into his embrace. Kisses and murmurs of love were exchanged as they found their way to the sofa, where Aiden pulled her onto his lap.

Drawing back, he laughed and said, "I take it that is a yes."

"Yes, yes, you impossible man!" exclaimed Margaret, kissing him again. Then it was her turn to draw back and say, "Couldn't you have done this when I was dressed and presentable?"

"I think you are perfectly presentable just as you are," he whispered before kissing her deeply.

Making a great deal of noise before actually entering the room, the rest of the family hurried to extend their best wishes. Clarence Tate opened the dusty bottle and poured glasses for everyone. Will took one sip and set it aside, climbing onto the sofa between his uncle and his Miss Margaret and smiling hugely.

"We did it, my boy," said Aiden, ruffling his nephew's hair and glancing up to see the love in Margaret's eyes.

Wriggling happily, Will said, "Now I have an aunt for my mother and an uncle, too."

"You have more than that, darling," said Margaret, hugging him to her. "You now have two cousins, Honoria and Harrietta, and a great-uncle Clarence."

"Jiminy," said the boy in awe. "I've got a whole, big family!"

The Perfect Mother, Retired

Jeanne Savery

Blinded by a sudden discovery, Lady Anne Forsythe raised a startled glance toward nothing at all. The last trunk lid half open, she half stood, utterly still.

How she wondered *had it happened?*

How had it come about that she would miss Beth and Thomasina? Her hand released the lid, which dropped with a dull thud. She straightened, still staring at nothing, unaware that a stray bit of lace, the hem of her best night rail, required tucking inside.

Anne had waited so long for this day when her duty as stepmother to her husband's three daughters ended and she could live her own life. It was, therefore, a shock to find that Beth and Thomasina, somehow, *some-when*, had engaged her affections.

Not Catherine. It would be a relief not to face Catherine's disapproval, her smug superiority. Anne had, again and again, sent a thank you winging heavenward that Catherine, the eldest of the three, wed her adored Beast, Lord Moreton-Smythe, well before Lord Forsythe succumbed to the disabilities acquired in the coaching accident that killed his first wife, the girls' mother.

At long last the two younger girls were also wed. All three were happily married—just as their father had decreed they should be. She had done her duty. Her work was finished and Anne was responsible to no one but herself.

Satisfaction filled her and—she chuckled softly as she realized it—she felt as smug as Catherine so often looked. Besides, if it was true she'd miss the two younger Forsythe daughters while traveling, then it would be equally true she'd miss them if she stayed home. So why stay in London where they were not when, now, finally, at long last, she was free to travel?

Anne brought her attention back to her packing and noticing the lace, tucked it in. She shut the trunk and, with something of a flourish, locked it. Then she counted. Three trunks, nine bandboxes, four hatboxes, and a travel desk with a hidden drawer for the few jewels her ailing husband had given her. All except the last would be transported to Dover. There they would await loading onto the packet on which she would sail to France.

Anne grinned, excitement making her feel young. She whirled around once, twice, and fell back onto her bed. The daughter of the village vicar and, finding herself a penniless orphan at seventeen, then accepting a marriage of convenience, Anne had known nothing but duty all her twenty-seven years. Finally, at long last, she meant to enjoy herself.

Anne sobered. She had expected to forget the past ten years as easily as she'd closed up her cases and trunks. It was, therefore, dismaying to find memories popping into her mind one after another. Seeking distraction, she rose and tidied her room—but the odd bit *would* intrude. Almost reluctantly, she admitted they'd not been *bad,* the nearly ten years of her marriage. She was, in fact, forced to admit that she had enjoyed a great deal of her life to date.

Still . . . while still in her teens she'd married a much older man, a man already suffering severe and chronic pain. He wed her because he expected imminent death himself and, by offering for her, *planned* for it. It was not the sort of marriage of which she'd dreamed, of which any girl dreamed. But the marriage saved her from the misery of being the poor relation in a second cousin's household and that fact alone filled her with gratitude toward Lord Forsythe.

There was nothing wrong with gratitude of course, but with it she felt a certain sadness. Perhaps, if she was honest, there was the *tiniest* bit of resentment, as well. She was, after all, grown too old to experience the romantic love for which her younger self had longed. Not only would she never know romance, but she was nearly too old to remarry at all—another marriage of convenience—in order to have children of her own.

Perhaps such resentment merely proved she was human?

In any case, what was past could not be changed and now she could organize her life to suit herself. That in itself was nothing at which one should sneeze, and for that, too, her husband deserved her gratitude, since his excessively generous settlements at the time of their marriage made it possible.

Firmly putting the past from her mind, Anne looked around. Her bedroom was neat, just as she liked it. Her housekeeper would need to do little before putting it under Holland covers, like most of the other rooms. Anne counted the trunks and portmanteaus again, nodded, and moved to the fireplace, where she yanked the bellpull. Footmen would remove the baggage to the cart hired to haul it to Dover. When she and her party arrived for one night at the Ship Inn, it would be there, ready to load onto the packet when, *the very next evening*, she and Milly sailed for France.

Finally, at long last, she could sail away to adventure!

Once again Anne whirled around the room—bringing herself to a sudden and embarrassed halt at the sound of a tap at her door.

The footmen had come.

Mrs. Millicent Seward, not long widowed, cast a fond glance at her friend, Anne, Lady Forsythe, who stood by the rail staring back toward England. Twice a day Milly thanked the good Lord for giving her such a friend, one who had come to her rescue just at the moment she realized her husband, a born gambler, left her next to penniless. All very well for dear Anne to insist she could not travel without a companion! Milly knew there were far more interesting people in the world than her country-bred self, many of whom would happily join Anne in her travels.

"We are leaving harbor, Lady Forsythe. Should we not go below?" asked Millicent gently.

"Hmm? Lady Forsythe?" Anne turned and leaned against the rail, her brows arching and a dimple flirting in her cheek from the smile she didn't quite smile. "You would go below, *Mrs. Seward*, leaving behind this bracing and salubrious air?"

Anne adopted a wistful look, fooling her friend—until Millicent saw the mischief lurking in Anne's eyes.

"We have known each other," Anne continued, "since before we sat at my father's knee learning our letters. Now all that that awful London formality is behind us, may we not return to the *informality* we knew then?"

"You mean now we are beyond the eyes and ears of those who would disapprove?"

Anne chuckled. "*Catherine's* long ears, for instance?"

"Poor Lady Moreton-Smythe," said Milly, "to fear the *ton's* judgment as she must."

Anne shook her head. "You do not understand. She truly *enjoys* proper form. She revels in it. Why, after her marriage, the first time she, quite properly went into dinner before me, you should have seen her expression."

"One of smug pride, I suppose."

"More that of having won, I think," mused Anne, her tone dry as dust. "The poor dear. Catherine competed with me for her father's attention from the moment he brought me home, a no one, a penniless orphan." Tiny lines creased Anne's forehead. "I wonder . . . Did the fact I never tried to best her in any way infuriate her."

"I think it might."

Anne recalled her last conversation with her eldest stepdaughter. Catherine, at her husband's prompting, had apologized, earnestly assuring Anne she would never again complain about the husbands Anne approved for her sisters, that she had been forced to realize her sisters were happy and that that was as her father had wished it.

It had been a difficult scene and Anne put it from her mind. The girls were no longer her responsibility. They were, *all three*, married. Their *husbands* would watch over them, keep them safe. . . .

So, finally, at long last, she was free.

A smile that might, by the uncharitable, be termed a rather unladylike grin, lit Anne's countenance. She was *free!* She enjoyed the sensation for a moment before turning to her friend. "You have not said we may use each other's names."

"Annie," said Millicent, her tone thoughtful. "You want me to call you *Annie* as I did when we were five?"

Anne chuckled. "Perhaps Anne, think you not?" She tipped her head. "Would you prefer Millicent to Milly?"

Milly grimaced. "You know how I love my name," she said. "*Milly* will do quite well. And now—" She spoke briskly, her hand covering her tummy as she eyed the rolling waves. "—do you not wish to go to our cabin?"

"My dear, you go. I will follow shortly."

"The . . . the waves do not bother you?"

Anne blinked. It had not occurred to her they might. Quite obviously, now she took a good look at her, Milly *was* affected. Anne's voice softened with concern as she asked, "Shall I come, too?"

Milly smiled a quick smile that faded just as quickly. She bit her lip. "I think," she said, averting her eyes in embarrassment, "I prefer to be alone."

"Then, in a little while, I will come see how you go on. Try to sleep," Anne suggested. "That might be best?"

Anne watched Milly until she disappeared down the companionway. She turned back to the rail and, for a moment, worried that perhaps she *should* attend her friend. Then, recalling Milly's independent nature, she decided against it.

France, she thought, looking forward. *In only a few hours we will be in France!*

It was her dream, travel. Many *many* hours were filled with reading and planning, with dreams. Dreams about when she would escape the responsibilities weighing on her, when she could see and do all those wonderful delightful things the future held for her. And now she could. *Now* she could go with a light heart.

But even though it was done, finished, her mind refused to be disciplined and insisted on remembering. The bit popping into her head just then concerned Thomasina's recent wedding. As Anne, steadying herself with a hand on the rail, worked her way toward the prow of the packet, her mind's eye filled with pictures of the bride. Radiant, the pale pink of her gown reflected unneeded color onto normally pale cheeks. The groom was nearly as visibly happy as he watched his bride's approach to the altar. Anne felt a mix of pleasure for her stepdaughter and something more—

—something she could not, or *would* not, admit was jealousy.

Perhaps one day a man will wait at the altar for me—a man deeply in love with me.

Anne smiled at the ridiculous daydream. The most generous of friends would admit that she was firmly upon that shelf to which spinsters were relegated. An ape leader! The notion caught her fancy, and she chuckled softly.

Anyone watching me will know me for a ninny, grinning at nothing at all.

She glanced around to see if anyone *had* noticed. A tall stranger stood a little farther on. Oblivious, deeply involved with his own thoughts, he ignored her, which was good, since it allowed her to continue dreaming silly dreams. Anne pretended to look beyond him.

A man to love me, she mused. *A man like that one.*

Surreptitiously, she studied the dark stranger even as she chided herself for playing the romantic fool. And then she told herself she didn't care if she was a fool. She'd been too busy when of an age to spin fantasies, first as a vicar's busy daughter and then as housewife, nurse, and surrogate mother.

Anne watched the stranger, carefully pretending to stare beyond him. The capes of his long coat flipped around him, emphasizing the width of his shoulders. He wore no hat and unfashionably long dark hair was flung into wild disarray by the wind speeding them across the Channel. A high forehead, a blade of a nose, and a starkly carved chin, darkened now by a beard he must shave more than once a day, all were thrust forward toward France. His legs were spread ever so slightly for balance, his hands behind him, the fists opening and

closing, opening and closing, unconsciously exposing a
tension Anne guessed he'd dislike having revealed.

Anne played a game of which she was fond. Since a
child she had made up stories about an unknown, anyone who caught at her imagination. Now she made up
a history for this man, a man so obviously impatient to
reach his destination.

Perhaps he is with the government, she thought. *Perhaps he
carries important documents to Wellington in Paris.* That
seemed apt, so having given him an occupation, Anne
went on to give him a background. *A second son? No,* she
decided, *that doesn't fit. Then he is the* eldest *son of an . . .
a marquess,* she concluded—but even that was not quite
right. She hesitated. *But . . . but illegitimate? One who must
make his own way in the world.*

She hid a sudden grin at that thought. The arrogance
of the stranger did not match the notion he was born out
of wedlock, so she set aside that bit of Gothic nonsense.

No, he is *the eldest son. Oh yes. And the heir of a marquess.
But why so tense? Why that brooding look?*

He did brood. The lowering brow, heavily shadowing
deep-set eyes, convinced Anne of it. *A runaway wife?* she
mused *One he must chase down and return to their home and
manage the whole without raising scandal? Or—Ah yes, far
more likely! A sister. Yes a much better notion.*

Anne nodded, happy it was his sister. For reasons she
didn't care to explore, the idea he might be married
bothered her.

It doesn't fit, she explained her feelings to herself. *He
doesn't have that married look. But he is ever so worried. . . .*

If she'd been asked what a married look might be,
Anne would have had a deal of difficulty explaining.

Why is he worried? Truly? she asked herself, knowing her
imagination had gotten a trifle out of hand. Anne's soft
heart worried right along with him until she realized that

he was upsetting her peace of mind and interfering with her anticipation of the coming months, the experiencing of new sights and tastes, and the satisfying of her curiosity about the people she would meet and customs she would observe. . . .

It is, she thought crossly, *too bad of him, making me tumble into the dismals because I must feel concern for his problems.*

Anne turned away from the stranger, and she, too, stared broodingly toward the unseen shores ahead. It was foolish to bother her head about the man. He was *not* her responsibility. It was merely *habit* to worry about another. About any other.

It is a habit I mean to break. Anne's little chin tightened up still more and she raised it a notch. *If I worry about anything at all,* she told herself, *then I will worry about myself.*

That decided, she immediately thought of Catherine's latest pregnancy, which had followed, Anne felt, far too quickly on the last. She wondered, again, whether she should speak to Catherine's husband of such delicate matters—whether she *could* speak about such things to a man.

Still debating the question, Anne went to the cabin and quietly opened the door. She peered in and, thanks to the lamp swinging from the ceiling, lit but turned low, she saw that Milly slept, a tiny frown marring her brow. Careful not to wake her, Anne put herself to bed, removing only her travel gown so that it would not be wrinkled beyond further wear.

Several hours later a knock at the door and a steward's shout warned that they had arrived, that the packet had unloaded while the passengers slept and that now all must debark.

Anne awakened from an exceedingly interesting dream. Half asleep, she regretted the loss of it. But then, her mind clearing, she remembered more details and felt a blush rise up her throat. She turned and found Milly sitting on the side of her bunk, yawning, rubbing her face with both hands.

"I see," said Anne as soon as she was certain her voice would not betray the odd warmth her dreams about the tall dark stranger had induced, "that you managed to survive the crossing."

"My tummy was not happy, but it didn't complain to the point of making me ill," said Milly. She yawned again. "My brother-in-law gave me a vial and told me that a sip or two before I tried to sleep would very likely do me a great deal of good." She lowered her voice. "Spirits, I fear," she said as if revealing a terrible secret. "I am almost certain it was brandy." She grimaced. "It tasted terrible but I must admit it did the trick."

"It helped?" asked Anne sympathetically. "Then think of it as medicine. Medicine always tastes awful."

Milly grimaced again and again scrubbed her face with her hands, ending by thrusting her fingers into her sleep-tossed hair. "Is there water in the ewer?"

There was and soon the two, finished with a sketchy toilet, helped each other back into their gowns. Donning coats, tying bonnets, gloves smoothed over wrists, reticules checked, and parasols tightly furled, they removed to the deck, where the courier Anne had hired to organize their journey awaited them.

He organized them so well that they were installed in their heavily loaded traveling carriage almost before they had taken in anything at all about the old port town. Rather bemused by the speed, they opened the basket he'd supplied and ate their breakfast while the driver tooled the horses down the road and away from Calais.

"*Paris,*" breathed Anne once her hunger was satisfied. Excitement gave her a glow.

"But not today," reminded practical Milly. "You will

not wish to leave your horses behind, so they must be rested often."

Anne nodded. "It is an extravagance, the carriage and the horses, but I was informed that hiring transport is a chancy thing and long delays are common. We will go slowly, but at least we will *go*." She dug into her overlarge reticule and pulled out a traveling chessboard. "Shall we play? To while away the miles?"

The play was erratic, both women often lifting their eyes to stare at the passing scene. When Milly made an extremely idiotic move, Anne looked at her friend, noted how distracted she was by the view, and laughed. Without asking, she cleared the board and put it away.

"You must say when you do not wish to do something. Just because I suggest it is no reason to agree to it if you do not wish it."

"I must earn my way, Anne. Do not treat me utterly as a friend or I will forget I am here to provide propriety and that you pay our bills. I might come to think I have nothing to do but enjoy myself."

"I very much hope you *will* enjoy yourself!"

"That is very like you, Anne, but you know very well . . . Oh dear. That poor man."

Anne leaned to look out her friend's window. "My goodness," she said, surprised. They were passing a tall dark man wearing a caped coat, who strode along the verge leading a limping horse. There was no mistaking that blade of a nose, that jutting chin—or the glowering frown. Anne pulled the string and her courier, seated by her driver, opened the flap.

"Stop," she ordered, "so that I may speak to that man."

"My lady!"

His look of outrage had her biting back another unladylike grin. "He was on the packet," she said, implying that she knew him.

"Oh. In that case . . ." said the courier and disappeared. The carriage pulled to the side of the road.

"Do not tell me," said Milly in a whisper, "that you spoke to a total stranger while on board."

"We did not speak, but he is English and he is in difficulties in a foreign land. We will take him up and Jeffery—" She referred to the footman-cum-groom, also a member of her entourage. "—may lead his horse into the next town while he rides with us."

"You do not know him. He might be a murderer escaping justice!"

"Nonsense. I am certain he is no such thing. I doubt he is the heir to a marquess but I am certain he is of the *ton*."

"Son of a marquess . . . Anne, what are you . . . ?"

But the door opened and the stranger stood there frowning still more deeply. "Madam, I do not know you," he said in harsh, not *too* badly accented, French.

"Nor I you," said Anne. Her French was much more the thing although still carrying a hint of an English accent. She continued in English. "Nevertheless, when I see a countryman in difficulties, I feel I must offer what aid I can. Will you not ride with us while my groom walks your mount into town?"

It was soon arranged, although Anne felt the stranger was reluctant to be under an obligation to her. When Milly moved to seat herself beside the silent maid on the rear-facing seat, Anne very nearly stopped her, but Milly shook her head at her, so she turned slightly in order to face the stranger who seated himself at her side.

"This is Mrs. Seward, my companion, and I am Lady Anne Forsythe."

The stranger nodded. "Elverston. *Mr.* Elverston," he offered, disappointing Anne, who had convinced herself he was a titled gentleman—although *not*, of course, heir to a marquisate, as in her invented history.

Conversation was stiff and formal and Anne found that disappointing as well. Her first effort to become acquainted with a fellow traveler appeared to be a failure. At the same time, she found herself still more impressed by Mr. Elverston, his looks, a faint scent of sandalwood that wafted her way whenever he moved, and a certain natural authority that, under other circumstances, she felt would give him stature beyond the excellent physique covered but not hidden by layers of clothing—that and something that was utterly male stimulated feelings in her she had never before experienced.

Although she discovered little of a personal nature concerning Mr. Elverston, it occurred to her that he drew from her a great deal of *her* history. Enough so that she felt a trifle awkward that he knew so much about her when she knew so little about him. Therefore, despite her curiosity, it was a relief to arrive where he could see to his horse. *Their* horses would rest while they enjoyed a luncheon and a stroll about the town.

Anne, enjoying her first stop in a foreign land, very nearly forgot her unsatisfying experience with the dark stranger. She and Milly strolled the streets, and she tried to take in everything, exclaiming to Milly about one thing, turning to see what her friend was oohing about, and, in her adequate if not always elegant French, asking questions of locals concerning the history of buildings and monuments along the way.

Her greatest delight was the church near the inn at which they'd lunched. It was not a cathedral—several of which were on her list of Things-to-See—but it was a delightful Gothic structure with much of interest in the way of stone and wood carving. She fell in love with one of the gargoyles decorating the exterior. There was, nearby, an impish little stone angel, perhaps a cherub, that, if she was not reading too much into it, was tormenting the gargoyle. The poor gargoyle appeared much put-upon but patiently resigned to the teasing.

Anne purchased a pad of drawing paper and pencils and settled herself on a bench to sketch. Milly, who was not artistically inclined, wandered here and there, never going far, and returning often to see how Anne progressed.

"Lady Forsythe," spoke a deep abrupt voice.

Anne glanced up, her eyes widening painfully. "Mr. Elverston!"

"I am sorry I startled you, but I wish to thank you, which I think I did not, for your help this morning."

He bowed, glanced at her work, and then took a better look. He smiled for the first time in their brief acquaintance, and she hoped no one noticed how the change in him made her heart race.

"You are very talented." He reached for the sketchbook, glanced up at the church, back to the page, and then grinned widely—making Anne's disobedient heart thunder within her breast. "Delightful," he said sincerely.

Anne took back her pad and, impulsively, tore out the page. She handed it to him. "I can draw another," she said, feeling a trifle shy.

He bowed, holding the sketch carefully. "I will treasure it," he said, and again it seemed to Anne that he meant it. "I must be off. I wish you the very best of travels," he added, bowed again, and almost at once was gone.

Anne, bemused, stared at the blank page before her and then, slowly, almost absently, began to draw.

That night she opened her sketchbook to the dark face, the slashing buccaneering grin, and shook her head, exasperated with herself for continuing to indulge herself in such obviously romantic nonsense. She tore the page out and was about to put it into the fire when she hesitated. With a sigh, she slipped it into the back of the book.

Facing her was her second drawing of the impish angel and the patient gargoyle. It made her smile just as the real thing had made her smile. It would make a happy memory . . . although exactly what that memory might include she refused to admit. She closed the book, putting it into the portmanteau from which she had taken her night rail.

From the bed, Milly asked, "Did you manage to get the image you tried for?"

"I think so." A vision of the stranger's dangerous grin hovered in Anne's head. "Yes, I think I managed something of what I saw there," she said.

She crawled into bed beside her friend and blew out her candle. Then, only the glow from the fireplace lighting the room, she stared at the ceiling. After a few moments, Milly's soft snores reached her ears, and smiling fondly, she turned her head. She was unused to having anyone share her room let alone her bed, and— even as she yawned widely—she wondered if her friend's soft night noises would keep her awake.

They did not.

When she woke up in the morning, she almost wished they had. Her dreams that night were not such that she would ever reveal them to a soul. When Milly was occupied behind the screen, washing, Anne once again found Elverston's portrait. Once again she very nearly put it in the fire.

And once again she returned it to the back of her sketchbook.

"You," she muttered to herself, "are very nearly as foolish as was poor Thomasina about that poet!" The thought made her smile. Thomasina had recovered from her brief infatuation and so, too, would she—and would cease to find her sleeping mind invaded by a stranger.

Anne, taking her turn behind the screen for her ablutions, muttered, "And the sooner the better, too. Very rude, to intrude on my dreams that way . . ."

"You said something?" called Milly from where she was closing up the portmanteaus.

"What? Oh—" Anne thought quickly. "—merely wondering how Thomasina is doing with her new husband."

"Worrying you mean. Now stop that," scolded Milly. "You spent a decade worrying about those girls. You worry about yourself for a change."

Anne instantly felt guilty that she had not had a thought in her head about any of the girls since sometime much earlier the previous day. From approximately the time they met a distressed English man along the road. . . .

The first day in Paris, Anne fidgeted around their sitting room in the accommodations her courier had had ready for them. It was a light and airy room, decorated in the latest style, with high windows looking out over a brand-new avenue where, at regular intervals, young trees cast small patches of brave shadow. She had told herself that she would, the moment she finished dressing, encourage Milly to join her in a long exploratory walk.

"So why do I not?" she asked fretfully.

For the third time she found herself approaching the escritoire. For the third time she turned away. But this time, instead of stalking the length of the magnificent room, she stopped and turned back. She growled in frustration.

"What is it, Anne?" Milly looked up from her personal lap desk, at which she was composing one of her regular letters to her brother, a vicar in a smallish village in the north of England.

"I swore that once I left its shores I would not give one thought to anything back in England!"

Milly chuckled.

"Yes, you are very right," continued Anne as if Milly had commented. "It seems I cannot, just like that, put aside the concerns with which I have been burdened for the past decade."

"Concerns, Anne?" Milly picked up her pen wiper, wiped her pen free of ink, and set it into the slot made for it. She quietly closed the lid and set the traveling desk to the side of her chair.

"You will never know what a terrible responsibility it was, following my husband's many directions—" Anne cast a dour look toward her friend. "—*some* of which *contradicted* others."

Milly laughed. "But you did it, Anne. And you did it well. Is there no satisfaction in that?"

Anne pushed her upper lip up with a pursed lower lip. Then she relaxed and heaved a sigh. "It had its compensations—and I do not refer to the fact I have been left very well-to-do. My widow's portion is generous far beyond my expectations, of course, but the girls, especially little Thomasina—well, you know how I came to love that minx—"

"And she you," inserted Milly.

"—and Beth nearly so well." Anne frowned. "I failed with Catherine, of course. I still think there must have been something . . ."

"She would have resented any woman her father married, but you, Anne, were only two years older than she herself."

Anne sighed. "Yes, well, something . . . ?"

Milly chuckled. "We have, I think, slipped away from what it is that bothers you."

Anne nodded. "I *swore* I'd not worry the teeniest tiny bit about any of them . . . and here I am, wondering how Tommy and her new husband get on, how Beth is coping with the loss of a favorite nursery maid who left to get married, and even how Catherine feels. She is in her fourth month, you know, which, she assures me, is not, for her, a pleasant time."

Milly nodded. "Anne, you spent the better part of ten years concerning yourself with their lives. You cannot rid yourself of that as one would brush up the ashes in a fire-place and throw them into the ash bin."

"So . . ." After a long moment, she cast Milly another look. "What do *you* suggest I do?"

"I suggest you sit down, write each of them a short but friendly letter, and that when you have finished we take ourselves out for a long walk this first full day in Paris."

Anne chuckled. "Even if I were not curious beyond belief, we need the exercise after two long days in the carriage. But how did you know that was my intention? The walk, I mean?"

"Have I known you since you were in leading strings or have I not?" asked Milly sternly.

"Not *quite* that long."

"Write your letters, Anne. If nothing else it is only proper you should send them notice of your safe arrival."

Anne cast a longing look toward the bright windows, turned to look at the escritoire, sighed, and dragging her feet to it in an exaggerated fashion that made Milly chuckle, went to open the desk.

That each brief note turned into an epistle of some length did not surprise Milly, who quietly went back to her own letter detailing their journey and describing their new residence, which Anne meant to retain for two months before moving on to Switzerland. Milly had, over the years, received many letters from Anne, and not a one of them had been less than two pages, crossed, and occasionally *recrossed*. She was certain she'd time to finish her own.

"There," said Anne at last. "I am finished. And you, Milly?"

"I have been sitting here with my bonnet in hand for hours and hours," teased Milly.

> *From a letter to Beth from Thomasina: " . . . wonderful how often she mentions that Elverston? I am so pleased for her. She has been alone far too long. I loved our father dearly, but you will admit he was not the sort of husband of whom one dreams . . ."*
>
> *From a letter to Beth from Catherine. " . . . I do not know what she can be thinking. No sooner does she leave the country than she takes up with some stranger. Now if it were the man my dear Beast remembers from their days at Oxford, why this Elverston would be more than acceptable. But a mere mister? After being Lady Anne Forsythe? It is not to be thought of and if it were not for my beloved Beast insisting I do no such thing, I would write to tell her so . . ."*
>
> *From a letter to Thomasina from Beth. " . . . Catherine's husband recalls the heir to a marquisate whose courtesy title was Elverston. He seems to have disappeared from society, a recluse. You don't suppose the man travels incognito, do you? Oh! Do not take me seriously, Tommy. I jest, as you well know . . ."*

Anne and Milly packed every day full of sightseeing, marveling at the scope and magnificence of Napoleon's plan for the city. Although it was still in the initial stages of construction, enough was finished one could imagine the majestic whole. Having accomplished so much so quickly, the two ladies decided it was time to slow down, enjoy the lovely spring weather, and some of the more *commercial* temptations offered by Paris.

Toward the end of the second week, Anne and Milly strolled the wide boulevard leading to the Place de l'Etoile, where Napoleon's unfinished Arc de Triomphe rose.

"Ironic, is it not?" asked Anne as they neared the arch. "It was he who ordered it erected but it is we who triumphed."

"Finally."

Anne nodded. "So *many* years of war. I do hope it is a very long time before we must worry so again."

As usual, the shops drew them. An hour later they were still moving slowly from window to window. The Parisian shopkeepers displayed their goods in such tempting arrays it was difficult to restrain oneself from opening one's purse again and again, but both, after an initial flurry of spending, were determined to be frugal.

They were, however, contemplating whether Anne could do without a certain very fine bonnet when someone behind them cleared her throat. Anne turned slightly and then completely, a smile on her lips and glad lights glowing in her eyes at the sight of the first friend she had made when her ailing husband introduced her to London, a shy and frightened eighteen-year-old.

"Lady Margrove! I heard you meant to remove to Paris, but I did not expect to see you so soon."

"My dear Lady Anne, I am *so* glad *you* are finally arrived. I hold a small soiree this *very* evening. I hope you are free to join us? Oh dear. Such *insultingly* short notice, but I was *unaware* you . . . ?"

"We arrived some days ago," said Anne, interrupting. Softhearted Lady Margrove could go on and on, with excuse after excuse, when she feared she had insulted or hurt someone. "We have not formally announced our arrival so you could not have known of it. May I present my friend . . . ?"

Ten minutes later Anne and Milly, promises to attend the soiree given, were free to continue their walk. Milly asked about the lady and listened with interest to Anne's discussion of how kind Lady Margrove had helped ease Anne's introduction to London society, and then chuckled when Anne finished, ". . . but she is just the teeniest—" She held her finger and thumb a fraction of an inch apart. "—bit the shatterbrain. Oh! But in the *nicest* way, of course."

Almost immediately upon their arrival at Lady Margrove's, they discovered another old friend. Major Michael Torrington had grown up near Anne and Milly's village. The third son of the local squire who must earn his living, he had chosen to go into the army and it was many years since the three had last met. Anne left Milly and the major talking animatedly and continued on to find their hostess. Lady Margrove was also speaking with animation—perhaps one might be forgiven the term "gushing"—with a tall dark stranger.

"My stranger," muttered Anne and felt a rosy glow at the way she'd phrased that thought. She then blushed still more deeply upon realizing that not only had she referred to the gentleman as hers, but had spoken the words aloud. She glanced around and breathed freely again when no one appeared to have noticed.

Lady Margrove beckoned, and Anne was obliged to join them. "My dear, here is an *old* friend from *our* corner of England. He's a bit of a *recluse* these days—the *sweet brute*—so it is likely *you* have never met *him*."

"But we have met," said Anne and held out her hand.

"Yes," said Mr. Elverston shortly. "Lady Forsythe was kind enough to take me up in her carriage when my horse lost a shoe on the road from Calais."

Lady Margrove's eyes bulged. "You *rode*! My *dear* Drake, is that not *just* like you when any *sensible* man would have *driven*—" Even as she chided Mr. Elverston, Lady Margrove searched the crowd for new arrivals. She gasped, interrupting herself. "—and *there* is Lady Venetia. I hadn't a notion *she* would come although I *did* send her an *invitation*. Oh, do, *please*, excuse me . . ."

Lady Anne shook her head ever so slightly as she fondly watched her hostess flit away, then glanced at Mr. Elverston and discovered he looked ever so slightly put out. At that, she frowned. "Something troubles you, sir?" she asked.

He focused on her. "Ah! I am rude, am I not? Forgive me. Do tell me—" He completely ignored her question. "—how you go on. Are your accommodations adequate? Do you find friends who have also settled in Paris? Have you succumbed and bought yourself a bonnet in the new French style?"

The questions were more than proper, but there was an abruptness and just a hint of coolness that irritated Anne. "Do you care?" she asked quietly.

It took perhaps half a second for her question to register. He blinked. Then he barked a short sharp laugh. "You find it unnecessary to mouth polite nothings when you meet a stranger at a gathering such as this?"

"I do."

He bowed, and when he straightened, eyed her with curiosity—really looked at her as he had not done before, not even when he'd ridden in her carriage or, later, when he'd spoken to her as she sketched. When she merely smiled slightly, eyeing him steadily, he blinked. "I had believed," he said, in that abrupt manner, "that such inanities were the proper way to go on, but if you disagree, then what *shall* we discuss?"

There was something of a challenge in his tone, something that was very nearly a dare. Anne, even as she wondered what he saw when he stared that way—so rude—was quite ready to take it up. "There are any number of topics that might be of interest to the both of us. For my part, I admit to being a bit of a bluestocking and enjoy talking about literature—especially the work of modern writers such as Sir Walter Scott or the playwright, Sheridan. Not, however, Byron, who has been discussed to such an extent the topic has become a bore." She paused but he said nothing. "If none of the first three "p's," prose, poetry, or plays, appeal, perhaps you have an interest in the fourth?"

He tipped his head, questioningly.

"*Politics,* sir. Can you, perhaps, tell me how Viscount Castlereagh goes on in Vienna, if he is any nearer achieving England's goal of a balance of power among the great states?" She eyed him. "Not politics," she said when he blinked. "Then perhaps you have a particular interest in the late war . . ."

He froze.

She tipped her head. "What did I say?"

"I lost a brother in the war," he said, his voice clipped.

"I am sorry for it," she said.

His brows rose. "You sound sincere."

"Why should I be insincere where such a terrible subject is concerned?"

"You don't know me. You didn't know my brother. In what way does it concern you?"

"You suggest that I cannot feel sorry for your pain, even though you are a stranger to me?" Her lips tightened and her gaze held his steadily. "You would believe me so heartless?"

"I have insulted you," he said quietly.

"You have."

He smiled a brief flickering smile. "Should I apologize?"

Anne's chin tilted just a trifle. "It is usual to do so when one makes such an error."

"Then I will. I do." He studied her, once again really looking at her. "To prove you accept my apology, will you consent to ride with me? Tomorrow?"

She relaxed. "I love to ride. My correspondents tell me there are lovely long rides where one may meet any number of friends and acquaintances. It would please me to experience it for the first time at your side, sir." Then, chagrined, she bit her lip. "But I fear I cannot. I have not set up a riding mare . . ."

Mr. Elverston bowed very slightly. "I will supply one." He discovered her address and suggested a time when he would bring around horses for the two of them. "Now I must leave you. I have not come to Paris solely to enjoy myself and I see two men with whom I must speak." He bowed again, said he looked forward to seeing her in the morning, and left her.

Anne's dreams that night included a knight riding a white horse along the sun-dappled grassy rides of an ancient forest—and a never-to-be-forgotten walk among incredible blossoms that could not possibly exist.

Perhaps because of the dream, the fact Mr. Elverston rode a white horse—having had a lady's saddle put on the back of the roan he'd ridden from Calais—did not surprise her. Too, their ride was all she had hoped it would be—and more. Mr. Elverston proved to be widely read and an interesting conversationalist. He appeared to think well of Anne, too, and Anne could not help but feel a tiny bud of gratification that it was so. She was so bold as to wonder if she invaded *his* dreams as he did hers—but not so bold she dared ask.

Another fortnight passed pleasantly. There were soirees, the mixed English and French guests leavened with a handful of Russian princes, foreign military gentlemen, and diplomats from every Allied country. Two grand balls were held during this period. Major Torrington was often among the guests. Anne smiled to see the growing friendship between Milly and their old friend.

And then, too, there was Mr. Elverston . . .

It was all very nearly as delightful as Anne had hoped, the sights and smells and tastes of this foreign land. Delightful, that is, until the bubble burst.

Mr. Elverston was decidedly chilly when he came to call one afternoon. He apologized—although he did not sound particularly apologetic—but it was imperative that he leave Paris immediately, and therefore he must cancel their engagement to ride out the following morning.

Anne blinked. "I hope it is not bad news," she said, hesitating ever so slightly.

"Bad news?" He laughed a rather bitter laugh. "You might say it is and it isn't."

Then, softening slightly, he explained that he was off to Hanover on that business that preoccupied him. "It has been enjoyable knowing you," he said abruptly, his tone again chilly. Then, abruptly, he bowed and left the room with a quick, determined stride—before Anne could even think to offer him morning coffee.

"Now what," she asked the empty room, "was that all about?"

Milly and Major Torrington returned from a walk along the Seine soon after and found Anne seated at her desk, the ink drying on her pen, and a pensive look in her eyes. Milly, realizing that the moment was not propitious for announcements turned a warning glance on the major before asking what was wrong.

"Wrong? Why should you think anything is wrong? I am planning the next stage of our odyssey, Milly. Count Leopold was telling me about Switzerland. His description of the Alps is such that I cannot believe such scenery exists. It has inspired in me a great desire to see for myself.

Then, too, I am told Lake Constance is especially lovely this time of year. What do you think, Milly?"

Milly cast another look at the major, who pokered up, his spine stiffening. Milly spoke quickly. "It must be your decision, Anne, but surely you cannot leave Paris all at once. Are we not invited to a ball at the end of next week? And you and Mr. Elverston mean to ride out tomorrow, do you not?"

Reminding Anne of Mr. Elverston was, although Milly could not know it, a mistake. Anne felt still more convinced that she could not bear to remain in the city where, in a very short time, she had come all too near to falling deeply in love.

Worse.

She might have fallen in love with a man who did not exist. The creature who spoke so coldly just a brief hour earlier had nothing in common with the warmth and gentleness, the intelligence and humor, of the man she *thought* she'd begun to know. A man who had had no difficulty following her little jokes, who shared her feelings concerning the sorry effect war had on those who had no part in it, the women and children, the poor and the aged . . . no, that man must have been a false image and she should thank her lucky stars he had tired of playing with her and gone on about his business.

"I think we might be ready to leave by Monday at the latest," mused Anne, not really looking at Milly.

If she had, she would have seen a moment's despair before her friend swallowed hard, squeezed Major Torrington's arm, and released him. "In that case," said Milly, "there are one or two things I still wish to see. Major," she said, turning to him and holding his gaze with her own, "are you free to escort me again tomorrow or will your duty keep you occupied?"

"I shall make myself free to accompany you," he said.

"And as often as you like in the days before you leave, of course."

Anne thought she heard a very slight grimness in his voice, but when she looked, his features were as bland and smooth as always. She tipped her head, looked from one to the other, but decided she must be wrong. They were just Milly and Michael, old friends of her youth.

"I must speak with Gerard," she said. "Reprehensible of me, to leave you two alone, but if I do not close the door—" She held it, her eyes twinkling as she looked back into the room. "—then it cannot be thought improper."

With that comment she gently *shut* the door, and whistling in an improper fashion as she'd not allowed herself to do for years, she sought out Jeremy, to whom she gave orders to locate the courier who was to come immediately to receive new commands.

There followed, for Anne, a number of boring days. She had not realized until he was gone just how firmly Mr. Elverston had taken up residence in her thoughts. She chided herself for her foolishness. Making a great effort, she threw herself into giddy pleasure at the last few entertainments she graced with her presence. Not that she *wanted* to attend, but she had accepted invitations from which she did not feel it proper to cry off.

Besides, if she *did* cry off, then someone would notice that Mr. Elverston was also absent and accuse her of moping. Worse. They might think she was pining for him. Which she was—but only in her dreams.

Letter to Beth from Catherine. ". . . very glad to hear that that Elverston person has gone from Paris. I do not understand your sympathy for Anne. You cannot have thought the connection suitable . . ."

Letter to Catherine from Thomasina. ". . . you are your usual proud and cold self. Have you ever truly thought

of another's hopes and dreams? Wished them happiness?
Or is it all pomp and ceremony with you . . . ?"

Letter to Thomasina from Beth. ". . . must not. Poor
Catherine cannot help being who and what she is. Mother
Anne does not need a knight errant and you do no good
scolding. But know that I too am concerned. Mother
Anne's last letter pretends an excitement I am convinced
she does not feel. I pray this move to the mountains will
do her good . . ."

Anne sat writing letters when Milly returned from her
last jaunt with the major. "Back so soon, Milly? I had a
notion you meant to be gone most of the afternoon."

"It has been the most of it, Anne. Do ring for tea, will
you not? I am parched."

Anne looked at the ormolu clock. "Oh dear. Where has
time fled? I am glad we need not go out this evening. I
have yet to finish my packing and I am not at all pleased
with Gerard's arrangements for our first day on the road.
I will insist he change the route so as to take in Chartres.
The cathedral, you know. I will not miss that . . . what is it
Milly? You are very quiet."

"Hmm? Oh it is nothing." Milly, with difficulty, had convinced the major that her duty lay with Anne until Anne
returned to England—but it had not been easy, and she
was no happier with the decision than he. "I must take my
bonnet to my room and return for tea which you—" Milly
pretended annoyance "—have yet to order."

Relieved by her friend's teasing, Anne chuckled.
"Hurry, or it will be cold."

"How can that be?" asked Milly with the faintest touch
of acid. "Unordered, it is unlikely to have arrived!"

* * *

They traveled so slowly it required more than two weeks to reach Lake Constance, where they settled into a new set of rooms. Milly had felt unwell that last part of the journey and to recoup spent the first few days lying on a sofa in their small salon.

Anne could not remain still. Reprehensibly, she took herself off to walk, alone, along the paving that fronted Lake Constance. Every so often she paused, laying a hand on the balustrade that prevented one from falling into the water. The view was breathtaking, the water a vivid blue one rarely saw—reminding her of Mr. Elverston's piercing blue eyes.

Cross with herself for thinking of the man when she only wished to forget him, Anne turned away from the lake and walked up an interesting-looking side street. It narrowed, but unwilling to return to her accommodation where her thoughts tended to be perverse, Anne persevered. She rounded a corner into a still narrower passage and, the more rounded cobbles giving her difficulties, picked her way carefully. More than once she used the ferrule of her sturdy parasol to steady herself.

Ahead was another corner. For a moment Anne considered retracing her steps. Then a shaft of sunlight lighted a niche at the end of the street, catching the eye. Anne continued on in order to see what, exactly, it held.

She discovered a small shrine to the Virgin, fresh flowers gracing the bowl set at the figure's feet. It was a lovely little marble statue, and Anne wondered who had sculpted it. Thinking she should return with her sketchbook, she drew nearer, enjoying the gently rounded, cloth-draped limbs, the down-turned eyes, the simple acceptance of duty and love.

Her approach brought her beyond the corner and a flash of movement to the right caught her eye. For a moment shock stilled her. Two men attacked a third and

the third, turning suddenly, was the one man she had
hoped never to meet again. Shock faded into anger that
anyone dared harm Elverston. Anne picked up her skirts
with one hand and raced forward. She brought her parasol down, hard, on the head of one of the attackers,
partially stunning him. At the same moment Mr. Elverston's fist connected with his other opponent's chin,
felling him. He turned back to the second, and that man
fell to the ground as well.

Only then did Mr. Elverston look at his unexpected
ally. His brows clashed together. "Lady Forsythe," he said,
bowing. His mouth formed a stern line when he rose to
face her, his eyes flashing with temper.

Her heart beating hard—although she could not tell
if it was from the melee or from once again facing the
man in her dreams—she spoke quickly. "I know what
you would say to me, sir, but should we not go elsewhere
before you ring a peal over my head?" She prodded one
of the men with her parasol. He moaned.

Elverston barked a short sharp laugh. "Yes, perhaps we
should—" He grasped her elbow and led her down the
narrow street at an uncomfortable pace. "—but do not
think to escape a scold."

"Did you know those men?" asked Anne, rather
breathlessly.

"No."

She ran a few steps in order to catch up with him after
they rounded a corner. "They meant to rob you?"

"Yes."

Another corner and then they were back in the sun and
on the promenade along the lakeshore. Anne breathed
deeply. If one were not a gentleman, one might have accused her of panting. She was glad that, in this respect,
Mr. Elverston *was* a gentleman. Finally she felt she had
recovered sufficiently to speak again.

"Was it," she asked, "necessary to rush us *quite* so quickly?"

"I didn't want either of those men seeing you and recognizing you and wishing you ill for interfering." He waved his hand in a chopping motion and changed the subject before she could comment. "I see a café just there. Will you join me for a coffee?"

Anne had been pleased to discover that women were allowed to sit at the little street-side tables set under colorful umbrellas to protect against the bright blue sky. There, in the open air, a lady could sip coffee or tea without her reputation suffering and watch the world pass along the paving. She decided not to suffer from pique that he seemed to wish to ignore their recent adventure and, suddenly elated to be again in his company, wanted nothing more than to drink coffee with him.

"I would like that," she said quietly, knowing she was feeding what had become an obsession but not caring a fig for what she would suffer when he disappeared again. As he *would* do.

Anne accompanied him to a table, where he seated her and then himself. Then Mr. Elverston stared out over the water, silent, as they waited for their coffee to arrive. When it did, he drew in a deep breath and looked at her. "I must, of course, thank you for your aid."

Obviously he was still reluctant to speak of their adventure but felt forced to do so. Anne felt her lips twitch. "But?" she asked politely.

"But what damn—" His voice grew deeper with each word. "—maggot did you get into your head to put yourself in such danger?"

Anne's brows arched, surprised he felt so strongly he'd swear at her. Very softly, she said, "I don't think it was maggots. I merely saw a fellow countryman . . ."

His voice joined hers and they finished as a duet.

". . . in difficulties and I could not simply pass him by."

"Any normal woman would have set up a screech," he said peevishly and added, almost as an afterthought, "or fainted."

"Then," she said with only a bit of asperity, "I am not normal. I have never seen the sense of screeches and if there is more useless behavior than a faint I don't know what it could be."

Her change of mood for the worse changed his for the better. He chuckled. "I agree, of course—" The frown returned. "—but that does *not* excuse you. You should *not* have put yourself into danger."

"Bah." She said it in something of an experimental tone, her previous show of irritation having improved his mood. She watched to see if it improved still more.

He eyed her for half a moment and then smiled ever so slightly. "Perhaps we should agree to disagree?"

Anne nodded, a regal movement of her head that surprised another chuckle from him.

"In that case," he said, after half a moment, "it is your turn to open a conversation."

Anne relaxed. "I hadn't a notion you meant to come to Switzerland," she said. "In fact—" She frowned ever so slightly. "—I thought you'd formed the intention of removing to Hanover."

"Ah! Then you did *not* go to Hanover?"

She frowned in earnest. "No of course not. We mean to spend the opera season in Milan, but it is yet too early in the year and, therefore, our intention is to take in the magnificent scenery along the way, traveling slowly and staying wherever strikes us as interesting. We remain here for some weeks and then move on, a day or two here and as much as a week there—you know the sort of thing I mean."

"Will you scold if I admit I am so much the cockscomb I wondered if you had followed me?"

Anne's spine, which had relaxed ever so slightly with his chuckles, stiffened. "I *follow* you? But *I* arrived here very nearly a week past."

"And I only yesterday. Perhaps——" His tone was more conciliating. "——you will accuse me of following you?"

"That would be gratifying if true, but somehow I doubt it." As Anne said it she knew she wished it *were* true. "Are you enjoying your travels?" she asked, fearing she'd give away her preference for his company if they did not change the subject immediately.

As she would have known if she'd only thought, it was exactly the wrong thing to say. His features took on a tense look and his eyes lost their concentration, staring over the water at nothing at all.

"I see," she said softly. "You are not. I am sorry."

Mr. Elverston didn't exactly shake himself, but it was obviously an effort to return his attention to her. "My journey, unlike yours, is not one of pleasure," he said. The words seemed to bring to mind something else, and although he moved not so much as a muscle, she had the sense he withdrew from her still more. "I've a duty to accomplish. I cannot think of . . . other things——"

He eyed her in a manner she could not interpret.

"——until I have managed to discover . . ."

He broke off sharply, his lips closing tightly. His gaze as cold as when she'd last seen him in Paris, he took his purse from his pocket, put some coins on the table and then rose. "I thank you again for your aid in that alley. When I return there, as I must, I will take someone with me to guard my back." He bowed, turned, and without another look, walked off.

Anne, blinking, stared after him. "That man is as changeable as a weather vane. What do I see in him that appeals to me so strongly?" She sighed, looked into her coffee cup, found there was one last swallow—but it was cold and unpleasant—so she, too, rose and walked away.

The other way.

Changeable indeed. The next day Milly, who had gone to post a letter, found him standing, looking undecided, in the small lobby outside the concierge's door.

"Mr. Elverston!"

"Ah! Mrs. Seward," he said. "I wondered if I had reached the right building." Still more abruptly, he asked, "Is Lady Anne in and might she spare me a moment of her time? Will you ask her to join me for a walk?"

"I am sure she is and that she will," said Milly. "I will go up and ask."

Anne frowned when the request was made of her. "Milly, do you think the man can be quite right in the head?"

Milly chuckled. Anne had regaled her with the preceding day's happenings, so she was well aware of what Anne meant. "You know he is," she said, scolding. "What you do not know is why he has come today. I suggest, my dear friend, that you put on your bonnet, pick up your parasol, and take yourself down and ask."

"I believe," said Anne, her features showing no sign of humor, "that is the proper way of satisfying one's curiosity."

She showed no sign of the excitement rising within her, but Milly knew her well and guessed. "You might also want to do something about that curl falling down your back—before you put on your bonnet."

Anne blushed and hurried to her bedroom, where she fixed her hair, found her bonnet and gloves, and hurried out again.

"Mr. Elverston," she said some minutes later. He turned from the foyer's window and smiled at her. "You look a great deal more relaxed than you did yesterday, sir?"

"I am. I've found what I think is important news leading to my goal." He sobered and held out his hand. "Lady Forsythe, I must leave immediately for my next destination, but I did not wish to go without speaking to you."

She put her hand into his, found it tucked under his arm and herself being led outside. Not that she minded. She would, she thought ruefully, go mindlessly wherever Mr. Elverston led.

Even—the still more rueful thought crossed her mind— *if it is up the garden path!*

"I am uncertain where to begin," he said. "Perhaps firstly, I want you to know that I admire you greatly. What you did yesterday revealed a courage and generosity not found in many. I know men who would have turned tail and run from such a situation."

"You exaggerate," she murmured.

"You know I do not," he said in a slightly scolding tone. "Now be still because I have little time to say all I wish to say . . . Yes?" he asked after a moment.

"Sir," she said. "I remain quite still!"

He laughed. "Intelligent. And a sense of humor. I like that." He patted her hand. And then, despite saying he had no time to spare, he walked on in silence.

Twice Anne peered around the side of her bonnet and up at him. Twice she very nearly spoke. Twice she bit her tongue.

"I have told no one why I crossed the Channel, but I feel it is safe to tell you," he said, and this time it was he who peered around the bonnet rim into her face.

She nodded, glad she'd waited.

"It concerns my family."

Again she nodded.

"Some two, perhaps so much as two and a half years ago, we received word that my brother was missing and believed dead. It was a terrible blow to our mother who loved him dearly. I will admit to a great deal of sadness myself. Timothy is—was—is?" He drew in a deep breath. "A rapscallion, our Timothy, and always falling into scrapes from which I found myself removing him, and one might have thought I'd have grown tired of it. Frankly, I thought so too—until word reached us that he was dead. Believed dead," he corrected himself.

Again they walked in silence, and again Anne managed, with great difficulty, to keep a still tongue in her head.

He sighed softly and continued. "Recently, a month or two now, an old friend drove miles out of his way to come to see me. He was perplexed . . . unhappy . . . confused . . . I don't quite know how to describe him. He had gone to Vienna to the Congress, and as he'd passed through Paris on his return, he saw a man he *knew* was Tim. He accosted the man, was spoken to in fluent and rather vituperative Italian, and then the stranger stalked off. Our friend saw this man again a day or so later and approached him more cautiously and was again responded to in what could only be called a belligerent fashion. My friend, however, is convinced it is Tim, that he did *not* die and that, somewhere in Europe, he is living the life of an Italian trader. You can see that I must find this man."

"Good heavens yes," exclaimed Anne. "The sooner the better."

He nodded gravely. "So you see, my dear—"

Anne's mouth fell open at the endearment, her eyes widening.

"—that I haven't the time to indulge myself. Or you. I have never been one to go into an affaire with a married woman, so this would be a first for me, but I am—" He turned her so that he held her by both shoulders. "—

drawn to you. I wanted you to know that I do not leave you, yet again, without reason."

With that he tipped up her face, kissed her warmly, and while Anne was still unable to find words, attempting as she was to disabuse him of two very different things at the exact same time, he left her.

"Mr. Elverston," she called and took a few steps after him—but it was too late. He had rounded the corner and disappeared. She could neither inform him she was a widow—Where *had* he come by the notion she was married?—nor tell him she'd no intention of indulging in an affaire of the heart. She wouldn't do that. Not even with a man such as himself, one who drew her in a way she'd never before experienced.

Despite that odd thought about garden paths . . .

Anne sighed and, looking about her, discovered she stood before her own building. She entered and climbed the stairs to their rooms, where she related the whole to Milly—except the revelations concerning the brother.

"He is a monster," said Milly.

"Nonsense. He thinks me married." Anne waved that away. "What I want to know is, *why* does he believe me married? Rather than widowed?"

"I don't know," said Milly, still angry on her friend's behalf, "but might it not be worse if he thought you have no husband in the background? He admitted he'd have no qualms at all taking you for his mistress if you were *not* married. I fear it will make no difference whether it is what *you* want—once he discovers the truth!"

"Oh, I wanted," said Anne slowly, blushing brightly. "He is so very much the sort of hero of whom I have dreamed—when I've had time for dreams, that is."

She looked so regretful that Milly managed to put aside the anger she felt on her friend's behalf and smile.

"I *wouldn't*, of course," said Anne hurriedly, wondering

if she would, "but I would so like to know him better. Perhaps, for the first time, I might fall in love . . ." The blush returned and her hands flew to her cheeks. "Oh! I am far too old for such romantic fancies. They belong to Thomasina, not to me."

"*Not* Thomasina. You forget. She is a married lady now!"

Anne laughed and relaxed. "So she is. Finally. But you know what I mean." She drew in a deep breath. "I am," she elaborated, in case Milly *didn't* know, "far too old to indulge myself in idiotic fancies. Shall we," she said, determined to change the subject and forget all about the intriguing Mr. Elverston, "request that a picnic be packed for us and that a driver be hired and we will ride in one of those odd little charavants up into the hills for a picnic?"

Milly smiled. "The ones in which the passengers sit back to back very like one does in an Irish jaunting car?" She was agreeable so that is what they did.

> *Letter to Beth from Thomasina.* "*Is it not wonderful? They have found each other again!*"
>
> *Letter to Catherine from Beth.* "*. . . in her letter she again sounded happy. You know our father thought that more important than anything else. Do you think him so selfish he'd resent her finding happiness? It is not as if she has not been widowed for years. It is four since Father died. A longer period of mourning than anyone should think necessary!*"
>
> *Letter to Catherine from Thomasina.* "*. . . are a beast. A nasty selfish ungenerous beast to suggest such a thing! Mother Anne would not indulge in anything sordid . . .*"

If Anne did not enjoy the following period so thoroughly as she'd hoped—the picnic or the boating party, an excursion to see the Chateau de Chillon, which they joined soon after, or, following that, a trek of several days into the heights, riding mules along paths with a fearsome precipice along one side—she refrained from saying anything to spoil Milly's enjoyment. In each place she added to her sketchbook—the cart and driver wearing the garb of his canton, a water view of the ancient chateau, delightful drawings of wild lilies, anemones, narcissus, and orange trees which grew in the high valley where, it had appeared to the visitors, the inhabitants lived on thick cream and brown bread. . . .

It was all very interesting, Anne decided—or would be if she could have shared her experiences and her thoughts with Mr. Elverston.

Anne wrote letters home and wished she'd receive mail from her stepdaughters, the receipt of which had been slowed by their unexpected exodus from Paris, and, most of all, she thought about the coming stay in Milan. The opera season would not begin for several months, but Anne's courier was finding them accommodations and preparing them.

The very next day a letter arrived—but not from a daughter.

"Milly, our courier has done his duty in Milan and rooms are ready for whenever we care to arrive. He will return to us here in a few days . . ." Anne looked up. "What do you think of beginning our journey through the Alps? A slow journey with many stops, staying wherever we find a thing that catches our fancy? I would like to cross the passes well before it is likely the weather will change, since I do not wish to take the least chance that we be caught in a freakishly early snowstorm. However I doubt it is necessary to go *this* early if you have reason to remain longer?"

Milly shook her head. "No reason at all," she said. "Shall I order our trunks brought up so that we may begin our packing?" And without waiting for a response, and clutching an open letter, she hurried from the room—to her own, rather than to where the concierge might be found who would know where the trunks had been stored.

Anne tipped her head thoughtfully. Was that bad news from home or could it possibly be still another letter from Major Torrington? Was it possible her old friends were falling in love with each other?

Anne bit her lip. If so, would it be better if she took Milly back to Paris, rather than to Milan? When Milly returned, sans letter, and blushing ever so slightly, Anne asked.

"Paris? Oh no. Why ever would you want to do that?"

"I don't," said Anne bluntly. "I thought perhaps you might . . . ?"

Milly's rosy cheeks grew still more rosy. "No of course not."

Deciding that only a blunt question would achieve her goal, Anne asked, "You do not wish to live near where Major Torrington resides?"

"Oh. Is that what you meant?" Milly chuckled. "Well, you see, the thing is, he doesn't."

Anne closed her eyes and grimaced in ever so nice a fashion. "Milly!"

Milly laughed again and explained. "His unit has been moved hither and thither and then yon and back again. He sounds ever so exasperated in the letter I just received. No sooner do they settle into quarters than they are ordered to pack up and moved elsewhere. You and I do very well going on as we are. But my next letter to him must include our Milan postal destination—if you'd be so kind as to write it out for me?"

Anne did so while Milly went down to request that their trunks be brought round. She also wrote three letters, one for each of her stepdaughters.

They will think me a veritable butterfly, I move so frequently!

* * *

Milan was all Anne had expected it would be, and she was relieved to reach it. The journey through the passes had been hair-raising despite the improvements Napoleon had ordered for military reasons. At one point they had no more than passed by when snow and rocks fell behind them, an avalanche that startled the horses, making them bolt on up a rather steep section of road—which their driver informed them, once he'd stopped them, was a very lucky thing. If they had been going *downhill* when he lost control, they would all be at the bottom of a gully and, if not dead, then badly injured.

Anne still felt unsettled by the near disaster when they reached Milan. Once unpacked, her first outing was to the Duomo in the piazza, where she wandered until she found herself drawn to the Altar of the Madonna. Although not Catholic, she spent more than a few thankful moments on her knees before she continued on. As she was leaving the Duomo she turned back for a last look down the long nave between the massive pillars. As she watched, a tall man turned from before the high altar and stalked toward her.

"Mr. Elverston," she murmured.

Soft as her voice was, it carried; the acoustics of the place were surprisingly excellent. The man looked up, a startled expression crossing features that were far darker than those she knew. Also, there was a scar cutting this man's brow. He scowled. In Italian she could barely follow, he growled at her, denying he was Elverston, denying he knew anyone by that name, and, finally, would perfect strangers cease calling him by that name! His voice rose with each sentence. His tirade became completely unintelligible to Anne, who stared at him, confounded that she could possibly have mistaken this man for the one she loved.

That revelation, unexpected self-knowledge, stopped her breath. Her eyes unfocused as she assimilated the notion. When she looked up, she realized a priest had rushed up to them and was speaking quietly to the stranger, who looked thoroughly embarrassed.

The stranger turned from the priest and bowed. "I apologize," he said in perfect English—and then, as if suddenly panicked, his mouth dropped, his eyes widened, his hand came up as if fending off a blow—and he very nearly ran from the Duomo.

Anne spoke a few explanatory words to the priest and apologized for being the cause of such a scene. And she, too, left, her deeply thoughtful expression leading perfect strangers to give her odd looks as she returned to her accommodations. She continued to feel extraordinarily preoccupied until, finally, Milly asked what was bothering her.

"I met a man today who looked very much like our Mr. Elverston."

"*Looked* like?"

"Very like. His behavior, however, was *nothing* like."

"You mean he was ungentlemanly toward you?"

Anne chuckled. "I cannot decide if you are appalled or look a trifle hopeful. Do you think I deserve to be accosted by ungentlemanly men?"

Milly smiled. "You may rest easy. My emotions veer toward the appalled! Anne, you really must not speak to strangers as you do. It is not done. It can, you know, be dangerous."

Anne nodded. "I was amply repaid for my error. Not," she hurriedly added, "that I actually spoke to him, but I did speak. He shouted at me," she finished on a thoughtful note.

Milly looked still more appalled, and there was no mistaking her expression for any other.

"Worse, we were in the Duomo."

"You were not!"

"Now—" Anne rolled her eyes toward the heavens. "—she accuses me of telling fibs!"

Milly blushed ever so slightly. "Not that. It is merely that to be yelled at is a terrible thing. But to be yelled at in *church!*"

"The man was scolded by a priest," murmured Anne, her eyes twinkling. "After all, I did not raise *my* voice." She got a thoughtful look. "Or perhaps I did. Just a very little? When I first saw him? It was rather dim and he looked so very much like Mr. Elverston. Beyond that— well, he *walked* like our Mr. Elverston—"

She heard a muttered, "*Your* Mr. Elverston."

"—and his voice has the same timber, despite his rudeness."

Anne's preoccupation returned and she wandered off. If this was the brother for whom Mr. Elverston searched, it would be dreadful to have seen him and not inform Mr. Elverston. She frowned. Was there a way of contacting him? When he left so abruptly, did he give any clue as to his next destination?

"Annie, something worries you and I don't think it is a stranger yelling at you. Tell me."

"I wish I could think how to get a message to Mr. Elverston. *Our* Mr. Elverston."

Milly shrugged. "Send the courier back to Switzerland. He can check on whatever forwarding address was left. Surely the British Consul has a record of such things. I know *you* left *our* new address with them . . ."

Anne hugged Milly so quickly and so fervently, Milly broke off what she was saying and laughed.

Milly asked, "You feel so very strongly that this might be Mr. Elverston's quarry?"

Anne had given Milly the bare information that

Elverston was seeking a certain man. "I think it possible. I cannot say if it was a relative he sought—" Anne felt Mr. Elverston's explanation had been in confidence and that she must not tell anyone what he'd said. "—but this man . . ."

"So very like?"

Anne nodded. "I believe I will write our consul and send an enclosed letter to Mr. Elverston which can be forwarded to him."

She set to work instantly and was, once the letter was on its way, very much the same person she'd always been. She and Milly explored, took short journeys to places of interest, and enjoyed good Italian food—or Anne did. Milly was a trifle less adventurous when it came to trying new and, to her mind, very odd viands.

Even though the Season would not begin for some time, Anne was impatient to experience the opening night of the coming opera season, and often she would stroll past the disappointingly plain exterior of La Scala, the opera house. One of her first actions upon arriving in Milan had been to oversee the purchase of tickets for herself and Milly. She meant to attend nearly every performance scheduled in the coming season.

Anne had loved good music all her life. Her greatest pleasure in London was attending all and every musical evening she could, from the opera and Concerts of Ancient Music to the most wobbly voiced young soprano performing for guests in someone's drawing room. Everywhere she had heard tales of La Scala, the Italian Opera House in Milan. Her appetite to go there and hear for herself had been whetted again and again, and now, impatiently, she awaited her chance.

And while she waited, she wrote long letters home about all the various little adventures she and Milly enjoyed, the brief trips, the picnics and as they acquired friends, the visiting back and forth, the invitations to grand entertainments.

> *Letter to Catherine from Beth.* ". . . yes, I agree. But is contentment enough for our Mother Anne? Surely you want more for her . . . ?"
> *Letter to Catherine from Thomasina.* ". . . thank you for apologizing. I didn't really mean half the names I called you—but you must admit suggesting Mother Anne would have an affaire with this stranger is outside enough . . . !"
> *Letter to Beth from Catherine.* ". . . We must hope that is the end of it. I can discover nothing about a Mr. Elverston. I cannot help but believe him an adventurer and Dear Anne is much better without him . . ."

One day followed another. Each was pleasant but something was missing. Anne could not put her finger on what it might be—although the fact she awoke each morning from dreams of a certain dark-haired blue-eyed stranger might have given her a clue if only she had allowed herself to admit it. That one brief moment of self-knowledge in the Duomo, when she had admitted she loved Elverston, was thrust firmly into the back of her mind where she made certain it stayed!

On this particular day Anne was unable to settle to anything. She moved from the window to the table by the door, where she moved a rose from one part of the bouquet to another and then to the mantel, where she shifted the porcelain shepherdess from one end to the other, trading it for the pig-herd boy who, when moved, stared off at nothing at all, instead of mooning at the simpering maiden.

Then Anne moved to the middle of the floor—where she stopped dead.

"What is it, Anne?" asked Milly, looking up from her writing.

Anne turned. "I don't know."

"Yes you do."

Anne sighed. "I don't want to admit it."

"But you will."

Anne stiffened. "I am not such a flitter-brained little idiot that I am pining for a mere man!"

"No of course not."

Her spine relaxed ever so slightly and her shoulders dropped to a more normal position below her ears.

"He is not," added Milly, "a mere man."

Spine and shoulders returned to their prior position. "You would say I am infatuated for the first time in my life and handling it badly." Anne drew in a deep breath. "There are still two months until the Season begins. I think we will go to Florence. Perhaps on to Rome. There is so much to see . . ."

"We will do no such thing," said Milly placidly.

"Why not?"

"Because if we left and your Mr. Elverston came, hot-foot, to discover what you know about this man he seeks, you would never forgive yourself if you were not here to tell him."

Anne sighed. *"Why does he not come?"*

"Very likely your letter to him is dogging his footsteps as he travels here and there seeking information concerning the fellow he wishes to find. If he would stay in one place for a time, then perhaps it would catch him up and he would come running to seek you out."

Anne sighed more deeply. "I am going quite out of my mind. The man I saw in the Duomo might have been merely passing through the city, you know. Seeing the sights . . ."

"You said the priest called him by name."

Anne nodded. "So he did," she said slowly . . . and her eyes gleamed.

Hurriedly, Milly warned, "Anne, you *cannot* . . ."

"Why not?"

"You would seek out a Catholic priest and insist he tell you about the man you saw? You cannot."

"You have yet to say *why* I cannot," said Anne cheerfully. Now that she had a goal in mind all her restlessness had fallen away.

"First of all, he is a priest. You are a good Englishwoman and have nothing to do with such as he."

"I might be Irish," teased Anne.

"You might be, but you are not." Milly looked, for her, quite stern. "Secondly, you would be interfering in the business of a man you admire but one you do not know at all well, one who might resent it very much if you were to interfere in such a way that his quarry took to his heels and disappeared."

Anne, who had begun by looking faintly defiant, felt the restiveness return with a rush. "Unfortunately, you have that right. The last thing in the world I would wish to do is, unwittingly, make things worse. Especially when my only intention would be to hurry things along, make it possible for Mr. Elverston to finish his quest as quickly as possible—"

A sudden vision of herself in Mr. Elverston's arms, hot feelings pouring into her, appalled Anne.

"—since," she finished rather hurriedly, "he is so terribly worried by it all."

"That," said Milly blandly, "is, of course, the only reason you wish him to conclude his business. Of course. I understand that. How could it be otherwise?" She raised her hand to hide a smile, but her eyes twinkled.

"You are laughing at me."

"Perhaps. A little. But only in the nicest way."

Anne sighed. "You are correct, of course. I want him to notice *me.*"

"I think we may say he *has* noticed you."

"*And*—" Anne glared at her friend. "—have the time and the peace of mind that we might . . . might . . ."

"Explore what might come of your mutual attraction?"

Anne, her cheeks flushed, nodded. "Milly," she said, her voice small, "I am not wrong, am I? He is a most unusual man, is he not?"

"Most unusual."

Milly had no intention of elaborating on that. She was still not completely certain she liked the gentleman's attitude toward her friend. That he had actually suggested an affaire did not bode well. Anne was not one to indulge herself in that fashion without experiencing heartbreak when the affaire ended. Milly decided that if she ever again was in a position to speak to Mr. Elverston, her first words would somehow disabuse him of Anne's status.

Perhaps, if he did not believe her married, he would think of a different relationship the two might explore. One that would make Anne as happy as Milly was herself. Milly looked down at her letter to Major Torrington. She dipped her pen into her ink and, writing furiously, outlined her concerns, her hopes and fears, with her dearest Michael.

Michael would enter into her feelings perfectly. What was better, he might have advice for her, good advice. He knew far more about the world than Milly did and she had every faith that he would tell her exactly how she should go on . . .

Anne watched Milly for some minutes. "I need exercise, Milly. I think I will go for a walk."

"Yes, dear," murmured Milly, not looking up.

Anne smiled. *What,* she wondered, *does Milly find to*

write in her endless letters to her brother? She had forgotten if she ever knew that by far the larger number of Milly's letters were *not* addressed to her beloved brother and that they never left the continent.

Anne was in her room, donning her newest bonnet, when she remembered that Milly did respond to the letters she received from the major. Green darkened Anne's eyes for a moment before she told herself it was exceedingly selfish to feel jealous of Milly. She should feel happy for her. Milly's first marriage had not been so very bad, but it had not, from what Anne could gather, been anything special. Milly hadn't been beaten or anything of that nature, but she must have been exceedingly bored by her sport-loving and often absent husband. Anne suspected a marriage between Milly and her major would not be boring, whatever else it might be.

Collecting Jeremy to accompany her, Anne set out. She hadn't a notion where she would go, nor an idea in her head of what she might do. She simply wandered, Jeremy trailing after her as was proper. She was exceedingly glad that he did, when, rounding a corner, she came upon a lovely young lady struggling in the arms of a foppishly dressed and exceedingly inebriated young man.

Anne, calling to Jeremy, rushed forward and, once again, made unusual use of her parasol, swinging it with both hands against the molester's shoulders and then, again, against his thighs, which startled him into releasing the young woman. Jeremy, coming up at a run, swung the fellow around and landed a facer that felled the man.

"Very well done, Jeremy," praised Anne. "I hadn't a notion you excelled at fisticuffs, but I am glad to discover you do. My dear child," she added, taking the shaking girl, who looked about to faint, into her arms. "Shush now," she crooned. "All is well. You are safe."

The young woman looked up at Anne with huge brown eyes and spoke in Italian.

Anne shook her head. "I cannot understand you very well, more's the pity." She glanced down at the man at their feet. "And I do not think we should remain here while we discuss the problem."

The girl spoke again, this time in French. "*Merci*, my lady. You cannot guess how very frightened I was."

Anne, also speaking French, asked, "Where, my child, is your maid . . . ?" She was not surprised to see a blush rise in the high cheek-boned little face. "I see. You will, I think, never again attempt to meet your beloved by sneaking off from your home, will you?"

The girl blushed more furiously. "I was very foolish, but I am so worried."

"Worried?"

"He has not been to see us for days and days."

"Hmm. And has he never been parted from you for days and days?"

She blinked. "Of course he has. When he is traveling he cannot come to see us. But he always does when home. Every day. My father—" A sad look darkened her expression. "—is an invalid. He cannot easily get out and about. Timos comes to him to discuss their business. Too, my beloved plays excellent chess and comes every evening to give my father a game or two. But he has *not* come." The chit actually wrung her hands. "I am so worried. I must see him, must discover what is wrong. He might have fallen. He might be ill. Oh, do you not see that I had to . . ."

"Hush." Anne put her fingers over the girl's lips. She was surprised when it stilled the escalating tirade. Staring into the large, pleading eyes, she sighed. "Very well. Where does your Timos live?"

"Just there. Just down the street to the corner."

"Jeremy, we will escort Miss . . ." Anne smiled. "I do not know your name."

"Signorina Rosita Maria Costello," said the girl shyly, holding out her little long-fingered hand.

"You may call me Lady Anne," said Anne, not willing to reveal her full name. "I do have one more question. Why do you think your Timos has not gone off on his travels as you say he does?"

"Why—" Her eyes rounded once again. "—because he and Papa always plan his journey. They plan where he goes and how long he will be gone. So we will not worry, do you not see?"

Anne felt just a trifle worried herself at that news. "I see. Come along now. It might be better if we were not here when that shagbag rouses himself."

"This word? Shag . . . ?"

"Hmm? Shagbag?" Anne smiled. "A word I should not have used and one you need not remember. I should have said that low shabby fellow need not see us when he comes to his senses!"

They reached the corner and Rosita Marie moved quickly to the steps into the small lobby, where she stopped, suddenly shy. "I do not know which rooms . . ." she admitted, looking embarrassed.

"Jeremy, that door is to the concierge's rooms, I believe. Knock, please."

Jeremy knocked, and almost instantly the door opened on a wizened little woman with deep-set eyes gazing suspiciously from one to the other. Rosita spoke in rapid Italian. The woman spat. Rosita spoke more conciliatingly. Anne, behind the girl's back, fished a coin from her reticule and held it up, turning it, looking at it thoughtfully. After a moment the woman spoke three harsh words. Rosita thanked her and turned to the stairs. Behind her back, Anne flipped the coin toward the claw-like hands held out for it, and then she, too, followed by Jeremy, started up the stairs.

She reached the hall down which Rosita had run and paused. The door opened to the girl's knock revealed a haggard-looking man. Rosita sobbed once and threw herself into his arms, arms that closed gently around her. Anne, from the shadows at her end of the hall, watched the door close on the two. She bit her lip, glanced at Jeremy, and then back toward the stairway. She hesitated to start down them.

"I believe the gentleman will see Rosita home," she said, uncertain whether she should or should not leave. She *wanted* to stay. She *wanted* to invade that room and demand answers from the man who lived there.

But she wanted, more than anything, to have Mr. Elverston at her side when she did so. The man who opened the door, his shirt open at the throat, his sleeves rolled well above his elbows, his chin dark and unshaven, dark hair falling over his scarred brow, had—for a moment—had her believing she, once again by accident, had found Mr. Elverston. But only for a moment.

The likeness was so very strong. Timos *had* to be the brother for whom Elverston searched. He *must* be. Anne thought furiously all the way back to her rooms. Once there, she went straight to her desk and penned a second letter to the consul, a second enclosure to Elverston, and this time sent Jeremy off to find the courier.

"What is it Anne?" asked Milly, coming in just then.

"I have seen that man again. It occurred to me that my first letter to Mr. Elverston must have gone astray. I mean to send another, but this time Gerard will take it to the consul, will discover where to take my letter, and will track down Mr. Elverston if it takes from now to doomsday."

"You are so certain?"

"I am certain." She described the scene when Rosita

opened the door, described her emotions when she watched *her Mr. Elverston*—as she'd momentarily thought—draw the child into his embrace. "It was only when I realized this was the man I saw in the Duomo that I realized he must be Elverston's—" She caught herself before she said brother. "—relative."

"Then I agree you must locate Elverston as quickly as can be. As I returned from my errand Jeremy was leaving. In search, perhaps, of the courier? He seemed to be favoring his right hand."

"Oh dear." Anne's eyes widened. "I forgot to ask him if he had damaged himself. I was so pleased with him, it did not occur to me he hurt himself when he felled that . . . that monster attacking Rosita."

"Attacking . . . *monster* . . . !*Rosita?*"

So Anne told her the whole story this time, finishing, ". . . and remind me to see if Jeremy's hand needs bandaging. If he broke a bone in my service, then I must see that it receives the necessary attention to make sure it mends properly." She turned back to her desk. "I think I will write the girls. I have not done so for some time now."

There was so much to tell them.

And, of course, so much more she could *not* tell them.

From a letter to Beth from Thomasina. ". . . have you heard? It has been so long since I last had a letter. What do you think it means? I cannot help but worry about . . ."

From a letter to Catherine from Beth. ". . . you have never believed Mother Anne capable of caring for herself. You have always thought of her as that naïve young girl our father married out of hand. Perhaps if you had not wed soon after, had remained at home, you would have seen her mature and discover her strengths as we did . . ."

From a letter to Thomasina from Catherine. "Beth

*assures me Mother Anne cannot possibly have fallen prey
to highwaymen in the mountains or slave traders in Italy.
We are, she says, indulging in Gothic nonsense. Actually,
I believe it much more likely she succumbed to a plausible
rogue, threw her hat over the windmill, and went off with
him. Very likely she will come home with a babe in her
arms . . ."*

Letter to Catherine from Thomasina. *" . . . may forget I
ever apologized. You are a beast. A nasty, jealous, scandal-
mongering beast and I have decided you are not a person
I wish to know. Do not bother to respond . . ."*

Feeling more depressed than any time since he had first
set out on this mission, Drake Elverston, Marquess of
Burnside, Earl of Elverston, Baron Elverston, stared out
the window of his room in the inn in the Austrian town
to which his last information had sent him. And then
nothing. A dead end. If his brother had deliberately done
his best to avoid discovery, he could have done no better
job of it.

Had it been deliberate? Had someone along the line
contacted Tim, warned him a search for him was in
progress? Drake considered that possibility and discarded it. The man he sought was reported, by all to
whom he spoke, to be nothing but a successful trader
in Italian wines and oils. He was admired for honest
measure and high quality. He was liked for his friendly
nature, for always remembering the wife's name, how
old the children were . . . a good man who made his
rounds erratically, but quite often enough one need not
worry he would be needed before he arrived.

And now he was not to be found.

An Italian, mused Drake. *Thought to be Italian . . .*

Drake mentally kicked himself for a fool. Why was he
traipsing all over northern Europe when he should be

searching Italy? He had a name. He certainly had a description. Several had called *him* Timos or, more commonly, Signor Victor, mistaking him for the dealer they knew. Signor Timos Victor. A name, then, and he need only point to himself in order to describe the man for whom he searched.

"Yes," he told himself. "I will go to Italy. Immediately. I will do what I should have done from the beginning. Or, at least from the point I had a name . . ."

That decision made, Drake's mood lightened and he actually looked at the scene beyond his window. He smiled. A festival was in progress. He watched a group of young girls dressed in full-skirted gowns held wide by lacy petticoats and with sheer fichus over the shoulders and pinned down over young breasts. They skipped, hand-in-hand, into a circle. One girl, slightly older, looked over her shoulder and nodded. Drake turned his gaze to where she had glanced and saw a small group of musicians. He quickly opened his window, leaning out at the first oompah from a brass instrument, the first scrape of a violin and tootle of a flute, the first beat of the drum. The joyful music soared up from the green to match his new mood of optimism.

For nearly half an hour Drake enjoyed his view of the dancing. Then the minx who had first nodded toward the musicians drew near, smiled up at him, and beckoned, nodding encouragingly. Impulsively, Drake drew on his coat and straightened his cravat. He strode down the stairs and out onto the green.

Much later, arm in arm with the local butcher and the local blacksmith, he kicked his heels high, hopped and skipped, and laughing freely, found himself actually enjoying a village celebration which every friend he had would say was quaint.

Much they know, he thought.

But, between the dancing, the drinking, but *not*, since

he'd reason to resist her, the nicely rounded body of the barmaid, it was far later the next morning than he'd meant to rise from his bed when he awoke. And when he did open his eyes, it was with a head that throbbed at the slightest movement.

There was no way Drake Elverston, Marquess of Burnside, was riding anywhere today. In fact, it hurt so much to open his eyes against the glare from his window that he rolled over and went right back to sleep.

And because the marquess had indulged a whim and, besides, indulged far more deeply in strong new wine than he'd meant to, Lady Anne's courier finally caught him up.

Unfortunately, so had winter in the high Alps.

"You are looking rather hagged," said Milly, eyeing her friend judiciously.

"My looks, I am certain, are in no worse case than the rest of me."

Milly's brows rose at Anne's rueful tone. "What is it?"

Anne's lips compressed and her eyes lost focus.

"That bad, hmmm?" asked Milly, with just a hint of a chuckle.

"Bad?" Anne's gaze sharpened. *"Worse."*

"Tell me."

"I cannot sleep. I have nightmares in which I chase a long-legged creature wearing seven-league boots. I never catch it up. We bound across the countryside, turning hither and yon and I wake more worn out than when I went to bed."

"I see. You fear the courier will be unable to trace Mr. Elverston."

"I suppose I do. Or when I do not think that, I think of all the things that could happen. It snowed last night in the mountains. It said so in our morning paper."

Milly had been astounded by how quickly Anne managed to pick up enough Italian to read the newspapers.

"The passes are closed. It is not thought that they will remain closed since it is early in the season, but what if Mr. Elverston was attempting them when the storm blew in? What if he was caught and unable to find shelter?" Anne's eyes opened widely as they stared at her friend.

"That is, of course, one possible tragedy. Another is that there was ice and his carriage slid over a cliff. Ah! But he rides, does he not? So . . . *bandits.* Anyone traversing the Alps *must* be wary of bandits. Let me see now." Milly put a finger to her chin and looked thoughtful. "I suppose he might have been caught in the middle of a plague and lie sickened unto death in some small smelly inn, abandoned by all and . . ." She ducked the apple Anne threw at her. "Missed me," she teased, laughing.

"Perhaps his bro . . . *relative* might go out on his travels again."

"Did I not mention that? Surely I meant to include it."

Anne bit her lip. "You feel I am being very foolish?"

"Anne, dear, they are problems worthy of an opera libretto!"

Both women were silent for a time. Then Anne sighed. "You are correct, of course."

The silence stretched again.

Once again Anne broke it. "Unfortunately," she said, "I doubt knowing how right you are will help me avoid nightmares." Anne turned away, moving toward the door.

"Where are you going?"

"A walk. A long walk. If I tire myself sufficiently, perhaps mere exhaustion will make sleep possible."

"Take Jeremy."

"Of course. Do I not always take him?"

Half an hour later Anne found herself standing before the open doors to the Duomo. The cathedral beckoned and Anne, a trifle reluctantly, climbed the steps and entered. She moved into the dimness . . . and then stopped and stared at a high window through which the sun beamed down. A man, standing in the brightness, moved slightly, catching her eye before shadows shrouded him.

Anne's eyes widened. It was him. The Italian. Should she approach him? Try to make him understand? The man turned, his head bowed, his hands behind his back. His shoulders were bowed under some heavy weight, a weight that seemed almost more than he could bear. Anne couldn't take her eyes off him. He approached her, not seeing her. Panicked, Anne wondered if she should move, should turn away, should get out of his way—or stand there and face him.

And then it was too late.

"You." He spoke quietly, wearily. "I must offer my thanks that you were there when my Rosy needed your aid. I do thank you."

"You speak English."

He smiled ruefully. "Yes, it seems I do."

"What is it?" asked Anne, suddenly filled with pity for the haunted-looking man.

"What is it? I do not know . . . I wish I did." He doffed his hat, and despite Anne's hurried demand he stay a moment, he walked out the wide high doors into the sun, ran trippingly down the stairs, and seated himself in a waiting carriage which instantly moved off.

Anne watched him go, her hand slowly dropping back to her side. A soft voice spoke from near her, a questioning tone to the words. She turned. The same priest stood there, a tall man with silvery hair, his cassock hanging straight to the floor from shoulders that had the arrogance to sport a many-capped driving coat.

Anne gave him an apologetic glance. "I am sorry. I

only speak English and some French." She repeated that last in French.

He smiled, teeth white in his olive-skinned face. In perfect French, he asked if she knew that young man.

"No. However, he is the image of a man I *do* know," she responded, also in French.

"He is a troubled man. I know a bit of his history. It is very sad."

Anne hesitated. "Is it . . . something you can tell me?"

It was his turn to hesitate. "I fear not. I learned it, as you perhaps guessed, in the confessional." He sighed. "But if *you* know something . . . ? Something that would help me help him?" he elaborated when she did not instantly confide in him.

"I know so little," she said. "I know my acquaintance seeks a . . . man. A . . . relative." She had promised to keep the secret. She could not say more. "Someone he thought lost to him. Someone who may be lost to him and not this man at all." It was Anne's turn to sigh.

"You have made promises that mean as much to you as the secrecy of the confessional means to me?" asked the priest gently.

The man's aristocratic demeanor, his arrogant posture, did not match the caring she felt coming from him, the sincerity. "That is so. I promised."

He nodded. "Promises are to be kept, of course. But if you remember something that would help me help my young friend, will you please bring me word?" He gave her his name and she realized he was not a simple priest, but had risen far in the hierarchy of the church. Her eyes widened and she flicked a quick glance down at his plain garment. He smiled. "You think it odd in me that I do not wear what are considered appropriate robes?" he asked, a twinkle in his eye.

"I suppose I do."

"It is a penance. I am a vain man. It does not do to feed that vanity."

She smiled. "I doubt the outergarb will hide that of which you are vain, Monsignor de Este."

He grinned, showing off excellent white teeth. "It is not proper of *you* to feed my vanity in other ways . . . child."

"Lady Forsythe," she offered, as she offered her hand.

"I am pleased to meet you, Lady Forsythe," he responded, and lifted her hand to place an airy kiss above her knuckles. He again gave her his full name and title. "Do remember that any information you may share would be valued. That young man has been very generous in his gifts to the poor. We would wish to do something for him in return."

"Does he come here often?" asked Anne.

"Every day," he said. And then he frowned. "Although there was a week or two recently when he did not come. Since he had not told me he was leaving Milan, I wondered if he was ill . . . but you saw him? Is it not obvious he was ill?"

Anne nodded, but she did not think it an illness of the body so much as an illness of the mind and heart. "Oh, I *do* wish Mr. Elverston would come!"

"I will pray he comes soon," said the priest, "but now I must go." With a nod of his head he moved off to speak with a bent old woman dressed from head to toe in rusty black. He offered the crone his arm and the two moved slowly, disappearing into the dusky dimness of the huge nave.

Anne watched him go. "A prayer cannot hurt and might be answered since it is not for myself I pray." She stared at a statue of an unknown saint and felt a faint flush rise up her throat. "Well, mostly not for myself?"

Prayer would not come there in the presence of so much her own church labeled popish—and, given where she was, no insult. Still, unlike her first visit, when she'd freely given her thanks for keeping them safe on their journey, she found she needed a different milieu for this particular prayer.

Anne returned to the piazza. What she wanted, she decided, was the countryside, an open field, an orchard or perhaps a garden. The nearest grass, trees, and flowers were too far away to walk.

"Jeremy, hire me a carriage. I would go into the country."

Half an hour later they halted near what Anne craved. The fields did not look like those she'd left behind in England, but they were dedicated to the same purposes, the growing of fruit and vegetables and the rearing of farm animals. She gave her hand to Jeremy and stepped from the rather odorous box in order to stroll along the lane leading from the main road.

Jeremy hesitated before telling the driver they would not be long. The man shrugged, pulled his hat low on his brow, settled himself, and—although Jeremy was gone too far to notice—soon snored softly into its brim.

Anne found a rustic gate solid enough for sitting on and climbed it. Jeremy paused a little distance from her and watched as Lady Anne stared across the fields toward an orchard heavy with ripe apples. Then she ducked her head, and from where he was standing to the side, he saw she closed her eyes. It wasn't long before she opened them and stared again across the field.

Soon she climbed down and smiled at her footman. "You are very patient with me, Jeremy, and I do not think it is totally because I pay your wages on time."

"We like you, Lady Forsythe. We'd all do whatever you wanted—up to killing anyone who attempted to harm you."

Anne's brows rose. She glanced at his hand, which was still wrapped in a white bandage. "I see." She spoke a trifle dryly. "I do hope the situation never arises, but I am happy to know I am so well protected. Let us return. I have been gone longer than I expected and Mrs. Seward will be concerned.

That night Anne slept well for the first time since she'd rescued Rosita.

And three days after Anne sent aloft her prayer that Mr. Elverston would soon arrive, he did. He was tired and cross and both hopeful and unwilling to allow his hopes freedom.

"What do you know?" he asked bluntly even before she offered him a seat.

Anne described her three meetings with the man who looked enough like Mr. Elverston to be his brother. Perhaps was his brother . . . ?

". . . so you see," she finished, "I had to contact you. I cannot promise this is the man you seek, but he has acted very strangely. May I make a suggestion?"

"Since you have yet to tell me where I may find him, I suppose I must listen, must I not?" There was a bite to that, revealing impatience and worry and even a touch of that hope to which he dared not admit.

"There is a priest who knows him and wishes to help. The man who looks like you comes to the Duomo regularly and is a regular donor to the poor box—or whatever it is called here. I believe there is a serious problem and that you should not confront your brother, if it is your brother, without support. Since the priest is his friend, then perhaps that is the help you need."

"Problem?" Mr. Elverston leapt on the word, ignoring the rest.

"When we first confronted each other, he spoke a few words of English and then looked appalled, shocked even, and lifted a hand as if to ward off evil. When we spoke this last time, and I mentioned he knew English, he said something like, 'it appears to be the case, does it not?' or some such thing, as if he could not believe it. Mr. Elverston, do you think it possible he does not *know* who he is? If so, then it will come as a shock to him when he learns, will it not?"

"You are worried about him? Even though he yelled at you?"

"I am worried about the both of you," she said quietly.

Mr. Elverston studied her. Then he sighed. "I have searched for months to find this man. I suppose I can wait another day or two. Will you take me to this priest? I would meet with him, judge him, for myself."

"You are afraid he has an ulterior motive for talking to me?"

"I don't know, do I? Frankly, he sounds too good to be true, wanting to do this Timos a good turn merely because Timos gives generously to the poor."

"Timos. Has it occurred to you how near that is to Timothy?"

"Instantly," he said and, for the first time, grinned. "Will you introduce me to your priest?"

"Not mine."

At that Mr. Elverston frowned. "No, and not Timothy's either. I suppose he attended church as often as the next man, but to go daily . . . this does not sound like my brother." He sighed. "I must not hope," he said with bitterness. "More than likely this is a mare's nest." He looked up from the tessera making up a mosaic patterning the floor, which he'd seemed to study although he'd seen nothing of the stylized fish and fruits making up the design. "When will it be convenient for you to introduce me to this priest?"

Anne smiled. "Why do you not merely tell me to get my bonnet so that we may go at once?"

He smiled, but it was a weak smile. "Lady Forsythe, go get your bonnet. We will go at once."

She chuckled. "Very well, Mr. Elverston. Happily."

She closed her bedroom door behind her and leaned against it, her eyes closing and a prayer of thankfulness wafting upward. He had come. He was here—

And then that truly struck her. *He is here.*

Anne's limbs shook so badly she wondered if she could walk so far as the bed where she might seat herself and recover.

He is here. He has come. I conversed with him.

Her heart beat so loudly she put a hand over it, as if to contain it within her chest.

He is here.

"Ah, you fool! You too must not hope," she told herself sternly. "Come now. Find your bonnet . . ."

Half an hour later they walked through the huge double doors into the Duomo. Anne hesitated. She looked around. "I haven't a notion where to find him," she admitted.

Mr. Elverston grasped her elbow and marched her toward a priest who stood near the altar, praying. They waited until the priest looked around. Speaking Italian that Anne guessed was less well accented than his rough French had been, Elverston told the man they were to speak with—And then, realizing he did not know whom that was, he turned to Anne.

Anne murmured the name and the priest looked startled, glanced at her, flushed, and looked quickly away. He spoke to Mr. Elverston and then repeated himself more slowly when Elverston said something—pretty obviously that he did not understand.

Elverston nodded, and his hand again at Anne's elbow, he led her toward a door to one side of the apse—not that Anne saw the door until they reached it since it was hidden behind a pillar. They went down steps and along a long hall to another building where Elverston repeated his question and was given further directions.

Twenty minutes later they were seated before the desk behind which sat their quarry. "I understand why Lady Forsythe felt the need to send for you, Mr. Elverston."

"The likeness is so very great?"

"You did not believe Lady Forsythe?"

Elverston grimaced. "I have not allowed myself to believe anything at all. If my brother is not dead, if this is he . . . it will be a miracle."

The priest nodded. "You speak lightly, I think. But, yes. A veritable miracle. As *I* believe it to be."

"You wish to be with me when I confront this man?"

The priest smiled. "I will be with you both." He rose to his feet. "Come. We will go immediately to his residence where, at this time of day, he should be."

"You know him so well?" asked Anne.

"We met by accident. A very troubled young man at that time. I found myself deeply interested in him. And then I found I liked him." The priest smiled. "He is a very likeable gentleman, you know."

For the first time Elverston smiled. "If it is my brother, then he is, yes, easily liked."

"A trifle mischievous?" asked the priest.

"More than a trifle," agreed Elverston, his eyes narrowing.

"Sir, I think we will delay no longer. I cannot bear the suspense. Lady Forsythe? Do you accompany us?"

Anne looked toward Elverston, who a trifle reluctantly, she thought, nodded. She turned back, smiling. "I would be honored to be allowed a part in this meeting," she said softly.

"I believe you deserve a part," the priest said and laughed. "You have done your best to bring it about, have you not?"

Anne felt herself blushing. "If this is the man for whom Mr. Elverston has searched, then I am grateful to have had a small part in finding him. I firmly believe, however, that Mr. Elverston would have found him himself before long. I have only given a slight impetus to the effort."

Elverston's eyes softened as he gazed at her. "You have done more, my lady," he said softly. "You have, more than once, lightened my way. Before I forget, I would thank you for that."

The blush deepened to a flush and Anne covered her cheeks with her hands.

"You embarrass her, sir," said the priest and threw a stole around his shoulders. "I have ordered my carriage," he added and Anne wondered when he'd done so and then saw a speaking tube attached to the side of his desk. "Yes," he said, although she made no comment, "it is an amazing contraption."

He led the way to a rear door where a groom wearing discreet livery and an unmarked carriage harnessed to two horses awaited them. The priest gave the lad orders and then helped Anne in. The two men followed her in and the carriage moved off. The priest spoke of this and that and didn't seem to expect any response—which was just as well since neither Anne nor Elverston could have made one.

Anne felt her heart beating hard, and she could see how tense Mr. Elverston had grown, a white mark around his mouth and lines deepening beside his nose. She wanted to offer him her hand, but they were not alone and she dared not.

Only the priest seemed relaxed and anticipating with a whole heart the coming interview.

They arrived and the priest alit, speaking a few words to the groom before turning to help Lady Forsythe down.

Mr. Elverston hesitated, his eyes gazing hungrily at the building before which they had stopped. Still he hesitated.

"Afraid?" asked Anne.

He turned his gaze toward her. "Yes," he said abruptly.

"Either it is or it is not," she said.

"Yes."

She smiled and this time she did offer her hand. He jumped down, grasped it tightly for a moment, and then, the priest clearing his throat, laid it on his arm before moving toward the entrance. "Which floor?" he asked.

The priest and Anne responded together and they moved to the steps.

"I hope Timos is home," said the priest, speaking lightly. "I fear the two of you will explode if he is not."

Anne smiled, but Mr. Elverston did not.

The priest knocked on a heavy age-blackened door. After a moment he knocked again, more loudly this time. A muffled voice from within called something they could not hear. Anne felt Mr. Elverston's arm tremble.

The door opened and the arm stilled. "Oh my God. Timmytoo," breathed Mr. Elverston, using a nursery name from long ago, "it *is* you."

Timos stilled. His eyes widened. He stared. And then, without warning, he fainted dead away, folding up and depositing himself on the floor without a sound.

As she knelt down beside the fallen man, Anne heard a sound of dismay from the priest. She pulled a vinaigrette from her ample reticule and uncapped it, waving it under the unconscious man's nose. "Come, come, it is a *good* thing. You are all right now," she crooned softly.

Timos's eyes opened and stared up at her. "I know you," he said in English.

"Yes. We do keep running into each other, do we not? Timothy?"

He closed his eyes. "I remember," he breathed. "Goosey?"

He pushed himself up, looking beyond her. "*Drake?* It is you?"

"*Goosey?*" she breathed, turning to look at Mr. Elverston.

"It is I," said Elverston, all his attention on his brother. "You *didn't* die."

"No. Almost, I think," said Timos–Timothy. He raised a hand to his head and rubbed his eyes. "Am I dreaming?"

"No. Something over two years ago we received word you were missing, believed dead. Then, some months ago, you were seen in Paris—but denied you were you. I didn't know what to think."

"Yes . . . I remember that. Owen, wasn't it?" Timothy spoke slowly, frowning. "Since then I've had terrible dreams. *Confusing* dreams. About things I didn't think I could possibly know anything about." He glanced at the priest, who stood quietly to one side. "As you know . . . ?"

The man smiled. "Yes. I thought perhaps it was a sign you were beginning to remember."

"Remember?" asked Mr. Elverston sharply.

"It is a long story," began Timothy and, with the priest's help, rose to his feet, where for half a moment he wobbled and then found the strength to stand alone. "I don't know what you were told about the work I did for Wellington . . . ?" He stared at his brother.

"Nothing at all. All we ever knew is what I said. Reported missing. Believed dead." More softly, he added, "Tim, the news very nearly killed Mother."

"Ah." It was a sad sound. "Drake . . . I'm sorry." He held out his hand and Elverston grasped it.

"Tim, we must return to England at once. She never truly recovered and now she awaits word of you. She has believed you were dead ever since that first report from Paris."

Anne saw instant denial in the younger Elverston's face. "Your work? *Rosita?*" she asked softly.

"Both," he said, casting her a thankful look. "Drake, I am the active partner in a rather large trading concern," he said. "And my silent partner is not well. I cannot leave it in his hands with no preparation. Then there is . . ." His voice trailed off.

"Rosita," said Anne again.

"There is Rosita."

"Tim . . ."

Timothy held up a hand. "Drake, I will write Mother instantly and will send the letter by private courier the quickest way he can go, but I cannot leave Milan immediately."

For a moment Anne thought Elverston would argue. Then he nodded. "You have a life here that you made for yourself under difficult conditions. You cannot simply forget you have lived and worked here for over two years."

"Thank God you understand," said Timothy fervently.

The priest spoke then. "The two of you have much to say to each other. I will escort Lady Forsythe to her home, leaving the two of you together, but I invite all of you, including Signorina Rosita and her father, to my home for dinner this evening. Yes?"

The men nodded, obviously glad to be left alone. But as they were leaving, Timothy moved suddenly and caught Anne into a bear hug. "You are an angel, I think, to have discovered me. I thank you." And then he kissed her, smacking kisses on each cheek. "Oh, it is wonderful." Suddenly it hit him, and exuberantly he swung her off her feet and in a circle. "I *remember*." And there was no missing the gladness in his eyes—or the suddenly frozen blue crackling in Mr. Elverston's.

Anne wondered about that last as she allowed herself to be led away by the priest.

* * *

"You have changed your gown twice," said Milly, laughing. "I forbid you to return to your room to change yet again!"

Anne blushed. "But I have never dined at a palace. Are you certain I have chosen the proper thing?"

"You are not worried about propriety. You are worried that Mr. Elverston will not think you pretty."

The blush deepened. "Nonsense," said Anne gruffly. "I am too old to be thinking anything of the sort. Far too old for such romantic nonsense. My twenty-eighth birthday is just around the corner."

"Such an old hag it makes you!"

"You cannot consider me a dewy young lady."

"No. I consider you a very attractive mature lady. There is no reason whatsoever that Mr. Elverston will not find you just as interesting tomorrow as he did yesterday."

"Yesterday he was not around and very likely had not thought about me for days and days."

"Yesterday he was hotfooting it directly to your side."

"Yes, but only because I had information he needed."

"And because he was glad it was you who had that information. Anne, it is not like you, this indecision and pessimism."

"Is it not?"

"No."

"Oh . . . I suppose I must hope for the best?"

"You must *expect* the best." There was a knock at the door and Jeremy opened it, announcing the arrival of Mr. Elverston and his brother.

"I do not wish to rush you," said Mr. Elverston with the faintest chill to his tone, "but my brother's partner and his daughter await us in the coach."

Anne blinked. She turned to Milly. "This is the best?" she mouthed on a breath of air. She turned back. Jeremy waited with her evening cloak and bonnet. She donned them, and when Elverston put her fingers on his arm, she swept from the room, pride keeping her head high.

The palace salon into which they were ushered was grand beyond Anne's dreams of elegance. Her eyes widened as she looked around.

Rosita, beside her, seemed to shrink. "It frightens me. What have we to do with such as the monsignor?"

"I think he is Timothy's friend and, frankly, I think him curious as to how all this will turn out."

"Timos," said Rosita quickly, defiantly.

"I am sure he will wish *you* to call him that," soothed Anne. She did not add that it was not the name with which he'd been born. She watched as Timothy gently helped Rosita's elderly father to a chair where, with relief, the gentleman seated himself. "Your father will be all right, will he not?"

"He knows what he can do and what he cannot," said Rosita firmly and then added with a touch of worry, "But he will be very tired tomorrow."

Monsignor de Asti swept into the room, welcoming them. "I know that Signor Costello cannot tolerate late nights, so I have directed my servants to serve our meal immediately. Come now. We will begin."

Instead of the grand dining hall which Anne had glimpsed as she followed Monsignor de Asti down a long hall, they were ushered into a much cozier room with a table of a size that no one need feel it necessary to behave formally. In fact, they were encouraged to speak to everyone who was sitting at the table, rather than merely to those on right and left. Monsignor de Asti began by speaking across the table to Timothy. "Did you, my son, find the answers for which you have searched?"

Timothy nodded. "My brother and I talked all the afternoon. I told him all."

"Is it something you can tell *to* all?" The priest's eyes

twinkled. "You must know, Timos, that I've a great curiosity and can wait no longer for the answers."

"Ah! That explains the invitation. Rosita wondered," teased Timothy. Rosita's cheeks flooded with blood, and she turned accusing eyes on Timothy, who chuckled. "Very well," he said softly. "I will be good." He turned back to the priest. "You know I have been in partnership with Signor Costello for some years. It was arranged for me by a mutual acquaintance who shall remain nameless. Signor Costello could no longer make the journeys necessary for getting orders and buying supplies. I could. It gave me the freedom to travel here and there, which was important at that time."

He closed his mouth with a snap, but everyone at the table, with the exception of Rosita, guessed he hinted at military reasons.

"Two years ago," he continued, "I was in Madrid, where I caught a fever. I was visiting one of our best customers there, someone I had come to know rather well, but who only knew me as Timos Victor. They nursed me and I recovered, but the fever affected my mind. I could not remember who I was or anything of my past. They told me what they knew, which was little enough, but enough that it allowed me to return here to Milan. Signor Costello and Rosita helped me come to terms with my life, but—" He looked straight at the priest. "—as *you* know, it never felt quite right. Also, I could remember nothing from before the illness. I didn't know if I had parents, if I had a wife awaiting me or worse, thinking me dead when I did not appear, *not* awaiting me." He shrugged and, after a quick glance at Rosita, swallowed. "Ethically and morally, I could make only half a life. Just in case."

Rosita cast an adoring look his way. "We," she said softly, "discussed all this. It was not easy, but I understood."

The priest smiled. "I remember the discussions *we* had

concerning the impediments to your marriage to Rosita. Have you learned there are none?"

"There are none. Thank the good Lord above," said Timothy and no longer tried to hide his feelings for the girl.

"Then, if Signor Costello does not object," said the priest, smiling broadly, "when we finish dining, we will adjourn to my private chapel and celebrate the rite of marriage which has been too long delayed."

"I have no objections," said Signor Costello, smiling softly at his daughter, who blushed delightfully, but made no pretense that *she* objected.

"But I do," said Elverston, rising to his feet. "Timothy is English. If you will pardon my saying so, he was not raised in your church, Monsignor de Asti. He is Church of England and, when he weds, will wed under those rites."

"Drake . . ."

"There is also the problem that—"

"Drake!"

"—he left behind a life, a commission in the British army which must be seen to before he is accused of desertion—"

"*Drake.*"

"What?"

"I have converted to Catholicism. I had to. I lived here. So far as I knew I was Italian, born and raised, even though it didn't feel right. The good father has spent hours with me. It was not something I did easily or without thought, but I have done it." He drew in a deep breath. "As to the commission, you are correct. We must go directly to the local British consul tomorrow where we will begin whatever must be done to clear our name of any taint." He held his brother's stern gaze. "As to tonight . . . I will spend it with my bride."

They dueled with their eyes, Rosita, looking worried, glancing from one to the other. Finally Elverston looked down. "I apologize. It is that I have just found you and feel that I am losing you all over again."

"You have not lost me. You will never again lose me." Timothy grinned. "In fact, I wonder if we should not expand our business into England . . . ?"

"Business."

Timothy grinned more widely. "You will find I am very good at it, Drake."

"*Very* good," said Signor Costello. "He has more than doubled our annual net profit. It was the best day of my life when we were introduced."

"You will have to accept you've a cit for a brother, Drake. Or—" Timothy sobered. "—you *will* lose me again."

"You have made your decisions very quickly, have you not?" asked Elverston mildly.

Timothy's eyes widened. "Ah! I recall that tone. You think me overly impulsive, that I will regret what I mean to do, but, Drake, I am no longer twelve or eighteen or even twenty-five. I *like* my life. I like what I do. And—" He pulled Rosita to her feet and into the protection of his arm. "—I love my little Rose. Very much."

Drake sighed. "I have not lost you, Tim, but I have not totally got you back, either, have I?"

Timothy nodded. "I am changed, if that is what you mean. But I suspect those changes began long before I lost my memory." He sobered. "War does that to a man, you know."

They all sobered at that. And nodded. War made great changes in everyone's lives, even among those who remained at home, knowing that loved ones faced dangers and horrors they could never know. But as the meal continued with the changing courses, the mood lightened. It ended with all being pleasantly content.

Soon after, they adjourned to the private chapel where Timothy and Rosita became man and wife.

> *From a letter to Beth from Thomasina.* ". . . *noted a change in her?*"
> *From a letter to Beth from Catherine.* ". . . *so worried. I wish it were possible to see what is going on with her.*"
> *From Beth to the both of them.* "*Mother Anne is a grown woman. Can you not allow her to know what is best for herself?*"

Several days passed and Anne believed Elverston had left Milan without so much as a note of good-bye. She found her appetite had taken a walk without her and not returned. The weather worsened, and her favorite occupation became impossible: She could not take long walks in the hopes of recovering—recovering a desire to eat if nothing else.

"You will waste away to nothing," scolded Milly.

"Nothing?" Anne picked at the truly excellent fish lying on her plate. "That is what I feel I have."

"Nothing? Anne, you are a relatively wealthy woman. You have two daughters you adore, several grandchildren, and another daughter who respects you even if the two of you argue constantly."

"Catherine and I have not argued for some time. We made an agreement we would agree to disagree."

"And Beth? Thomasina? They are nothing?"

"You remind me I am selfish and think only of myself."

"You are not selfish. You are in love."

Anne blanched. She had taken great care to avoid admitting, again, that she was in love with Elverston. "He is a prig and a prude. Do you know that he objects to Timothy remaining in business? Why should he care? It is not as if he were some great noble whose name would be besmirched by his brother's behavior."

Behind her, Jeremy cleared his throat. "You have company, my lady." He glanced at the card. "The Marquess of Burnside," he said, looking bemused. "I showed him into the salon," he added and then closed his mouth tightly.

Lady Anne rose from the table, patting her mouth with her napkin. "I do not know a Marquess of Burnside. Do you, Milly?"

"No." Milly finished her wine, and she, too, rose to her feet. "Since it is a stranger, I will join you," she said and then tipped her head to one side when Jeremy started to shake his and then didn't, his mouth tightening into an even firmer line. "It *is* a stranger, is it not?" she asked the footman. He cast her a look of chagrin. "Never mind. Shall we go, Anne?"

Anne sighed, too preoccupied with her unhappiness to notice the byplay. "I suppose we must. I do not understand why we've been honored by a total stranger's visit . . ."

Jeremy hurried to open the salon doors, and the two women entered. Anne looked idly across the room. She stiffened. "You."

Elverston grimaced. "I suppose it was not the best way to inform you I've traveled incognito, and now that I have found my brother and all is well, I must return to my own identity." He shrugged, settling his coat more comfortably. "I would know you better, Lady Forsythe, and, therefore, it is only right you should know me as well."

"I see." *Except,* she thought, *I do not see.*

He glanced at Milly, silently suggesting she leave them. Milly, stubborn, stood her ground. "We need to talk," he said softly. Turning, he held Anne's gaze.

"Before you have this talk," said Milly, her hands

folded tightly before her waist, "*you* should know something about *Anne.* She is a *widow.* Has been for over four years." Elverston's head swung away from Anne toward Milly, his eyes widening ever so slightly and a smile beginning to form. "And *now* I'll leave you so you may indulge in that talk."

Anne had forgotten that Elverston, no, *Burnside,* had come very near to offering her a slip on the shoulder when they were still in Switzerland. Milly's tone indicated it was that of which she warned him. Anne stiffened. "I am not sure we *do* have anything to say to each other," she said, backing toward the door in Milly's wake.

Drake was doing some very rapid recalculations and coming up with a sum total that surprised him. "Oh yes we do," he said, and smiled.

"No." *Oh, that buccaneering smile . . . !* Her mouth firmed. "I am very nearly certain we do *not.*" Anne turned smartly and ran from the room.

She didn't see the hand held out to her or the look of horrified disbelief on the face of the man she left behind, and very likely, if she had, she would have misunderstood. Anne could not bear for him to ask her to become his mistress. She could not bear it.

How could a marquess—

Memory struck hot coals.

—not even the son *of a marquess, legitimate or illegitimate, as I once pretended, but a* marquess *in his own right—How could he ask anything else of me? I am so far beneath him. A mere village vicar's daughter—oh, it would* never *do.*

Not marriage.

Not to a man who objected to his brother's intention of remaining a businessman, who objected to his brother marrying a Catholic in a Catholic ceremony. He would never look seriously at the daughter of a village vicar—

not even if she had, almost by accident, become the wife of a wealthy baron. Was the baron's *widow* . . .

Fairytales did not happen in real life. For a village maiden to contract a marriage of convenience with a baron had been difficult for the *ton* to swallow. That she might rise still higher in the peerage was beyond belief.

As she lay on her bed, staring at the ceiling, Anne's thoughts circled wildly. Her door was locked against Milly's good-intentioned demand for entrance and her tears a hot burning behind the dam she kept up against them. She would *not* cry.

A fleeting thought even made her smile, if only weakly: Catherine would *never* forgive her if she married Elverston—*Burnside*—because it would mean that Anne would once again go into dinner before her stepdaughter, who was a mere countess!

It must have been two in the morning when Anne's stomach finally made it clear that it must have food. She recalled the bowl of fruit that stood on the sideboard in the dining room and rolled from her bed. She found one of the shoes she had kicked off before flopping down, but sweeping the floor, first with her foot and then her hand, she could not locate the other.

Anne sighed and scrabbled around her bedside table for the tinderbox and lit her lamp. She stared around her. The shoe had found its way across the room and partially under the flounce covering the legs of the slipper chair set near the window. Recovering it, Anne sat in the chair to put both shoes on and then, for a moment, just sat there feeling exceedingly sorry for herself, utterly without interest in anything at all—except that her stomach insisted that she show a *bit* of interest, at least, in supplying it with food.

* * *

Giving in to the growling demand, Anne unlocked and opened the door—and instantly closed it, turning and leaning against it. Surely she hadn't seen what she thought she'd seen? Very carefully she opened the door an inch and peered into the hall. She had. There was no mistake. In the hall was a comfortable chair. Sprawled in it, fast asleep, his legs extending almost to her door, was Elverston.

Burnside, she reminded herself. *But why? Why is he sitting there? How long has he been sitting there? What does he want? What does he think he'll gain by waiting for me to leave this room?*

Softly she shut the door, her thoughts circling round and round, making her feel dizzy. She straightened, blinking. "And why," she wondered out loud, "has Milly *allowed* him to remain there?"

That thought put a stop to all the rest. Milly was not one to be intimidated by a title. Nor would she allow herself to be bullied into doing something she believed she should not. If she had wanted that man gone, willy-nilly, he'd be gone.

"So . . ." Anne murmured.

She put a finger to her chin, her eyes going out of focus. *What is in Milly's head?* The finger drifted up between her lips, her teeth nibbling at the nail. She removed it and dropped her hands to her side.

"And why am I merely asking *myself* questions when I should ask them of *him?*"

That thought frightened Anne into turning and staring at the door. He was there. Just beyond that door. The man to whom she'd given her silly heart with all the fervency of Thomasina doting on her poet—except, Anne had concluded, it was unlikely she'd find a way to retrieve it as Thomasina had hers.

"*Could* I become his mistress?" she asked softly. "Could I bear it?"

And if I did, what would I do when he tired of me? Left me to live the rest of my life without him?

"And if there were children . . . ?"

That thought very nearly solved all her problems. Anne wanted children. Her own children. They would be compensation, would salve her wounded heart, when he finished with her.

"But they would be bastards . . ." she said softly.

I cannot do that to an unborn child. Anne sighed and, restless, paced. What was she to do? How could she resolve this chaos scrambling her mind into a jumble of thoughts and feelings, the fears and the joys?

"Ask him," she said, but immediately shook her head. Not when she was feeling so fragile, so . . . so . . . needy?

What a stupid word, she thought crossly. *But he could talk me into anything the way I feel right now, and I must not allow that. I must decide for myself what I want.*

But she knew what she wanted. She wanted her Mr. Elverston. She wanted him to love her and marry her and the two of them to fill their nursery quickly with as many blessings as the good Lord would give them. . . .

But he was *not* Mr. Elverston.

He was Drake Elverston, Marquess of Burnside. Anne sighed. Since she could not have her Mr. Elverston, then she should send the marquess away. Her mouth firmed and she turned to do just that . . . and stared at the door, horrified. She watched it inch open. *I forgot to lock it!*

"Anne?" He peered in, saw her standing like a rock, and tipped his head. "Will you listen to me?"

Anne shook her head.

"Why? You are an intelligent woman. You are as brave a woman as I've ever known. What is it you fear?"

"I am afraid of myself," said Anne, her chin rising.

He blinked. "How odd. Can you explain?"

"My emotions are too wild for logic to control them—"

"Good."

"—and I will not . . . What did you say?"

He smiled. "I am glad you are feeling *something*. I would hate to be the only one." But then he frowned. "Or did you mean emotions like hate and dislike and wishing we'd never met?"

"You did not think your brother should wed his Rosita."

He nodded. "Our mother will be deeply unhappy not to have attended her younger son's wedding. My brother should have waited. Should have taken his Rosita home with us and introduced them. Should have allowed the chit to enjoy the bride parties, a ball announcing their engagement, the buying of her trousseau. She has missed all that."

Anne blinked. "I thought you were against his marrying her at all. Against his marrying her in a Catholic wedding."

"I freely admit that I am not happy about that. On the other hand, Tim is fully adult. That was his choice, one I could not make for him." He smiled again. "Especially since I was not here to help him when he needed help and that priest was and did!"

"You didn't know . . ."

"No. I didn't know. Anne . . ."

"No!"

"I would do my best to make you happy," he said softly, approaching her.

Anne backed up. "I cannot."

"Did I misunderstand Mrs. Seward? Was it *not* a marriage of convenience? Do you still love him so very much?" With each question he came a step or two nearer.

Anne stiffened her spine and denied the urge to turn and run from him. "You were not wrong and, although I had great respect for my husband, I did not love him."

"But you do love me," he said softly.

"Do I? I begin to wonder," she said, speaking with a touch of bitterness.

His hands landed on her shoulders. "Anne, I love you. Please do not say me no."

"Do not ask it of me. You know I cannot."

He frowned. "Why, Anne?"

Why? Her mouth dropped open. *Are we so different as all that that he can ask me why I cannot become his mistress?*

He sighed. "It is very late, is it not? Perhaps you can explain to me tomorrow." He stared down into her face for a moment . . . and then, with a groan, pulled her into his arms, found her mouth, captured it, and devoured it. His hands moved on her back, up, down . . . down . . . and pulled her into him until she could not avoid knowing how he felt, what he wanted.

And that frightened Anne all over again. Because it was what she wanted too. She pushed away and was slowly released.

"I should not have done that," he said, contrite.

"No," she said. "You should not have."

He glanced toward her bed. "Especially not here."

"Not at all," she said, speaking sharply and turning her head the other way so that she avoided altogether any chance of seeing the bed.

"You will not forgive me?"

"I'll not forgive myself. Mr. Elve . . . *My lord Burnside,* you must go. Please."

"Drake," he said.

"Burnside," she repeated.

"You will not give an inch."

"If I did, you would take a mile!"

He grinned. "Very likely I would. Come"—he held out his hand— "you must lock up after me."

At the outer door he turned. "I will come tomorrow, Anne. We are not done with our conversation."

She didn't object because it was true. They had not finished.

"This time you will not run from me, will you?"

Anne smiled softly. She shook her head.

She rose late, but Milly was waiting for her in the breakfast room, toying with a cup of hot chocolate. Or what had once been *hot* chocolate. "He wants to marry you," she said. She had already begun her packing, meaning to return to her major as soon as Anne was safely wed.

Anne had not believed her. Not at first. But Milly convinced her and now she faced Drake with a singing heart. "I thought you meant to ask me to . . . to . . ." She bit her lip and flicked a quick look at him.

He half frowned, half smiled, his brows pulled in a bit. Unsure of her meaning, he waited.

"You might be a trifle more helpful," she said and pouted.

"I cannot help what I do not understand."

She sighed an overly elaborate sigh. "I thought you meant you wanted to have an affaire with me."

His eyes widened and his mouth lost any semblance of a smile. "No. No . . ."

"You did once," she said, the faintest accusation in her tone.

He nodded. "When I thought you still wed, traveling to escape an elderly husband once you'd married off his last daughter. I will admit to eavesdropping on two ladies when still in Paris. Obviously I misunderstood something they said."

"I *did* marry off his last daughter and I *am* traveling. I am now free to travel whereas before I was not."

He nodded. "I know that now. Anne, before we are in

the midst of an argument and I've no notion how we got there, will you first tell me you will wed me? Soon?"

"Before I have met your mama? Enjoyed a ball announcing our engagement and the buying of my bride clothes?"

"Minx," he said smiling. He opened his arms and she ran into them. "You have not said you will," he said, holding her tightly.

"I will," she said—and brazenly lifted her face to his for his kiss.

From a letter to Beth from Catherine. ". . . cannot believe it possible. Not only is it my dear Beast's old friend, Elverston, but he is now Burnside. Married. So far from home. How can she have done such a thing . . . ?"

From a letter to Thomasina from Beth. ". . . obviously happy and he means to indulge her with the opera season in Milan followed by a long wedding journey. I am so pleased for her . . ."

From a letter to Catherine from Thomasina. ". . . a marchioness. Is it not delightful?"

From a letter to Beth from Thomasina. " . . . such a cat. She has her comeuppance, does she not? Think! Mother Anne outranks her again! And do not say it is terrible of me to feel gleeful. Who knows? Catherine might become a better person for such a setdown."

In the long run, many years later, the most wonderful thing of all was that Anne's son and Catherine's third daughter fell in love and were married, finally reconciling Catherine to her stepmother forever after. Anne, in her great happiness, had long before forgiven Catherine for every nasty thing she'd ever said or done, so everyone (even Catherine in the end) lived happily ever after.

More Regency Romance From Zebra